W9-CEI-331

A CATERED THANKSGIVING

Books by Isis Crawford

A CATERED MURDER

A CATERED WEDDING

A CATERED CHRISTMAS

A CATERED VALENTINE'S DAY

A CATERED HALLOWEEN

A CATERED BIRTHDAY PARTY

A CATERED THANKSGIVING

Published by Kensington Publishing Corporation

A Mystery with Recipes

A CATERED THANKSGIVING

ISIS CRAWFORD

KENSINGTON BOOKS
www.kensingtonbooks.com

Longely is an imaginary community, as are all its inhabitants.
Any resemblance to people either living or dead is pure coincidence.

KENSINGTON BOOKS are published by

Kensington Publishing Corp.
119 West 40th Street
New York, NY 10018

All Kensington titles, imprints and distributed lines are available at
special quantity discounts for bulk purchases for sales promotion,
premiums, fund-raising, educational or institutional use.

Special book excerpts or customized printings can also be created to
fit specific needs. For details, write or phone the office of the Kensington Special Sales Manager: Kensington Publishing Corp., 119 West
40th Street, New York, NY, 10018. Attn. Special Sales Department. Phone: 1-800-221-2647.

Kensington and the K logo Reg. U.S. Pat. & TM Off.

Library of Congress Control Number: 2010932962

ISBN-13: 978-0-7582-4738-4
ISBN-10: 0-7582-4738-9

First Hardcover Printing: November 2010

10 9 8 7 6 5 4 3 2 1

Printed in the United States of America

To Anna Jae and Mila Isabella
The world is a better place because you're in it.

ACKNOWLEDGMENTS

To DJM, for his great ideas and his willingness to share them, and to Larry, for reading my work and sharing his opinions. Don't know what I'd do without you guys.

A CATERED
THANKSGIVING

Prologue

It was two days before Thanksgiving, and five members of the Field family were huddled around the fireplace in the study off of the living room. It was a dismal space. The furniture they were sitting on, cheap to begin with, was literally coming apart at the seams, while the walls of the study were covered with a bamboo-textured wallpaper that had turned an unappetizing shade of yellow over the years.

A flickering overhead light did little to dispel the gloom of the late November afternoon. Each one in the room was wearing his or her coat. Most had wool scarves wound around their necks. Two of the people were wearing gloves.

"It's colder in here than it is outside," Lexus, Monty Field's blond trophy wife of three years, complained.

"I'm sure it's in the fifties," Melissa, Field's daughter from his first marriage, said. She was four years younger than Lexus, thirty pounds heavier, and not half as attractive.

Perceval, Field's older brother, whipped out the leather-covered temperature gauge he'd taken to carrying around and consulted it. "It's fifty-one, to be precise," he told everyone.

Melissa buried her chin in the neck of the sweater she had on over her nurse's uniform. "We should turn up the thermostat," she said.

"At least you have your fat to keep you warm, Melissa," Lexus said.

"Lexus!" Ralph, Field's younger brother, exclaimed.

Lexus turned to Ralph. "I'm not saying that in a bad way," she told him. "Everyone knows fat people are warmer. Right now I envy Melissa."

Two red spots grew on Melissa's cheeks. "That's good," she spat out, "because personally I wouldn't want to look like a walking skeleton."

Lexus fluffed her hair out. "I like being lean, Melissa."

Melissa sniffed. "Is that what you're calling it? I call it bulimia. Such an attractive form of behavior. We had two people in the ER room with that this week. Rotted their teeth right out of their mouths."

Ralph interrupted. "Ladies, please," he said. "Let's get down to more important matters." He gestured to the thermostat on the far wall, encased in a heavy plastic box. "Do you have the key to the lockbox?"

"I wish," Melissa said. "You know Dad always keeps it on him."

Ralph shook his head. His skin looked bluish in the cold. "My brother is pathologically cheap. He always has been, always will be."

"Except when it comes to his art," Lexus said bitterly as she fingered the black down coat she was wearing. It made her look at least twenty pounds heavier. She'd seen a really nice one at Barneys, but Monty had said it was ridiculous to spend money on something like that when she could get one at Marshalls for one-thirtieth of the price. He didn't understand that she deserved to look good. "Screw the American Impressionists."

"I mean, look at this furniture," Ralph continued, ignoring Lexus's comment. He indicated the mishmash of sofas and chairs scattered around the room. "It looks as if it comes from the Salvation Army."

"Actually, Dad got those three chairs off the street," Melissa volunteered, indicating the plaid rockers near the bookcase. "It was so embarrassing. He made me help him put them in the car. I said, 'Dad, what are you doing?' And he said, 'We need chairs and no one is going to see them except the family, so why waste money when there's something that's perfectly good right here?'"

"Yes, why waste money on us?" Perceval said. "I mean, for all we know, the chairs could be harboring roaches or mice." His face took on an expression of horror. "Or bedbugs."

Ralph unwrapped a cough drop and put it in his mouth. "It's too cold for bugs."

Geoff, Field's son, shivered as he cursed himself for forgetting to pack his long underwear. "The hell with the furniture," he said. "At least we should be able to start a fire."

"That would mean we'd need wood, and the old man would never pay for that," Melissa said.

"We could always burn the furniture," Geoff suggested. "I vote for starting with the purple club chair over in the corner."

"The chimney hasn't been cleaned. We'd just smoke ourselves out." Lexus wrapped her coat more tightly around her. It was like wearing a sleeping bag, for heaven's sake. She should be wearing ermine or mink at the very least. Monty had promised her a full-length fur coat before he'd married her. But, afterward it was like he'd forgotten he'd ever said anything like that. "This is ridiculous," Lexus said.

"I agree," Perceval replied. He looked at his temperature gauge again. "We're down to fifty. I mean, we should count for something, right?"

"This is just wrong," Lexus said. "People in the projects are warmer than we are."

"My house, my rules," Geoff said, repeating his father's mantra. "If you don't like them, get out."

"At least you don't live here," Lexus said to him as she surveyed the room. Why had she thought she could get Monty to change? *Delusional* was the word that came to mind. Of course, he had bought her a three-carat diamond engagement ring, but that was when he was courting her. And he had furnished her bedroom completely to her specifications. But again, that was premarriage. She hadn't realized at the time that everything he did, he did for show.

"Thank God, I don't," Geoff replied, remembering the lock on the refrigerator door. There'd been no between-meal eating in his father's house! When he was seven, he'd taken a bowl of vanilla ice cream out of the freezer without permission and been confined to his room for two days. His therapist said that was why he had weight issues. Then Geoff added, "I hate family holidays."

"I think we all do," Perceval said as he rubbed his hands together to keep his circulation going.

"Then why are we here?" Melissa asked.

"Don't be stupid," Geoff said. He started humming "Money Makes the World Go Round."

"Stop it," Melissa told him.

Geoff put on an innocent expression. "Why? What am I doing?"

"Stop humming that song."

"You know what they say," Geoff retorted. "If the shoe fits, wear it."

"That is completely unfair," Melissa told him.

"You really think no one knows what's going on?" Geoff demanded of his sister.

Melissa shook her head. "I don't know what you're talking about."

"Don't be so disingenuous," Lexus said to her stepdaughter.

Perceval snickered. "Disingenuous. That's a big word for you, Lexus. Is that the word of the day on your calendar?"

Lexus glared at him. "What's wrong with improving oneself?"

"Nothing. I just thought your attempts at self-improvement centered around buying the latest lipstick."

"There's no need to be unpleasant, Perceval."

"I wasn't being unpleasant, Lexus. I was being factual."

"You know," Ralph said as he glanced at himself in the mirror to make sure he'd buttoned his shirt properly, "I think we should stop bickering. My brother likes to set us against each other. We only play into his hands when we do."

Perceval sighed. "You're right. Let's face it, some people add nothing to the world. In fact, they take things away, and I'm sorry to say that my brother is one of those people."

"What kind of things?" Lexus asked. "You mean like stockpiling rice?"

Perceval managed to keep from rolling his eyes. "No. I'm talking about intangible things, like pleasure and good feelings. I'm talking about people who spread negative energy everywhere they go."

"The world would certainly be a better place without my dad," Geoff observed, speaking with feeling. "That's for sure."

"I agree," Ralph said. "You might say that putting him out of his misery would be a blessing. He's miserable, so he wants everyone else to be miserable, too. When I think about it, I can't remember my brother ever smiling. I don't remember him ever spending a single penny if he didn't have to. At least not on creature comforts. He's either saved his money or invested it. Basically, he's always been a cheap son of a bitch."

"Well, it must agree with him," Lexus informed them. "Because he just had a checkup and he's in great shape. He told me yesterday his blood pressure is lower than mine. I bet he'll live to be a hundred." She wound her scarf more tightly around her neck before burying her hands in her coat pockets. "God. Another thirty-five years. I'm not sure I can do that. No. Let me rephrase. I know I can't do that."

Melissa snorted. "That's so unfair. I mean, he slathers mayo on everything and he doesn't get more than four or five hours a night sleep. I thought he'd have heart disease or some other old person thing by now."

"Thanks," Perceval and Ralph said simultaneously since each one had had his arteries roto-rooted out in the past year.

"Cheer up," Perceval said. "Maybe he'll get hit by a car."

"Or blown up," Ralph added. "A little gunpowder is a wonderful thing. Maybe he'll have an accident down at the bunker."

Geoff laughed. "We certainly have enough of that stuff down there. A couple of Roman candles go off at the right time and it's good-bye, Monty."

"Yeah," Ralph said. "We could blow this whole place to kingdom come if we wanted to. A little gunpowder here, a switch there, and kerblewy." Ralph laughed. "All gone."

"But we don't," Lexus snapped.

"Of course we don't," Perceval replied. "We wouldn't want to hurt the cat."

"Or the art collection," said Ralph. "That's worth, what? Thirty million?"

"Forty," Geoff said, "and that's leaving out the blue and

white Chinese pottery collection. That's another two mil right there."

"Well, I think that's a disgusting way to talk," Melissa said.

"So you don't want him dead?" Geoff asked her.

Melissa didn't say anything.

"You don't think he deserves to die after what he did to Mom?" Geoff asked.

Melissa stiffened. "I thought we agreed not to talk about that."

"You're right. I'm sorry." Geoff leaned forward and caught her gaze. "But come on, sis, tell the truth for once in your life. Don't you want your inheritance?"

Melissa studied one of the posters on the wall. It was a cheap reproduction of *Nighthawks*. "Well, yes, of course I do," she finally admitted. "But I'm not going to do anything bad for it."

"Jeez, neither am I," Geoff said. "You know I'm not a hands-on type of person." He leaned back in his chair. "No, what we should all do is pool our money together and hire a hit man. It would be worth it. I mean, how much could it cost? Ten thousand? And that would be if we got a top-of-the-line one."

Melissa scowled. "That's really not funny."

Geoff held up his hands. "I was kidding. Why do you always have to take everything so seriously?"

Melissa sniffed. "Because I never know whether you're joking or not."

"Well, I was," Geoff said.

Perceval sneezed. "No one is doing anything to anybody," he said after he'd wiped his nose. "We may want to, but we won't."

Ralph leaned forward, crossed his arms over his chest, and hugged himself. "Of course we won't," he said. "Too high a probability of being caught. We'd be the primary suspects, right? It's always cherchez the money."

Perceval corrected him. "No, Ralph. It's cherchez la femme and follow the money."

"Whatever, Perceval."

A deep silence fell over the group. A moment later Perceval got up.

"I don't know about you," he said, "but I'm trundling off to bed."

"Are you sick?" Lexus asked.

"Why do you ask?" Perceval replied.

Lexus put her coat collar up. "Because it's three in the afternoon."

"True," Perceval said. "But my bed happens to be the warmest place in the house at the moment. It's probably the cold that's making everyone's thoughts turn homicidal."

"I thought it was heat that was supposed to turn people into crazed lunatics," Ralph said.

Perceval shrugged. "Both extremes are equally unpleasant."

"Let's look on the bright side," Geoff said.

Perceval cocked an eyebrow. "And that would be?"

"Well, at least we don't have to endure Alma's cooking anymore," Geoff said. "At least, we're going to have a decent Thanksgiving dinner."

"What happened to Alma, anyway?" Perceval asked Lexus. "When I asked Monty, he pretended he hadn't heard me and walked away."

Lexus stood up and stretched. "The INS came and scooped her up. Isn't that right, Melissa?"

Melissa nodded. "It was terrible."

"But why now?" Ralph asked. "She's been here forever."

Lexus shrugged. "Obviously someone called."

"But who?" Perceval asked. "She never goes out."

Melissa lowered her voice. "I think it was my dad."

Everyone turned to her.

"You're kidding," Geoff said.

Melissa shook her head. "I overheard him yelling at her about taking money that didn't belong to her. He was really, really angry."

Perceval patted his hair down. "I could see my brother calling."

"Unfortunately, so can I," Ralph agreed. "What happened to her kid?"

"Roberto?" Melissa replied. "I think he's staying with some relatives or something like that."

Ralph moved his feet up and down to get the circulation going in them. "Monty's course of action was entirely unnecessary," he announced in a tone of voice that left no doubt about his opinion on the matter. "But, then, he's never been one to use a firecracker if he can use a bottle rocket to get the job done."

"Well," Perceval remarked while he rubbed his hands together, "not to state the obvious, but compassion has never been one of our dear brother's finer virtues."

Melissa stood up, as did Perceval.

"I'm just surprised we're not cooking dinner ourselves," Melissa said. "I can't believe Dad actually hired someone to cater it."

"He didn't. We did," Ralph said.

"We?" Melissa repeated.

"We," Perceval said firmly. "We're all chipping in."

"But you didn't ask me," Melissa protested.

It was Ralph's turn to rise. "We most certainly did," he said.

Melissa glared at him. "You most certainly did not."

Perceval stifled a yawn. "Dear, you can't escape responsibility forever, you know."

"Meaning what, Perceval?"

"It's fairly obvious, isn't it, Melissa?"

"Not to me," Melissa snapped.

Ralph opened his mouth to reply, but before he could,

Lexus stepped between the two of them and said to Melissa "Would you prefer to do the cooking yourself?"

"My sister can't even make a grilled cheese sandwich," Geoff observed. "The only things she's good at are blowing things up and losing money at the casino."

"Exactly," Perceval said. Then he quickly turned and left the room before Melissa could reply.

Ralph, Geoff, and Lexus followed him out, leaving Melissa standing by herself. A few moments later she left, too.

The figure left, as well. The figure had been listening to everything. The conversation merely reconfirmed the decision that had been made. It had been a long time coming. The figure had waited and waited. But the time was right. That was the important thing.

Chapter 1

Sean Simmons peeked out of the kitchen door into his daughters' shop, A Little Taste of Heaven. They were definitely over their occupancy limit. The space between the front door and the counter was jammed with so many people waiting to pick up their orders that a line was beginning to form out the shop door. The counter people, Googie, Amber, and the new hire, were working at light speed, but they couldn't keep up with the crush. The day before Thanksgiving was always crazy, but this one, Sean decided, outdid all the others.

Ever since A Little Taste of Heaven had gotten a one-line mention in the *New York Times* food section lauding their pies, the shop's phone had been ringing off the hook. Naturally everyone wanted one thing. Pies. You'd think that Westchester didn't have any other bakeries. His daughters, Libby and Bernie, had been baking around the clock, and they still had 150 orders to finish before the end of the day. They both looked exhausted, but they weren't going to be able to catch a breather, because they had to cater the Fields' Thanksgiving dinner the following day. Now, that was a bad idea on several levels, if you asked him, which no one had. It was probably just as well that he was going to his sister's, Sean reflected as he leaned against the door frame to give himself a little extra support.

That way Bernie and Libby could come home from the Field house and collapse, instead of having to take care of him. Not that they had to—he could always eat a bowl of cereal for dinner—but they would never allow that to happen, especially not on Thanksgiving.

As he looked at the people milling in front of the counter, Sean felt bad that he couldn't help out. Back in the old days, he'd always pitched in when his wife, Rose, was swamped, but now he was just thankful that he could walk around with a cane, instead of being confined to a wheelchair. Standing for long periods of time was out. And he couldn't even mix up the fillings or peel the apples. His hands weren't steady enough for that.

Basically, he was useless for anything other than giving advice and counting and banding the money. God, when he was younger, he could practically leap tall buildings with a single bound, and look at him now. Who would have thought he would have ended up like this?

No, the best thing he could do right now was stay out of his daughters' way, Sean thought as he took a bite of the pumpkin walnut scone he'd lifted off the baking sheet. The scone was perfect. It had a good crumb and just the right amount of sweetness, which was balanced by the tang of ginger and the seductive taste of Vietnamese cinnamon. He took a sip of his coffee.

His girls were the best bakers he knew. They didn't cut corners, and they used only the freshest ingredients—just like their mother had. Their pie crusts were made with butter; their pumpkin pie filling was made from sugar pumpkins, which they baked instead of boiled to get maximum flavor; their apple pies were made from a mix of Cortlands, Northern Spys, and Crispins; and they ordered their spices online to make sure they weren't stale.

This year the girls had not only made their own mincemeat, but they'd reintroduced an old holiday favorite—nesserole pie, the recipe for which Libby had found in one of his wife Rose's recipe books. There was no canned anything in any of their pies. It was an expensive way to do things, but judging from the mob scene outside, people were willing to pay the price—even in economic hard times like these—for quality.

"Your mother would be proud of you," Sean told Libby and Bernie as they came up behind him.

"She probably would have had something to say about the mincemeat," Bernie said. "I substituted applejack for brandy."

Sean laughed and brushed a few scone crumbs off of his shirt. He was dressed for Florida in khaki pants, a white knit shirt, and sneakers. "I'm sure she'd understand, Bernie."

"I'm not," Bernie said. Her mother had been a stickler for following recipes to the letter, whereas she tended to take a more free-form approach to baking.

"Well, she wouldn't be able to argue with the sales figures," Sean pointed out. It seemed to him as if the shop was going to have its best day ever. "So you must be doing something right." He looked at his watch. "Marvin will be here to take me to the airport in ten minutes."

Libby gave Sean a hug. "I wish you weren't going."

Sean patted his daughter on the shoulder. "I'll be back on Saturday."

Libby bit her lip. "It'll just feel weird not having you here for Thanksgiving."

"But you're catering the Fields' dinner, anyway," Sean told her.

"Which we wouldn't be doing if you were going to be here," Bernie pointed out.

In her mind, Thanksgiving dinner was sacrosanct. It was a law their mom had enforced, and Libby and Bernie had continued that tradition. Except for this year. This year their dad was going to visit his sister down in Florida. Bernie and Libby had been invited as well, but they'd had to decline since from now until after New Year's was one of their busiest times of the year and they couldn't just take off, even though by now both women would have liked nothing more.

Sean sighed. "I couldn't very well say no, could I?"

Bernie retied her apron strings. "Why not? You haven't seen Martha in twenty-nine years. What's another three months?"

Sean gave her "the look." Which Bernie ignored. As per usual. It had worked with his men. It had worked with the guys he'd arrested. It had never worked with his daughters or his wife.

"Well, it's true," Bernie reiterated, putting her hands on her hips. "She calls and you go running."

"Flying, actually."

"Not funny, Dad." Bernie tapped her fingernails against her pant leg. "I just don't see why we can't all go down to Orlando . . ."

"Sarasota . . ."

"Whatever . . . in February."

"Because Martha invited us for now," Sean said.

"What happened between you two, anyway?" Libby asked before her sister could say anything else. The last thing she wanted was for Bernie and her dad to have a fight before he left. "Why did you guys stop speaking to one another?"

"To be honest, I don't even remember anymore," Sean lied. In his opinion, not everything was for sharing.

Bernie favored her dad with an appraising look. "Why do I so not believe that?" she said.

Sean was going to tell her that was what happened when you got old—your memory failed—when Brandon, Bernie's boyfriend, walked through the door.

"Evening, Mr. S," he said as he gave Bernie a hug. "All ready for Florida, I see."

"That I am," Sean said.

"Don't worry. Marvin and I will keep an eye on things when you're gone," Brandon assured him.

Bernie put her hands on her hips. "We don't need anyone to keep an eye on anything, thank you very much."

"Sure you do. Isn't that right, Mr. S?"

"Absolutely, Brandon," Sean said. "Appreciate it."

"Listen," Bernie began, but she didn't finish, because at that moment Marvin pulled up in his Volvo.

Brandon grabbed Sean's suitcase, and they all trooped out to the car. Marvin already had the trunk open. Brandon stowed the suitcase while Sean hugged Bernie and Libby and got in the car. Sean rolled the window down.

"I'm counting on you," Sean told Brandon.

"Don't worry about a thing," Brandon told him.

"I always worry. That's what I do," Sean replied as Marvin pulled away from the curb.

Bernie turned to Brandon. "Keep an eye on things?" she said when Marvin had turned the corner. "What was that about?"

Brandon grinned. "It made him feel better, so what's the harm?"

"I guess you're right," Bernie said.

"I'm always right," Brandon said.

Bernie turned and punched him in the arm.

"That hurt," Brandon complained.

Now it was Bernie's turn to grin. "It was supposed to."

Chapter 2

"Poor Marvin," Libby said, once she and Bernie were back in the shop. She was thinking of Marvin driving with her dad. "We should have taken Dad to the airport. That way we could have spared Marvin an hour and a half of hell." Her dad was a notorious backseat driver.

"We can't take Dad." Bernie indicated the line in front of the counter. "We have one hundred and fifty more orders to finish up. Marvin will survive. He always does. Besides, he likes Dad. Don't ask me why, but he does. And then if we took Dad, he couldn't smoke, because we're not supposed to know that he smokes, and he's going to want to because he's nervous about the flight."

"How could he think we wouldn't know?" Libby asked. "I can smell it on his clothes, for heaven's sake."

Bernie shrugged. She'd thought the same thing when she'd started smoking at eighteen. Her mother, however, had quickly banished that notion.

"Anyway, he shouldn't be smoking," Libby said.

"Are you going to tell him not to, sister dear?"

Libby snorted. "No."

"Well, neither am I."

The sisters walked back into the kitchen. It was cold

and damp outside, and they could feel the late autumn chill through their clothes.

"Forget the smoking thing," Libby said. "It just feels wrong not to see Dad off."

Bernie rolled her eyes. "He's only going to Florida, for heaven's sake. He'll be back on Saturday."

Libby glared at her sister. She was tired and irritable and not in the mood for attitude. "That's not the point. The point is he needs help."

Bernie bent over, picked an apple peel off the floor, and put it in the trash. "Marvin will help him."

"I realize that." Libby paused to take a piece of chocolate out of the pocket of her flannel shirt, unwrap it, and pop it into her mouth. "But we should be doing it."

"Maybe, but I think Dad actually prefers Marvin's help, even though Marvin's driving makes him crazy," Bernie observed as she went over to the sink and washed her hands.

"But why?" Libby asked.

Bernie shut off the water and wiped her hands on a paper towel. "Because he doesn't want us to see him needing help if we don't have to. It humiliates him."

"Maybe," Libby replied. She finished her chocolate and reached in her pocket for another piece. "But what if that storm they're predicting hits? What if he's stuck someplace? What then?"

Bernie brushed a stray wisp of hair off her forehead. "He'll manage. He always does."

"How can you be sure?"

"I can't, okay? But he's going, so let it alone. For heaven's sake, you sound like Mom," Bernie pointed out.

Libby bridled herself. "No, I don't."

"Yes, you do. You're a worrier, just like she was." Bernie went over and gave her sister a quick hug. "It'll be okay, Libby," she said. "It'll all work out. You'll see."

"I suppose," Libby conceded.

"No, definitely," Bernie reiterated. "If I didn't think he could make the trip on his own, I never would have let him go. However, *we* are going to be in trouble if we don't finish up those pies. Now, that I can guarantee." By Bernie's count they had sixty apple, twenty-five apple-cranberry, fifty pumpkin, eight mincemeat, and five nesserole pies to finish up. She flexed her fingers to work the cramps out. "You know," she said to Libby, "if I never see another pie, it won't be too soon for me."

Libby sighed. Her back was aching from bending over the table, and her feet hurt from standing. "You say that every Thanksgiving."

"But it's never been like this. We're going to have to take on an extra baker if it's like this next year. It's amazing what one line in the *Times* can do."

"Why did they have to mention our pies?" Libby lamented. "Why couldn't they have mentioned our cheesecakes instead? Those are so much easier to make, not to mention so much more profitable."

"This is true," Bernie said.

A while back she had added in their labor costs to the pear-and-almond tart that they made, and the results had been so dismaying that she'd never done it again with similar products.

Libby stifled a yawn. She'd been up since four in the morning, and they weren't even halfway through the day yet. "I mean, we make a great pumpkin cheesecake, and we've only had four orders for those."

"Maybe next year," Bernie said, looking at the mound of apples waiting to be prepped. "Yes, why can't people have something else for dessert?" she mused. "Something like a pumpkin mousse, or a sweet potato torte, or an assortment of cookies and chocolate, or an ice cream cake, or some sort of pudding? If I had time to sleep, I'd dream about pies."

"Or at least have one pie and a cheesecake," Libby said,

taking up the conversation where she'd left off as she started ladling pumpkin pie filling into the shells she'd made earlier. "All I know is that I'm going to have carpal tunnel syndrome if this keeps up, not to mention a bad back and flat feet."

"All I know," Bernie said, "is that I'm going to fall asleep on my feet."

Libby stopped ladling and went to put the water on to boil so she could make a fresh pot of coffee. "The only saving grace is that the Fields' dinner is going to be relatively easy to do and then we've got Friday off."

Bernie sighed. "And they're eating at five, so we can get a little bit of sleep before we have to be there. We could be there even later if we could cook the turkey here," Bernie observed.

Libby shrugged her shoulders. "What can I say? They wanted the smell of the bird cooking. One of the brothers . . ."

"Perceval . . ."

"They both look the same to me. . . ."

"Perceval is the one with the comb-over and the jowls. . . ."

"Fine. Perceval said, and I quote, 'The aroma of the roasting bird was one of his favorite parts of the holiday.'"

Bernie put down her paring knife. "I wonder if they have a spray with that scent on the market. I bet they do."

"It's probably called Holiday," Libby said, beginning to measure out the coffee. "Or Pilgrim's Progress."

"They didn't eat turkey the first Thanksgiving. That came later."

"Well, in any case we should dress warm," Libby said, changing the subject because she wasn't in the mood to listen to a history lesson at the moment.

"Believe me, I will. . . ."

"Because I am," Libby said.

"You always do. I think you support the flannel industry."

"Ha. Ha. Ha."

Bernie started on another apple. "I bet it's fifty degrees in that place."

Libby laughed. "At the most. Old man Field could afford to heat that place, if he wanted to."

"I believe the salient words are 'if he wanted to.' How can anyone be that cheap?" Bernie asked, having heard Marvin's story last night at RJ's about Monty Field not wanting to pay for an extra large casket for his wife.

Libby shrugged. Her mom had been frugal, but certainly nothing like Field. "It's a sickness."

"Personally, I think it's a lack of generosity, which is entirely different." Bernie peeled two more apples, cored them, sliced them into eighths, and dropped them in a bowl of acidulated water before continuing. "Maybe it doesn't run in the family. His brothers are spending a fair chunk of change with us," she continued.

"And they have given us some leeway menu-wise," Libby pointed out.

"Thank God." Bernie waved her paring knife in the air to emphasize her point. "But not enough."

"Thanksgiving menus are always traditional."

Bernie wrinkled up her nose. "Some traditions should be dispensed with. Like marshmallow and sweet potato casserole. Yuck."

"Be happy they don't want something like cocktail franks and grape jelly," Libby said.

"You're kidding, right?"

Libby shook her head. "I read that in one of Mom's old food magazines."

"That's beyond disgusting."

"Maybe it's not," Libby said, even though she shared Bernie's opinion on the matter.

"Why are you trying to pick a fight?" Bernie asked.

"Am not," Libby replied.

"Are too," Bernie said, lapsing into her childhood sing-song voice.

"No. I'm not. It's just that you don't need to be such a snob," Libby told her.

"In food, I don't think that's such a bad thing, and anyway, you know you are, too," Bernie retorted. "What did I hear you say about using canned pie fillings yesterday? That they're an abomination?"

"I said that they were inedible."

"Same thing," Bernie pointed out.

"Not really," Libby said as she got ready to roll out the next batch of pie crusts.

"Of course it is," Bernie said.

Libby looked at her and stuck out her tongue. Bernie laughed and the moment of tension was over.

"I'm just tired," Libby explained.

Bernie rubbed her hands again. "Me too."

The two women went back to work. They could hear the hubbub of the crowd out front over the strains of Simon and Garfunkel coming from Bernie's iPod. For some reason, these days Libby liked cooking to them. Maybe because she found their music soothing and she had an abiding belief that food always tasted better when you weren't rushed making it. Food, like people, needed attention to bring out its best.

On the whole, Libby thought that all their customers were being remarkably patient and well behaved. Of course, as the day wore on and people became more stressed, they would probably become less so, especially if what they wanted wasn't there.

"I wonder how Dad's meeting with his sister will go," Libby said after five minutes had gone by.

Bernie looked up from the apple she was peeling. "Mom always said she wasn't a very nice person. I guess Martha told Dad that Mom was beneath him when he told her they were getting married."

"How do you know that?"

"I overheard Mom telling Mrs. Feeney that one day. According to her, Dad never spoke to Martha again."

"Then why did you let me ask him that if you already knew?"

Bernie shrugged. "I just wanted to hear what he was going to say."

Libby didn't reply immediately, because she was busy concentrating on putting the pies in the oven. Usually, she put the pie shells in the oven and then filled them to minimize spillage, not the other way around. The fact that she'd reversed the order just showed her how tired she was—not that she needed more proof.

Libby gently closed the oven door. "There must have been other stuff going on between Dad and Martha, as well."

Bernie shrugged. "I expect there was."

"Maybe Martha's mellowed. Dad has."

"Let's hope so, for Dad's sake," Bernie said.

"She has to have," Libby said. "Otherwise, she wouldn't have invited him."

Bernie looked up. "Possibly. But in my experience people don't get better as they get older. They get worse."

Chapter 3

It had started snowing in earnest on Thursday by the time Bernie and Libby gathered up the supplies they'd need to cater the Fields' Thanksgiving dinner. They'd gone to bed as soon as they'd closed the shop at nine o'clock, and slept straight through until seven o'clock the next morning. They probably would have slept later if one of their customers hadn't pounded on the shop door and asked if they had any desserts they could sell her for tonight.

Fortunately, Bernie and Libby had an order that hadn't been picked up yesterday, so Libby had slipped on her robe and trundled downstairs to sell Mrs. Haldapur three pies—two pecan and one juiced apple. Then she'd made a big pot of coffee, toasted some cinnamon bread, added a tub of fresh butter from one of the local dairy farms to the tray, and brought everything upstairs. Bernie had already turned on the TV, and she and her sister sat there watching the Macy's Day Parade and sipping coffee and eating buttered cinnamon toast for a little while.

"It feels funny not having Dad here," Libby noted as she ate her third piece of toast.

Bernie looked up from yesterday's edition of the local paper. "I hope things are going well."

"Me too," Libby said. "I mean, he sounded okay when he called. Unless he was putting on an act."

Bernie closed the paper. "I guess he'll tell us when he gets home."

"Even if the visit isn't going well, he won't tell us."

Bernie checked the clock on the wall. It was time to get going. "This is true," she said as she stood up.

Bernie showered, dried herself off, and slipped into a white long-sleeved T-shirt, followed by a black merino wool turtleneck sweater and her dark green cargo pants. Normally, she wouldn't wear something like that in the kitchen, as it would be too warm, but she figured, considering the temperature at which Monty Field kept his house, she'd be okay. Then, to be on the safe side, she put a cotton long-sleeved turtleneck in her tote in case she had to change. She finished her outfit with a pair of heavyish green and yellow striped socks under some ankle-length black Dr. Martens. Libby, in turn, put on a white cotton turtleneck shirt, a black cardigan sweater, a pair of black slacks, and a pair of sensible black shoes.

"We're not serving the food," Bernie told Libby when she took a look at her outfit.

Libby looked puzzled. "I know that," she said.

"I wasn't sure, because you look like a waiter in those clothes."

Libby shrugged. At this point she was too tired to care. Her clothes were clean. They fit—kinda. And they were unobtrusive.

"You should get some new pants," her sister added. "Those should be retired. The seat is bagging out."

"I plan to on Friday," Libby lied as she closed the door to the flat. She hated shopping.

"And not from a catalog, either. You have to try them on."

Libby just grunted, annoyed that Bernie had called her out. But she didn't say anything, because there was no point. She'd tried, but she couldn't get Bernie to see her point of view. She didn't care about clothes. Not in the slightest. Unlike Bernie, who was a fashionista. On this issue they had to agree to disagree.

Libby was thinking about how one mother could have produced two daughters so opposite in their tastes as she and Bernie went downstairs and began gathering the supplies for the upcoming meal. The shop seemed especially quiet after yesterday's commotion, and as Libby passed the ovens on the way to the cooler, she could almost hear them sighing in relief. She ran her hand over the counters, then lightly touched the kitchen witch hanging over the window by the sink, something she did every day.

Libby remembered her mother buying the good luck charm at a craft fair two years after she'd opened A Little Taste of Heaven, and even though the witch was now more than a little worn, and she'd had to restitch the seams a couple of times, Libby wouldn't let Bernie take it down. Not that she was superstitious or anything, but why mess around with something when it was working, especially when the business you were working in was so precarious?

They'd had good luck so far, and Libby saw no reason to change things up now. Besides, the witch reminded her of her mom. She was thinking about her and how she'd always worn an apron in the shop kitchen—a different colored one for every day of the week—as she glanced out the window.

The weather reports had predicted light flurries, but this was more. This looked like a storm. Great. Just what they didn't need. Oh well, they'd better get a move on. The roads would be bad, and it would take them longer than usual to get to the Fields' house.

Longely was a great town and Libby was happy to be

living here, but the town wasn't very good at snow removal and the shop's van didn't have its snow tires on yet. Libby made a clucking noise with her tongue as she pondered the possibilities for disaster. After she'd come up with several scenarios, she decided it was better to try to think positively—an ability that had unfortunately eluded her since childhood.

And on that note Libby continued on to the cooler, opened the door, and slid the box containing the turkey out. It was an eighteen-pounder, which was rather large for the number of guests coming, but Perceval Field had said that they wanted enough for leftovers, which this would surely do. In fact, both she and Bernie had tried to convince him that a twelve-pound bird would do the trick, but he'd remained adamant on the subject, and so they'd bowed to his wishes under the rubric of the customer is always right—something that was so not true. In fact, he'd even specified the brand of turkey he'd wanted them to buy.

That had irritated Bernie no end, although it really shouldn't have. In Libby's humble opinion one brand of frozen turkey was as good as the next. No. Her fear was that since they hadn't gone to the Fields' house and seen the oven in the kitchen, the turkey might be too big for it plus the other dishes they had to fit in.

Perceval had assured them that that wasn't the case, and Libby figured they'd have to go with that. It was not as if they had a choice. And if that were the case, they would figure something out. They'd have to. Lately, Libby had come to realize that in a funny way cooking and baking were all about problem solving. You had the ideal, which was the recipe, and then you had reality. Reality was when you had the oven that wasn't calibrated correctly, you had the wrong-sized pans, you had ten eggs when you needed a dozen. The trick was to bring about some sort of amalgamation between the two and get a good result.

"I hope that oven is big enough," Bernie said, echoing Libby's thoughts as she watched her sister take the turkey out of the cooler, where it had been defrosting. It wasn't even fresh-killed, for heaven's sake, but this was what Perceval and Ralph Field had wanted and this was what they'd gotten. Both of them had claimed that this kind of turkey was what their brother wanted, and who was she to dispute that?

"I hope the oven is big enough, too," Libby said as she carried the box to the van.

It was snowing harder now, the snow coming down in thick, fat flakes. Bernie turned and studied the window of A Taste of Heaven. The window had come out well, if she had to say so herself. Mrs. Fowler's fifth-grade class had made a diorama of the first Thanksgiving meal between the Indians, or the first Americans, as they were now being called, and the Pilgrims. This formed the main element of the window design.

Bernie had had something else in mind, but her dad had told Mrs. Fowler that his daughters would love to display the classroom work in the store window, so what could she do? Bernie hadn't had the heart to contradict him. And, anyway, it was good community relations. But once they'd gotten the diorama in the window, it had become obvious that it was too small, so Bernie had surrounded it with old-fashioned paper turkeys with scarves wrapped around their necks, ears of corn with faces painted on them, and gourds wearing hats.

What she had was your standard kitschy Thanksgiving holiday window, but then she'd taken some pies, both big and small, lacquered them, and hung them from the ceiling. Somehow the whole thing worked. Maybe, Bernie mused, that was why they'd sold so many pies this year. It wasn't the one-liner in the *Times* at all; it was the window sending out subliminal messages. She was decid-

ing that next year she'd decorate in cheesecakes when
Libby came up behind her.

"Thinking about what you're going to do for Christmas?" she asked.

Bernie laughed and brushed the snowflakes out of her
hair. "Well, I'll tell you one thing it's not going to be. Pies."
She turned back to the van. "I can't believe it's snowing
like this in November. What ever happened to global
warming?" she asked.

"Well, wherever it is, it's not here," Libby replied as she
tromped back into the kitchen to get more supplies.

Bernie joined her. They loaded up the boxes with sweet
potatoes, onions, celery, peppers, garlic, pearl onions,
string beans, two types of mushrooms, butter, heavy
cream, freshly baked corn bread, Parker House rolls, a bag
of marshmallows, two pies and one cheesecake, and
whipped cream, along with five different types of cheese, a
variety of crackers, olives, spiced pecans, and walnuts, as
well as dried dates, figs, and apricots. And that wasn't
even counting all the other stuff they were bringing.

As Bernie moved the box that contained the turkey to
the side to make room for the other boxes, she said, "Why
these people insisted on having a battery-raised turkey, I
don't know," she groused. "They're tasteless."

"You tried to suggest alternatives and they didn't listen," Libby said.

Bernie sighed. "It's just that, popular opinion to the
contrary, this kind of turkey is difficult to cook well. They
tend to get mushy or extremely dry, and they're flavorless.
Except for the skin, of course."

Libby put the box with the pies in the van and wedged it
between the other two boxes so it wouldn't slide before replying. "*Chacun à su goût,* as they like to say in French."

Then she and Bernie went back inside for another load.
What with attending to a few last-minute details, it took
them another fifteen minutes to load up the van. Then

Libby took out her list of ingredients and read them off while Bernie looked to see that they had packed everything. This, they had painfully learned, was the best way to ensure that they didn't forget anything. "No ingredient left behind," was Libby's motto.

That accomplished, they both got in the van and fastened their seat belts. Bernie put the key in the ignition and turned it. The van made an odd clunking sound as it started up.

"This van is like an old lady," Bernie observed as she pulled out into the street. "It's always got something new wrong with it."

"I hope that something isn't anything serious," Libby said.

Bernie crossed her fingers. "Me too." Bernie knew they needed to get a new vehicle and soon, but whenever they'd saved up enough money, another emergency came along and they were back where they started again.

Libby stared out the window as the van puttered along at thirty miles an hour. For the moment, the town looked deserted. All the shops on the main drag were closed, and there were just two or three other cars on the street besides theirs. It seemed as if everyone was either traveling to their destination or had already arrived. And, of course, the storm didn't help things.

"This is what it would feel like to be the last person on earth," Libby opined right before she spotted a figure in a parka and snow pants being pulled along the sidewalk by his or her golden retriever.

Bernie didn't respond. She was too busy concentrating on driving. The van was a little wobbly at the best of times, but when it was fully loaded, it got more so. Especially since the van's all-weathers were almost bald. She slowed down to twenty-five miles an hour, and the van stopped sliding. The snow was coming straight at them now, and in addition to everything else, Bernie found it difficult to discern where the road ended and the sidewalk began. She hadn't seen this kind of snow since she'd been caught in a blizzard in Buffalo ten years ago.

"This is bad," Libby said as they turned right on Ash Street.

Bernie just nodded. Then she reached over and turned on Pat Benatar. She needed the music to distract her. The driving got worse as they left Longely, the snow sweeping off the fields and across the roads, creating whiteouts.

"Why don't you see what the weather channel says?" Libby suggested after fifteen minutes had gone by.

"What's the point?" Bernie snapped, squinting to better see the road. "I know what it's going to say. That we're in the middle of a friggin' blizzard."

"How long do you think it's going to take us to get to Field's house?"

"At the rate we're traveling? Another ten or fifteen minutes." Bernie patted the van's dashboard. "I promise I'll feed you premium gas if you get us there," she cooed.

Libby laughed. "It's the getting back that's worrying me."

"Hopefully, the storm will have blown itself out by then," Bernie responded as she turned onto Beechcroft Road. "I mean, this has to stop sometime, right?"

"Right," Libby said as she looked at the veil of white enshrouding the car.

Bernie took one of her hands off the wheel to rub the back of her neck, which had grown stiff with tension. By her calculations, they had five more miles to go until they got to their destination, and it was definitely going to be a white-knuckle ride. The road went up and down a series of hills. In the spring Bernie was sure it would be a beautiful drive, with green fields on either side and a vista of the valley down below. Unfortunately, that was not the case now. The wind had piled the snow up across the road, making it hard to negotiate.

Every time the van had to go up a hill, it spluttered and coughed, and every time it went down the hill, it slid from side to side, forcing Bernie to ride the brakes all the way. By the time they arrived, Bernie was exhausted from the effort of keeping the van on the road, and although she didn't say it, she was beginning to wonder how they were going to get out of there and back to Longely by the time they were supposed to leave.

They arrived at their destination half an hour later.

Libby looked around. From what she could see, the Field compound consisted of two buildings, the house, which was a standard cedar-shingled Colonial, and a second building, which bore a striking resemblance to a concrete bunker.

"I bet that's where they make their fireworks," Bernie commented as she drove by it.

"Used to," Libby said. "Remember, Marvin told us that when Penny's father started his fireworks business, he manufactured them here, but the business grew, so Monty Field moved the manufacturing end of it somewhere else, about the same time he moved the old man to an old-age home."

"Charming," muttered Bernie, who didn't remember the conversation her sister was alluding to at all, possibly because of the two Long Island iced teas she'd had.

"However," Libby continued, "according to Marvin, Field still uses the bunker as his headquarters and R & D locale." She shuddered. She certainly wouldn't be happy living next to all those explosives. "If it were me, I wouldn't be able to sleep just thinking about all that gunpowder." Fireworks scared her. She didn't like the noise, the smoke, or the flashing lights and hadn't ever since she could remember.

Bernie grunted. This was something she could never understand. Bernie loved them and never passed up the opportunity to see a fireworks display whenever possible. This had caused a certain amount of conflict when they were little, Bernie crying if they didn't go to the show, and Libby crying if they did.

"Then I guess it's lucky we're not catering a Fourth of July party for them, isn't it?" Bernie said as she brought the van to a stop in front of the house. There was probably another road that led to the kitchen door, but she couldn't see it.

"We wouldn't do that," Libby said.

"Not even for fifty thousand dollars?" Bernie teased.

"Not even for a million," Libby said.

"Maybe they celebrate Thanksgiving with fireworks," Bernie said, getting out of their vehicle.

"Ha. Ha. Ha. Very funny," retorted Libby as she jumped out and headed to the back of the van.

Bernie joined her a minute later. Libby was opening the door and lifting out the first box when she heard an explosion. She shrieked and jerked her arms up and then down, thereby tipping the contents of said box onto the ground. *God, don't let it be the pies,* Bernie prayed as the door to the bunker flew open and Geoff and Melissa came flying out.

"That was a good one," Geoff said.

Melissa made a face. "No. It was stupid and unnecessary. You could have burned my jacket."

"So what?"

Melissa stroked the lapel of her starter jacket. "So, it's my lucky jacket."

Geoff snorted. "Give me a break."

"Seriously. It is."

"Well, given the way things are going for you these days, maybe you should trade it in at the school rummage sale and get a new one." Geoff was about to say more when he spied Bernie and Libby and the fallen box. "Oops," he said, coming to a dead stop.

Melissa, who was slightly behind her brother, bumped into him, which propelled him forward. "What the hell?" Then she saw why her brother had stopped. "Sorry," she said to Libby and Bernie. "I didn't know anyone was out here."

Chapter 4

"I'm so, so sorry," Geoff said to Libby for the third time. "I didn't realize you were so sensitive to noise."

Libby's cheeks began to burn. She felt like a fool for reacting the way she had. "I'm not," she retorted. "The noise just startled me."

"It could be worse," Bernie said, finding herself to her surprise consoling Geoff, who, she decided, looked like a puppy that had just gotten hit. "Someone could have gotten hurt."

Libby glared at her. She couldn't believe her sister was siding with the people who had frightened her. Talk about loyalty.

"Well, it's true," Bernie hastily said.

"I told him not to do what he was doing," Melissa informed Libby as she stood and watched her brother root around in the snow for fallen vegetables. "I told him it was dangerous. I told him it wouldn't work, but he never listens. He's always playing around with that stuff."

Geoff brushed the snow off of a bunch of celery and handed it to Libby before replying to his sister. "I wasn't playing around," he objected. "I was trying something new. Pyrotechnics is a competitive business, and you always have to have the next best thing. People get bored with the same old, same old."

Melissa stuck her hands in the pockets of her jacket to warm them. "That's fine if you know what you're doing," she told her brother.

Geoff brushed a snowflake off the tip of his nose. "Of course I know what I'm doing."

"No, you don't," Melissa retorted.

"I most certainly do. It's in my blood."

Melissa pointed to Geoff's hand, which bore the obvious marks of skin grafts. "Need I say more?"

Geoff scowled. "I was young when that happened, okay." He turned to Bernie. "I'm more careful now," he explained. "And, anyway, it's like the mark of the clan."

Melissa rolled her eyes. "*Puh-lease*. Let's not over-dramatize."

"Well, it is," Geoff insisted. "Everyone around here has gotten stung by the dragon and usually more than once. You work with this stuff long enough and it's gonna happen. That's just the way it is."

"Dragon?" Libby asked.

"Explosives," Geoff clarified.

Melissa rolled her eyes again. "Don't listen to him," she told Bernie and Libby. "It's the mark of stupidity is what it is. He's lucky to have a hand."

Geoff gestured toward the bunker with his chin. "Like you haven't had any accidents in there, Melissa."

"Not like that I haven't," Melissa snapped back. "And you know why? Because I measure. I don't just throw things together to see what happens."

"Sounds like cooking," Bernie noted.

"Well, in a funny way it is," Melissa replied as she spotted an onion that Libby had missed sitting in the snow by the van. She walked over and picked it up.

As Bernie watched Melissa, she thought once again that at least Libby hadn't dropped the box with the pies. Thanks

be to heaven for that. You could always wash off a vegetable, but you couldn't reassemble a pie. Or a cheesecake,
for that matter.

Melissa held the onion up. "What do you want me to
do with this?" she asked.

Bernie nodded toward the back of the van. "Just throw
it in one of the cartons."

Melissa nodded. "That's a lot of food," she commented
as she inspected the contents of the boxes sitting in the van
before tossing the onion into the nearest one.

"What do you expect, sis?" Geoff asked. "After all,
there are nine of us and this *is* Thanksgiving."

Bernie stopped brushing the snow out of her hair and
thinking about how she wanted to get inside the house,
where it would be marginally warmer. "Nine?" she said.

"Nine?" Libby repeated, halting her search for the orange bell peppers, which had mysteriously vanished under
the snow. "I thought there were only supposed to be six
for dinner." In fact, she knew there were only supposed to
be six for dinner. She might make mistakes, but not like
that.

Melissa turned and looked at Libby. "There were, but
now we have three more coming. Why, is that a problem?"
she asked sweetly.

Bernie was just about to say, "Problem? Why should it
be a problem? We'll just snap our fingers and get whatever
we need. So nice of you guys to let us know." But before
she could, Libby answered.

"Fortunately not," she replied after making a mental in-
ventory of the menu.

In truth, it would have been a disaster if they'd been
serving single-sized portions of something, like steak, but
they were serving an eighteen-pound turkey instead, so
three more people wouldn't be a big deal. In fact, they
could feed ten more people if they needed to. And the new

dessert Libby was planning on making wouldn't hurt, either. On the way out of the door she'd decided that the menu needed something a little lighter in the dessert department, which was why she'd grabbed some extra pears, another bottle of red wine, and the brioche that hadn't sold yesterday.

She was going to poach the fruit in red wine flavored with orange and lemon peel, a touch of cloves, and cinnamon, then reduce the wine and serve the reduction and the fruit over slices of brioche sautéed in butter. That would be quite tasty, actually, and a nice change from the usual holiday fare, although Libby had found that when it came to food and holidays, most people did not like change in their menus—not even the smallest amount. Witness the menu they were serving today. If that wasn't a poster child for culinary conservatism, she didn't know what was.

"How much are the extra people going to cost, anyway?" Melissa asked, interrupting Libby's train of thought. "Because I don't think I should pay for them, since I haven't invited them."

"First of all," Geoff said, rounding on his sister, "that isn't these people's problem. You should talk to Uncle Ralph and Percy about that."

"Well, I don't see anything wrong with trying to keep track of money."

Geoff smirked. "Coming from you, that's a laugh."

Melissa drew herself up. "And what's that supposed to mean?"

"Exactly what I said, and money aside, these people are your cousins."

Melissa sniffed. "I know who they are, for heaven's sake. I just wonder what they want. I mean, they practically invited themselves."

"Maybe they want to mend fences with us, Melissa."

Melissa put her hands on her hips and scowled at her

brother. "And maybe it has to do with the business, Geoff. Maybe they want Dad to invest in another of their lame-brained ideas. Have you thought about that?"

"Their last one didn't do so badly."

"That's not what I heard."

"Either way, what difference does it make?"

Melissa gave an incredulous laugh. "It means there will be less for you. What are you? An idiot?"

"First of all, don't call me names, because I'm not greedy like you."

"That's a laugh," Melissa shot back.

Geoff pointed to the house. "And second of all, lower your voice, Melissa," he hissed. "They're inside."

"Don't be ridiculous," she snapped. "They can't hear me."

"They can if they're standing near the front bay window. I don't think you realize how loud your voice is." Geoff blinked. "Oh, oh," he said. "Here they come."

Libby followed his glance. She saw Melissa's father, Monty Field, coming out of the front door of the house. Two men and a woman followed him. Libby couldn't help noting the expression of extreme dislike that crossed Geoff's and Melissa's faces before they plastered smiles on them. But their eyes still held sparks of hate that they couldn't conceal as their father and their cousins approached them. This was not, Bernie decided, going to be a pleasant meal people interaction–wise. But at least no one would be able to say anything bad about the food.

"Why are you all standing around like lumps?" Monty Field snapped at his children.

Bernie hadn't seen him in a long time, and he looked even skinnier than she remembered. He was wearing an ill-fitting Harris tweed sports jacket that was probably twenty years old, a dingy white shirt, and a pair of corduroy pants that looked to be of a similar vintage to the jacket.

In contrast, Geoff and Melissa's male cousins were both

dressed in expensive suits and sheepskin jackets, while the woman had on a designer puffy jacket, one of those fox Sherlock Holmes–style hats, and enough make-up on her face for a glossy photo shoot. Bernie figured the three cousins to be in their late twenties, early thirties. And whatever business they were in, judging by their appearance, they were obviously doing well.

"Why isn't the van by the kitchen door?" Field asked his children.

"Because we can't get there," Libby replied, answering for Melissa and Geoff.

Field rounded on her. "I wasn't talking to you."

Libby blinked. "Excuse me," she said.

Field waved his hands in the air. "Sorry if I was rude. It's this dratted weather that's making me crazy. I hate being closed in." He turned and pointed a finger at Geoff. "Didn't I tell you to shovel a path to the kitchen so these people could use the back door?" he demanded. "Isn't that what I sent you out there to do?"

Geoff gestured toward the snow coming down. "But, Dad, there's a blizzard out," he protested.

"So what?" Monty Field shook his head in disgust. "You really are worthless," he said to his son.

Geoff's face got red. Bernie could see him clenching his fists.

"And you are, too," Field said, turning to his daughter. "Can't you even do a simple thing like shovel properly? Is that too much to ask of you? Evidently it is," he replied, answering his own question.

Melissa scowled. She put her hands back on her hips. "What's the point?" she demanded of her father. "It's snowing too hard. Given the circumstances, that van couldn't make it to the back door even if there was a path."

"How do you know if you don't try?" Field demanded. "Answer me that? That's right. You don't," he said to Melissa, who was now kicking at the snow with her boot.

The taller of the male cousins tapped Monty Field on the shoulder. "Do you want me to shovel?" he asked. "Bob and I would be happy to."

"Don't be ridiculous, Audie," Field told him before turning and going back in the house. "You're my guests. And, anyway, since when have you and Bob ever done anything even remotely like physical labor? You're too wussy for something like that."

Audie made clucking sounds with his tongue as he watched Monty Field disappear into the house. "I swear, he gets worse every time I see him."

"And he wasn't that good to begin with, right, Greta?" Bob said.

Greta gave a noncommittal grunt.

"I only hope we're not stuck here tonight," Bob continued. "I think I'll die of hypothermia."

"And boredom," Audie said. "Monty doesn't even have cable. He told me it's not worth the money."

Greta pursed her lips before carefully rearranging her cashmere scarf around her neck. "Personally," she said, "I've always gotten along with Monty. I don't understand what the problem is."

"The reason you get along with him is because you're his spy and his lackey," Geoff told her. "You do whatever he wants."

Greta shrugged. "You can think whatever you want, little man," she said.

"Little man?" Geoff squeaked.

"Did I say that? Oops." Greta put her hand to her lips. "I'm sorry. I must have slipped."

Bob and Audie smirked. Greta turned to them.

"Come," she said. "There's no reason for us to be standing here. Let's go back inside, where it's warm and dry." Then she linked arms with the two men and led them toward the house.

Geoff stood there, watching them go, while he clenched and unclenched his fists. "I hate that bitch," he finally growled just before he stalked off toward the house with Melissa in tow, leaving Bernie and Libby standing in the snow beside the van.

"What now?" Libby asked as she watched the front door slam behind Melissa.

"Now we ring the doorbell," Bernie said as she grabbed a box and marched through the snow. "Either we go through the front way or we don't go through at all. I mean, there's no way I'm walking through the snow with boxes to get to the side door. If they don't like it, too bad. We'll just turn around and go home."

Libby looked at the snow on the ground. It was halfway up the hubcaps. "*If* we can go home," she said. "The way things are going, we may be sleeping here tonight."

"Heaven forbid," Bernie said, thinking of the people inside the house. "I'd rather sleep in the van."

Libby sighed. Her feet were cold and her hair was wet. "Don't even think something like that, much less say it." She blinked the snow out of her eyes. "Maybe this wasn't such a good idea, after all."

"Maybe not," Bernie conceded. "But we're here now." She glanced at her watch. "Come on," she told her sister. "Let's get the show on the road. We've got to put the turkey in the oven now. We're already running late."

"You think I don't know that?" Libby said, and she grabbed a box, marched up to the door, and rang the bell.

Chapter 5

Two minutes later Perceval answered the door.

"Sorry, but there's no way we can use the side entrance," Bernie told him as she stepped inside.

Libby followed her sister, shutting the door behind her. The hallway floor was marble, while the walls were papered with chinoiserie wallpaper, the kind, Libby knew from reading her sister's decorating magazines, that cost at least 120 dollars a roll, if not more. A round, inlaid rosewood antique table sat in the middle of the foyer, supporting a large blue and white Chinese porcelain vase filled with an expensive arrangement of exotic blooms.

We should have charged them more, Bernie thought as she took in the whole setup. "Nice flowers," she observed. "Where did they come from?"

Perceval let out a long sigh. "Bogart's."

Bogart's was one of the premium flower vendors in Westchester County.

Then Perceval sighed again. "Only the best for my brother will do." And he gestured at the wallpaper.

"So I see," said Libby, who was also thinking that they should have charged Ralph and Perceval more.

"Usually," Perceval said, continuing on, "we have people like you—"

Bernie interrupted. "Like me?"

Perceval gave a vague wave in the air. "You know, tradespeople—"

Libby interrupted. "Now, there's an expression I haven't heard for a long time."

Perceval shrugged. "As I was saying, we usually have tradespeople go in the servants' entrance. However, due to the weather, Monty is prepared to make an exception in this case."

"How nice of him," Bernie said, not having gotten over being addressed as "you people." She could feel her temper flare.

"Uncharacteristically so," Perceval replied, choosing to ignore the sarcasm in Bernie's voice.

Libby said nothing, preferring to concentrate on signaling to Bernie that she should let the comments go. For her part, she was just glad to be in out of the snow.

"My brother is really very peculiar about certain things," Perceval informed them as he studied his reflection in the gilt mirror hanging on the wall. "Obsessively so, really."

"It's so quiet," Libby noted just to have something to say as she wiped her feet on the entrance mat.

Perceval patted his hair down and picked a piece of lint off his jacket before replying. "That's the way my brother likes it," he said as he gave his hair another tweak. "Not that the rest of us do," he confided in a lower voice after looking around to make sure no one was there. "Monty doesn't even have cable in this place. He says the programming isn't worth the money. He says it's all garbage. I feel as if we're back in the nineteenth century."

"That's a drag," Bernie observed at the same time Libby said, "Sounds good to me."

Perceval scowled. "I'm definitely on your side," he told Bernie. He was about to say something else when he heard footsteps. "My brother," he said, straightening up. "Here. Let me show you the kitchen." And he set off at a brisk pace, with Bernie and Libby trailing behind him.

As they walked, Bernie noted that the hallway looked like something out of *Architectural Digest,* with its deep-gloss eggplant-colored walls and ornate gilt mirrors hung every twelve feet or so. The living room and the dining room had been furnished by someone with an English country house fixation. There was chintz on the sofa, leather on the armchairs, oriental rugs on the dark wood floors, and what looked to Bernie's eyes like a really good selection of paintings hanging on the walls. She was sure she'd seen some of the artists in the Met.

"American Impressionists?" Bernie asked Perceval.

"They're my brother's passion," he answered, slowing his stride.

Bernie halted and pointed at a portrait of a woman. "Is that a John Singer Sargent?"

"Yes, it is," Perceval replied.

"Wow," Bernie said. "I'm impressed. I've just seen his work in museums."

Perceval gestured vaguely toward the rooms on his right. "I'm told that all the paintings in the house are of museum quality. Stupid waste of money, if you ask me, but then no one has. Now, if you will please come with me." And he continued on.

As Bernie followed him, she couldn't help noticing that the farther away they got from the foyer, the smaller the rooms became and the shabbier everything looked. Rooms shot off at odd angles from each other, while corridors meandered without any seeming direction. Bernie began to feel as if she was in a maze.

And then there was the paint job. In contrast to the front of the house, the back end appeared not to have seen a paintbrush in years. The walls were scuffed, and there were water stains on the ceiling. The rooms that she and Libby went by were furnished with pieces that looked as if they had been bought at a rummage sale and thrown in higgledy-piggledy without a thought to their arrangement.

"Well, here we are," Perceval announced when they got to the end of the hallway. He pointed to an unpainted wood-laminate door that had smudge marks around the door handle. "This is your kingdom."

"Kingdom?" Bernie asked.

"Kitchen," Perceval clarified. "Now, Monty likes to keep this door closed when not in use," he explained. "It cuts down on the draft." And he leaned over, grasped the door handle, and pulled it toward him. Libby felt a blast of Arctic air come barreling out. "Hopefully you will do the same. You can open the heat vents if you want," Perceval said. "Although Alma never needed to."

Poor Alma, Libby couldn't help thinking. She probably had to go home every night and soak in a hot tub to get the chill off.

Perceval wrapped his scarf more tightly around his neck. "And, anyway, I don't think it will do much good. And now, if you don't mind, I have business to attend to." At which point he took off, leaving Bernie and Libby to enter the kitchen by themselves.

"We should have worn long underwear and heavier socks," Bernie muttered as she took a step inside. It felt as cold in here as it had outside. "And face masks."

"Maybe it'll be better when we light the ovens," Libby suggested.

"Maybe," Bernie said. But she didn't think so, and she could tell from Libby's tone of voice that she really didn't think so, either.

Chapter 6

"God," Libby said, looking around at the room she was standing in. "I don't think this kitchen has been remodeled for thirty years."

Bernie put the mushrooms she was holding down on the counter. "At the very least," she said. "Give it another ten, and it'll become retro instead of merely outdated. You can tell that no one but the maid ever set foot in this place."

Over the years Bernie had observed that people who had people cooking for them rarely bothered spending the money to update their kitchens. Why should they? They weren't going to benefit. In fact, some of the oldest, grungiest kitchens Bernie had ever worked in had belonged to some of the fanciest houses.

Libby gave an absentminded grunt of agreement as she went over and opened the door of the oven. It needed a good cleaning, but she thought that she could get the turkey, the sweet potato casserole, and one of the stuffings they were making to all fit in there. Hopefully, the oven was correctly calibrated, because she'd found that lots of times they weren't. Not that it mattered if you used your oven every day. Then you knew whether it ran hot or cold.

Unfortunately, there was no one here they could ask about the oven's propensities. They'd just have to do more checking.

"We did bring the meat thermometer, didn't we?" she asked Bernie.

Bernie nodded. "It's in the box with the apples. Even though, theoretically, we don't really need it, since the turkey has that pop-up button thingy."

"I hate those things," Libby announced with a vehemence she normally reserved for prepackaged white bread. "They're totally inaccurate. Pay attention to those and your turkey will turn out dry and lifeless or undercooked." Neither of which was acceptable.

"Maybe," Bernie said, "but lots of people love those pop-up buttons. Don't ask me why. They just do."

"They're a symbol of what's wrong with America," Libby announced.

Bernie stopped counting the onions. She was sure they had three more. "How's that?"

"Overreliance on technology."

Bernie laughed.

"Seriously," Libby said. "You should know if the turkey is done by feel and smell alone."

"But you are using a thermometer," Bernie pointed out. "I'm sure that was considered radical in its day."

Not being able to come up with an immediate answer to that statement, Libby decided a change of subject might be politic. "Where are the oysters?" she asked. "I know we packed them."

"Yes, we did. I checked them off."

"Then where are they?" Libby demanded.

Bernie started rummaging through the boxes. After a moment she was forced to conclude that the oysters weren't there. She cursed silently. "I bet we left a carton in the van," she said and she went out to look.

Libby put the loaf of bread she was holding down and studied the kitchen again. No toaster, she realized, not that it really mattered, because she'd have to toast the white bread for the corn-bread stuffing in the oven, anyway. If she used a toaster, she'd be standing there for the next half an hour. She guessed she'd find out if the oven was properly calibrated or not sooner rather than later.

The countertops were absolutely bare. There wasn't a blender or a mixer or a Cuisinart in sight. Libby decided that they were probably all stored in the cabinets. She began to look through them to see what she could find. It wasn't much. She found a stash of camping food; old coupons; a manila envelope, which turned out to have building plans, which, as far as Libby could tell, had never been implemented; some old dented cans of corned beef hash; bags of chips; salsa; and a few sprouting potatoes and garlic that had gone soft.

Finally she found what she was looking for—an old blender, a handheld mixer, an eggbeater, and several other kitchen implements that looked as if they were at least twenty years old. Which was a good thing, Libby reflected, considering that there was only one electrical outlet in the whole kitchen. She had an idea that if she plugged in a blender and a mixer together, she'd probably blow all the fuses.

She sighed as she looked at the acid green Formica counters and the backsplash and the dingy white linoleum floor that had become scratched and pitted from years of use. Someone had painted the walls an unattractive shade of mustard yellow, not that mustard yellow could be attractive under any circumstances, and the fluorescent lights overhead just made the color even more hideous.

The walls themselves were barren of decoration except for two calendars from the local gas station. Libby knew this because A Little Taste of Heaven got one every year for Christmas. But they kept theirs on the desk in the office and changed it every year, unlike these. One was five years old and the other was seven.

Libby studied the refrigerator and the dishwasher. They looked as old as the stove and in about as good shape. Libby walked over and opened the refrigerator. There was practically nothing in it except for a pack of diet soda, a package of cream cheese, a jar of mayo, two containers of yogurt past their expiration date, and a container of moldy strawberries.

Well, Libby thought, *at least we won't have to make room in the frig for our supplies—not that they really need to go in there.* Given the room temperature, everything could stay out on the counter and would be fine. Still, Libby thought as she got the onions and the celery ready to be chopped, what did these people eat? They had to put their food somewhere.

Fortunately, Libby had brought her own knives, because she could tell from looking at them that the knives in the kitchen drawer were dull and of inferior quality. Too bad she hadn't brought her pans as well, because the ones here were cheap and cooking with cheap pans just made things harder. *Oh well,* Libby thought as she got ready to make the stuffing for the turkey. They would just have to do.

She was making two, one as requested. That was the oyster stuffing. The other one was Libby's personal favorite—a corn-bread stuffing. She liked it because unlike the oyster stuffing, it had a fresh, light taste. And, anyway, she really didn't like oysters.

Not that she'd ever admit this to anyone, but they grossed her out, which was a totally nonfoodie thing to say. But it was true. Cooked or raw, they still looked disgusting to her. Oyster stew sounded very good with all that cream and butter, and if you could disguise the way the oysters looked, it would be perfect. In fact, she wasn't a big fan of raw clams, either. She liked her shellfish cooked, thank you very much.

Or maybe she didn't like oysters because she'd nearly bisected her hand opening one, thought Libby as she put the loaf of white bread she'd made a couple of days ago on the counter and started slicing and cubing it. She needed ten cups for the oyster stuffing and ten cups for the cornbread stuffing. Making the bread into evenly shaped cubes settled her down, and she stopped thinking about all the pitfalls that the dinner they were about to make could hold and started concentrating on possible solutions to said problems.

She was almost done with the bread when Bernie walked inside, carrying the two cans of oysters.

"I come bearing gifts," she said.

"Thank God." Libby put her knife down. Having oyster stuffing without the oysters just wouldn't do. "Where did you find them?"

"In the back of the van. Somehow they managed to get wedged in the back next to the tire. On a different note, I ran into Field on the way in."

"Really?" Libby said. "What did he have to say?"

"He said he'd be in in a while to see how the turkey is doing."

"He's probably coming in to see if we turned the heat vents on or have the door open," Libby groused. "Living with him must be like living with Ebenezer Scrooge. He's not even paying for this dinner, and it's in his own house."

Bernie leaned over and stole a bread cube off the counter. "No. He seriously likes to check on the turkey's progress— at least that's what Ralph told me after his brother left."

Libby spread the bread cubes on the two small dented baking sheets she'd found in one of the cabinets. "I'm surprised he even sets foot in this place."

"I think it's a one-time event," Bernie said, surveying the scene in front of her as she formulated her plan of attack.

Chapter 7

For the next half an hour, Libby and Bernie worked side by side as they chopped the celery, onions, garlic, and parsley for the two stuffings. Then Libby found the biggest sauté pan that the kitchen had and melted two sticks of butter in it. First, she sautéed half the vegetables and poured the contents into a bowl. Then she put in two more sticks of butter and sautéed the next batch of vegetables. She crumbled corn bread into the bowl, then added ten cups of cubed bread, lots of black pepper, and some more butter.

"You can never have too much butter," she said in answer to Bernie's raised eyebrow as she set the stuffing aside.

"I'm sure the AMA would disagree with that," Bernie replied.

"Then screw 'em," Libby said, opening the cans with the oysters and adding them to the other bowl, which held the remaining toasted, cubed bread and sautéed vegetables. "This is holiday food, and you should be able to eat what you want on the holidays."

"Amen to that," Bernie said as she cleaned out the turkey's cavity, salted and peppered the inside, and placed the turkey in the pan, thinking as she did about the time one of her roommates out in Cali had roasted a chicken with the little packet of entrails still in the bird, because Bernie hadn't been there to tell her not to.

Next, Bernie took the oyster stuffing that Libby had prepared and put it inside the turkey's cavity. Then she took the heavy needle and thread that she'd brought and sewed the cavity shut and tucked the legs close to the breast. "I hope you'll be delicious and you won't have died in vain," she said to the turkey as she put it breast side down in the pan so all the juices would flow into it.

Of all the methods Bernie had tried for roasting a turkey—basting it every fifteen minutes, putting an aluminum tent over it, covering the breast with cheesecloth—this one seemed to work the best. You roasted it breast side down and then turned it breast side up for the last three-quarters of an hour of cooking time so the skin could brown. Bernie rubbed the skin with a mixture of butter, oil, salt, pepper, and paprika and slid the bird into the oven, which Libby had already preheated.

"Here we go," she said to Libby as she set the timer she'd brought with them.

Libby just nodded as she began peeling the potatoes for the sweet potato casserole. She loved sweet potatoes. They tasted great, were extremely good for you nutrition-wise, and came in pleasing shades of orange and yellow. What was there not to like? But putting marshmallows on top of them? No. She didn't think so. She realized it was an American tradition, but a relatively recent one. After all, marshmallows didn't become popular until the 1930s. They reached their high point in the 1950s, their use waning in the 1970s, when the food revolution hit American shores.

However, in those forty years they managed to find their way into a multitude of places they didn't belong. Libby still remembered a particularly ghastly salad she'd encountered that had been made with tomatoes, romaine lettuce, blue cheese, and marshmallows, and since the person who had made it had been an aged relative, she'd had to eat it and smile. Even worse had been the scrambled eggs and marshmallows her best friend's mother had whipped up for a late night snack.

She still shuddered at the memory of that. So really, looked at in that context, a sweet potato marshmallow casserole wasn't so bad. And even if it was, it didn't matter, because the truth was that in this business you gave the customer what they wanted—within reason, of course. Otherwise, you'd be out of business.

Bernie looked over to see her sister staring off into space. "What's going on?"

Libby shook herself. "Nothing. I was just thinking that if we had enough sweet potatoes left over after the casserole . . ."

"Which we do," Bernie said.

"I was being rhetorical. Anyway," Libby continued, "I was thinking that we could sauté the extra potatoes up with some pickled ginger and serve them as another side dish."

"I didn't see the pickled ginger in the cartons," Bernie objected.

"I tucked it in my backpack on the way out the door. It was kinda a last-minute thing."

Bernie laughed. "Well, the dish seems a little avant-garde for the Field family, but why not? The worst that can happen is that they won't like it."

"My thoughts exactly," Libby said.

Bernie gave her sister an appraising look. "You know, you do have this missionary streak in you when it comes to food."

Libby shrugged because it was true. She fought against it, but for better or worse, it was there. "I'm not denying it," she said. "I think I get it from Mom."

"I think you do, too," Bernie agreed, remembering her

mom's story about how she'd gotten their dad to eat garlic.

And on that note she and Libby went back to work.
They spent the next hour making a pumpkin bisque,
which they planned to serve in small sugar pumpkins with
toasted croutons floating on top; peeling chestnuts and
combining them with Brussels sprouts, to be finished off
on top of the stove; making a salad of arugula, endive, and
watercress with a sprinkling of toasted hazelnuts; plating
the hors d'oeuvres they'd brought from the shop; and getting the dining room table set up, which took some doing
because they couldn't find a tablecloth that fit.

"That's why I hate these kind of events," Bernie grumbled as she gave up looking through the linens and decided
to overlap two smaller white Irish linen tablecloths instead. "From now on in, we're just dropping the food off
and leaving."

"Works for me," Libby said as she located a silver plat-
ter for the turkey and a silver dish for the corn-bread stuffing. "We lose money every time we do this," she noted,
holding the serving pieces up. "Bernie, what do you think?"

"I think the sizes are right, but they need to be pol-
ished," Bernie replied.

Libby plunked the serving pieces on the sideboard and
opened up the top of the silver chest she'd found in the top
drawer. She sighed in dismay as she studied the contents.
"As does the silverware."

Bernie let out an indignant snort. She hated polishing
silver. Always had, always would. "That is not in our job
description," she groused.

"Too true," Libby agreed. "But Mom would be happy."

For some reason their mother had always loved polishing silver. It had relaxed her, as had ironing. At least that
was what she'd always told Libby and Bernie. This, however, was a concept that neither one of Rose's daughters
understood. Not even vaguely.

"We could always use plastic stuff," Bernie suggested. "I think I saw some in the kitchen."

"We may have to if we can't find the polish," Libby retorted as she gathered the silver up and walked back into the kitchen. "Obviously, Alma was slacking off."

Bernie cleared a place on the closest countertop for Libby to put down the silver. "Maybe that's why Monty fired her."

Libby stifled a yawn as she looked out the window. It was still snowing. If anything, it had gotten worse. "Ralph told me it was because she stole money. Not that it really matters, because we still have to get this stuff cleaned up."

Bernie shook her head and pinned a loose strand of hair back up. "Just another thing to do."

Libby and Bernie were searching for the silver polish in the kitchen utility closet when Monty Field came traipsing in.

"Ladies, how's the turkey doing?" he asked.

"Cooking along," Bernie said.

Monty Field rubbed one of his hands along the side of his beaklike nose before bringing it back down to his side. "I thought I'd check on the bird."

Libby nodded toward the oven. "Be our guest."

"This is my favorite part of the holiday," he confided as he walked toward the oven. "Alma always told me that the turkey would roast without my help," he said with a smile. "But I don't believe it. Actually, I don't think she liked me in her kitchen. Not one single bit. I know her son certainly didn't. He'd glare at me every time I came in." And he gave a self-deprecating laugh.

"I can't imagine why," Libby said as she and Bernie laughed with Monty to be polite. "After all, if you're not entitled to be here, who is?"

"That's what I told him," Monty replied. "He was better behaved after that." Monty bent over and opened the oven door. "But she did make a good turkey," he continued. "I'll give her that."

"Hopefully, ours will be, too," said Libby.

"Better than your mother's chicken, at any rate."

"Excuse me?" Libby said, thinking she hadn't heard Monty Field correctly.

"You were not my first choice," he informed them. "However, since I'm not paying, I acceded. Perhaps you will prove me wrong, although in my experience the apple never falls far from the tree."

Bernie and Libby were both too flabbergasted to speak. They simply watched as Monty reached over and pulled the rack containing the turkey out a couple of inches. Then he bent down even farther and inhaled.

"Smell that," he said, using his hand to waft the aroma up to his nose. "There's nothing like it. They should bottle it. Don't you agree, girls?"

But Libby wasn't listening to what Monty was saying. She was focusing on the turkey. She didn't get it. The turkey had been roasting breast side down, but now it was breast side up. That made no sense. The only possible explanation was that Bernie had turned the bird. But why? It wasn't time yet. She turned to Bernie to ask why she'd done that, but before she could get the words out, Monty reached over and tapped on the pop-up button embedded in the turkey's breast with the forefinger of his right hand.

He went tap, tap, tap.

On the third tap the turkey exploded.

Chapter 8

Bernie and Libby stood there with their mouths hanging open. They were too stunned to move. Or speak. Their ears rang. They couldn't believe what they were seeing.

Finally Libby said, "Tell me that isn't what I think it is."

"It is." Bernie pointed to the oven.

Monty Field lay sprawled half on the floor and half on the oven door. His head had been turned sideways by the blast. The upper half seemed to be gone.

Libby put her hand to her mouth and averted her eyes. She didn't want to look, but Bernie couldn't tear her eyes away.

"Ugh," Bernie said as she gingerly stepped around the blood dripping onto the floor. Monty's eyes seemed to follow her as she reached over and turned off the heat. "Death by turkey," Bernie said, the words flying out of her mouth before she could stop them. "That's a new one." Then she gave a nervous giggle, which was something she always did when she was extremely upset. "Who would have thought?"

"Who indeed?" Libby took a deep breath. She still hadn't moved from the spot she was standing in. Her legs felt wobbly, and her stomach was doing odd flip-flops. "I told you those pop-up buttons were no good," she wailed.

"Evidently not," Bernie replied. She was still having trouble thinking clearly.

"We killed him," Libby continued. "The stuffing made the turkey explode, and we killed him. I can't believe it."

"Don't be silly," Bernie said automatically.

"No. We did," Libby insisted.

"That's ridiculous," Bernie told her.

"Well, can you come up with another explanation?" Libby demanded.

"Possibly." Bernie studied the oven and the area surrounding it.

Of course, there was another explanation. There had to be. It was just a matter of reading the scene and coming up with one. She put aside her queasiness and told herself to focus.

"Well?" Libby said after a minute had gone by.

"No oyster stuffing," Bernie finally said.

"No oyster stuffing?" Libby repeated. "What do you mean, no oyster stuffing?"

"Exactly what I said."

"Which makes no sense," Libby said, raising her voice.

"Calm down."

"I am calm. I just want to know what you meant by 'no oyster stuffing.' Under the circumstances I don't think that's too much to ask."

"I meant exactly what I said, Libby," Bernie replied in a voice that Libby found infuriating. "There's a lot of other stuff on the walls"—Bernie didn't think she needed to be more specific—"but I don't see any oyster stuffing, do you?"

Libby looked around for a moment. She saw turkey and sweet potato casserole and corn-bread stuffing and some pieces of what she thought might be Monty Field's head—

better not to speculate on that—but Bernie was right. No oyster stuffing. Or so it would appear. Frankly, she didn't want to get close enough to find out.

"Maybe, there isn't any stuffing," Libby conceded. "But so what?"

"Well, then, where did the stuffing go?"

"Who cares?"

Bernie rolled her eyes. "You should care. Our insurance will care."

"Maybe it got atomized," Libby suggested. "Maybe the explosion turned it into tiny particles that we can't see."

Bernie waved her hand around the kitchen. "Nothing else did."

Libby put her hands on her hips. "So, Bernie, exactly what *are* you saying?" she demanded.

Bernie rocked back and forth on the heels of her boots. "It's obvious, isn't it?"

"Not to me."

"I'm saying that someone took the stuffing out."

"So?"

"So think about it, Libby."

"I am."

"Think harder."

"I hate when you do this."

"You need to pull yourself together," Bernie told her.

Libby had to admit that was true. She chewed on her lip while she thought, but she couldn't focus on anything. She was too rattled to think. She took a couple of deep breaths. That didn't work. No. What she needed was a piece of chocolate. Which she'd had the foresight to pack. Actually, she never left home without it. Who knew when a chocolate emergency might arise? Some people had tranquilizers. She had chocolate.

After she'd eaten a couple of Lindt's extra dark truffles and taken a couple more deep breaths, she began to understand what Bernie had been saying. "I get it," she said.

"Someone took the stuffing out and replaced it with an explosive device. And that's why the turkey was breast side up. Because whoever did it was in a hurry and they put the turkey back in the pan wrong."

Bernie nodded her approval. "Exactly." Then she had another idea. "Or they might have substituted an already roasted turkey, which they'd jerry-rigged with a bomb, for ours," she posited. "Smell that?" she asked.

Libby sniffed. "Now that you mention it, yes." She'd smelled it to begin with, but with everything going on, it just hadn't come to the fore of her consciousness.

"That's gunpowder," Bernie said. "That's what they use in fireworks."

Libby offered a truffle to Bernie, who took it—a mark of how upset she was. Then Libby took one, too. In her opinion, sisters never let sisters eat chocolate truffles alone. For a moment, both women stood there, allowing the chocolate to melt on their tongues and coat their mouths.

"Whoever did it must have done it when we were in the dining room, setting the table," Libby finally said.

"Had to have been," Bernie agreed. "We were in the kitchen the rest of the time."

Now that the shock was wearing off, Libby was indignant. "We could have been killed," she said.

"Indeed, we could have. Although," Bernie said thoughtfully, "it was tapping the pop-up button that set the device off."

"Maybe we were the targets," Libby said.

"No," Bernie said. "I think Field was."

"Are you sure?"

"Of course I'm not sure," Bernie said. "But first of all, I can't think of any reason why anyone here would want to kill us, and secondly, neither one of us would have tapped that button. Think about it. It's not something people usually do."

Libby made a clicking sound with her tongue. "I wonder if that's something that Field usually did."

"Yes, it was," Bernie said, remembering a conversation she'd had with Perceval. "It was one of Monty's foibles."

"Foibles?"

"Shtick."

Libby absentmindedly reorganized the Parker House rolls in the breadbasket. "Well, it's good that this isn't our fault," she added.

"Not even remotely our fault," Bernie said. "Turkeys do not explode without a lot of help. At least not like that they don't."

"There was the 'exploding snail in the puff pastry' incident that happened somewhere in upstate New York a couple of years ago," Libby pointed out.

"That was different," Bernie told her. "That was a temperature–air pocket thing. That was completely different than what happened here. And the lady just got a minor burn. She didn't get her head blown off. No, we have no liability with this whatsoever."

Libby decided Bernie was probably right. She gave a sigh of relief. Even though Bernie had already mentioned the insurance thing, she wasn't going to admit to her that one of the first things that had occurred to her after the explosion was whether or not their insurance policy would cover this. What clause would something like this fall under? she wondered. Sometimes she couldn't believe how crass she was.

"Who do you think did this?" she asked.

Bernie shook her head. "Some pissed-off Field family member," she said.

Libby rubbed her hands together. She was beginning to feel cold. It could be shock, or it could be the temperature of the house. "I wish Dad was here," she blurted out.

"Me too," Bernie said.

"Maybe we should call him."

"And tell him what? That Monty Field died from an exploding turkey?"

"I guess," Libby answered,"when you put it like that, there's really no point in worrying him. I mean, it's not as if there's anything he can do from Florida. He'll insist on coming right back."

"Exactly." Bernie tapped her nails on the kitchen counter. "Not to mention the fact that we're going to have to hear how he told us not to take this job every day for the next year."

"Two years, at least," Libby said.

"The police can handle this," Bernie said.

"I don't envy them their job," Libby commented.

"Me either," Bernie said. "Everyone here knows about fireworks, everyone has access to them, and everyone here apparently dislikes Monty."

Libby looked around and shuddered. "I'd hate to be the one that does that cleanup."

"Well, they're definitely going to have to get rid of the oven," Bernie said as she went over and fished her cell out of her tote bag so she could call the cops. "I can't imagine ever baking anything in it ever again."

She'd just started to dial 911 when Ralph and Perceval came running into the kitchen.

"We heard a noise," Perceval said.

"It sounded like an explosion," Ralph added. Then he caught sight of the blood and his brother lying half in the oven. "Oh my God," he cried. "They've killed Monty."

There was no doubt in Libby's mind that the "they" Ralph was referring to were her and Bernie.

If there was any doubt at all, it was dispelled when Perceval turned to her and Bernie and said, "Why did you do this?"

"Us?" Bernie countered. "You're kidding me, right?"

She would have said more except that Lexus came running in, took one look at her husband's body, shrieked, and commenced a graceful swan dive onto the kitchen floor, after she'd picked a spot where she wouldn't stain her white cashmere sweater and slacks.

As Libby watched Lexus do a bad imitation of a woman fainting from grief and fear, it occurred to her that as improbable as it might seem, she and Bernie were being set up to take the fall for Monty Field's death. The whole thing had been preplanned, and they'd walked right into it. At least, that was how it looked to her at the moment, she thought as she watched Perceval take out his phone and call the police.

Chapter 9

"I wish I hadn't given up smoking," Bernie said as she brushed the snow off her pants.

"I wish I had started," Libby told her as she did likewise.

"Well, one thing is clear. We're not getting out of here now," Bernie said, gloomily surveying the van's wheels, which were buried under the snow.

"Not without a snowplow and snowshoes we're not," Libby agreed, amazed at how much effort it took to walk in snow up to her knees.

Bernie studied the blizzard raging in front of them. She figured the wind was gusting at a good forty miles an hour, making visibility impossible. They couldn't see the road they'd come up on, much less the fireworks bunker near the house.

The moment Libby and Bernie had gone outside, they'd known they weren't going anywhere, but they'd cleared the snow off the van and started it up, anyway. It had been a futile gesture. The wheels had spun around, digging deeper into the snow, and the windshield wipers hadn't been able to keep up with the onslaught.

Then they'd called Brandon and found out that even if

they could get the van out and make it down the hill to the highway—which was extremely doubtful—there would be no place to go. A state of emergency had been declared for Westchester. All the roads were closed, and people were being told to stay off of them.

"We're stuck," Libby said, stating the obvious.

"No kidding," Bernie replied.

"This is not good."

"Why?" Bernie asked. "Just because we're stuck in the house with a corpse and the person who made him one?"

"There's that and the fact that whoever killed him is trying to pin the murders on us," Libby countered.

"I say it's the entire family. Witness Perceval's and Ralph's whole 'Oh my god, you've killed Monty' scene and Lexus's 'Oh, the horror of it all' after she revived." Bernie bracketed the word *revived* with her fingers.

Libby grimaced. "Yes. That was some of the worst acting I've seen since the Longely Playhouse rendition of *Our Town*. I mean, if you're going to do something, do it right."

"Well, they did it right with Monty. I'll give them that."

"Maybe they all killed him," Libby said.

"An attractive thought, but I don't think they trust each other enough to be able to coordinate something like that."

"Any chance it could have been an accident?" Libby asked.

Bernie looked at her. "Yes, someone just happened to lose an explosive device, and by some quirk of fate, it ended up in the turkey. It happens every day."

"Maybe it was supposed to be a joke."

"In other circumstances, I'd say that might be the case, but not in this one. All these people work with explosives. They know what they can do. If they wanted it to be a joke, they would have put something small in the turkey, not something that would blow off Field's head." Bernie stamped her feet up and down to keep the circulation going. "Just thinking about it makes me want a drink."

"Me too," Libby said. "I bet Monty kept a really good liquor cabinet."

Bernie gave a wistful sigh. "A shot of decent brandy would be incredibly nice right now."

"Yes, it would be," Libby agreed, despite the fact that she usually didn't drink. However, she was willing to make an exception in this case.

Suddenly Bernie's cell phone rang. Both women jumped at the noise. Bernie took it out of her pocket and looked at who was calling. She frowned.

"It's Dad," she said.

"That's bad," Libby replied. Their dad rarely made calls on his cell unless it was an emergency.

Bernie tried to reassure her sister. "He's probably just calling to wish us a happy Thanksgiving," she told her as she moved to the shelter of the doorway to shield the phone from the snow. If there was one thing she'd learned over the years, it was that water and electronics didn't mix.

Libby moved next to her so she could hear both sides of the conversation. "He did that this morning," Libby reminded her just as Bernie pressed the talk button. "He knows. Clyde called and told him."

"What does Libby say I know?" Sean asked Bernie.

"She was saying you know about the storm," Bernie told him in the most cheerful voice she could muster.

Libby gave her a thumbs-up for fast thinking.

"But don't worry about a thing," Bernie continued. "We're fine. How's it going in Florida?"

"I guarantee that it's going a lot better down here than it's going up there," Sean said. "And I'm not referring to the weather, either."

"You're right. He does know," Bernie mouthed to Libby.

"When were you going to call and tell me about Monty Field having his head blown off?" Sean demanded.

"Soon. We just didn't want to interrupt your family re-union and all that bonding that must be going on," Bernie said.

"Really?" Sean said.

Bernie winced at the sarcastic tone. "Don't worry," she told him. "We have everything under control."

"You consider being accused of murder having everything under control?"

Libby made a face. "I told you we should have called him immediately," she whispered.

Bernie raised her hand, signaling for Libby to stop talking. The connection wasn't that good, and she was having a hard time hearing her dad, let alone figuring out what to tell him, as it was.

"Clyde was exaggerating."

"I hope so," Sean said.

"He is," Bernie replied. "Perceval was hysterical."

"The boys at the Longely police station seem to be taking it pretty seriously."

"Well, Perceval called them up and retracted the statement after he'd calmed down fifteen minutes later. So I don't know what their problem is."

"Their problem," Sean said, "need I remind you, is that the chief has been gunning for me for years, and this offers him a perfect opportunity to embarrass me by putting you in jail."

"That's ridiculous," Bernie said.

"You don't know Lucas Broadbent like I do," Sean replied.

"I think you're exaggerating," Bernie insisted.

"Are you so sure? I thought not," Sean said when his daughter didn't answer. "Well, you know what I'd do if I were you?" he said.

Bernie moved farther into the doorway, with Libby at her side.

"What?" Bernie asked.

"I'd see if I could find out who killed Monty Field before the Longely CID gets there."

"Piece of cake," Bernie said.

"I'm serious," Sean replied.

"Funny, but we were just thinking about doing that," Bernie lied, although they would have come around to that conclusion eventually. Maybe.

Sean coughed. Bernie could hear the sounds of people talking in the background. "Given the way Clyde described the storm, I figure it'll take the police at least a day to get up there. That should give you plenty of time. And I'll be there as soon as I can," their dad said.

"No, Dad. You don't have to do that."

"Yes, I do," Sean replied. "I take care of my girls."

"We're perfectly capable . . ." Bernie began, but it was too late. Sean had already hung up. Bernie stared at the phone for a moment before slipping it in her jacket pocket. "Damn Clyde," she said. "I love him, but I wish he hadn't called Dad."

"I didn't even think Clyde was around to tell Dad," Libby said. "I thought he and the missus were out in Arizona, visiting his kids."

Bernie sighed. "Well, I guess you were wrong."

"Evidently," Libby said. She shook her head. "I wonder if you can get fingerprints off a turkey," she mused.

"Probably not. I don't think that turkey skin is a good vehicle for retaining fingerprints, but they might be able to get DNA off of it. Not that they would bother."

"But it would be bad if they did since we handled the bird."

"Lots of people have handled the bird."

"But if it was a substitute bird, then our DNA wouldn't be on it."

"This is true," Bernie told her. She looked out at the storm. It gave no hint of abating. "We should go inside. I'm freezing."

"Me too. Although it isn't much warmer inside," Libby pointed out.

"But it's drier," Bernie said.

"Maybe we can sleep in the van," Libby said, thinking ahead to the coming night. Any vain hope she'd had that they could get out of there was now gone.

The prospect of bedding down in the house did not thrill her, for obvious reasons. First, there was the whole "murderer on the loose" thing, and then there was the issue of random exploding objects. In Libby's book, neither one of those things made for a restful night's sleep. At this point, she'd give anything to be back in her snug flat above the store.

"Do you really want to sleep in the van?" Bernie asked her sister.

"It's probably not a good idea," Libby admitted. "We'd turn into Popsicles."

Bernie put her arm around Libby's shoulders and gave her a squeeze. "Come on. It won't be so bad."

Libby looked at the falling snow and sighed. "I guess Dad is right about trying to find out who killed Monty Field," she said.

"You know he is. It's not like we have a choice."

"And we're not going to get out of here for a while."

"No, we're not," Bernie said. "This is definitely going to be a memorable Thanksgiving."

Libby sighed again. "But not in a good way. This is like a setup for one of those bad horror movies."

"Woo," Bernie said, wiggling her fingers in front of Libby's face. "Watch out. I'm coming to get you."

"Ha. Ha. Very funny." Libby yanked her hood up for emphasis. "And to make matters worse, I'm all out of chocolate."

Bernie put her hand over her heart. "Oh, the tragedy of it all."

Libby frowned. "Well, it is. And I hate to admit this, but I'm also really hungry."

"Well, we do have plenty of food inside."

"Yes, but we have to go into the kitchen to get it," Libby said. "Which I am not anxious to do."

"Not a problem," Bernie replied. "I want to take another look around in there, anyway." She might be many things, but squeamish wasn't one of them. "What do you want to eat? I can bring it out to you if you want."

Libby thought for a moment. "Some pumpkin bisque and a little bit of Brie and some of the stretch bread I baked yesterday would be nice." Soup seemed like a soothing thing to have at a time like this, and Brie's creamy texture always cheered her up. "And maybe a thin slice of apple pie."

"You got it," Bernie said.

But the sisters never made it to the kitchen.

They got distracted along the way.

Chapter 10

Bernie and Libby could hear the raised voices the moment they stepped back into the foyer.

"Interesting," Libby whispered to Bernie as she listened to what was being said.

"Very," Bernie whispered back, wiping her feet on the mat. Then she took off her jacket and hung it over the hall closet doorknob.

"Forget the food," Libby murmured as she did likewise with her parka. "We need to check this out first."

"You want us to eavesdrop?" Bernie said in mock horror.

Libby grinned. "Heaven forfend."

"I'm shocked, shocked and appalled. Suggesting we listen in on what is obviously a private conversation. Tsk. Tsk." Bernie swept a loose strand of hair off of her forehead and pinned it up. "Okay. You win. I guess I'm going along because we're tradespeople and tradespeople have low morals."

"I'll tell that to Brandon," Libby said.

Bernie laughed and punched Libby in the arm. "He already knows. That's why he loves me."

"Then what did you hit me for?"

Bernie shrugged. "Because I can."

She leaned over and gave her sister a quick hug. Libby hugged her back. Then both women slowly tiptoed in the direction of the conversation, if that was what it could be called. *Arguing* seemed like a more appropriate term to Bernie. So did *quarreling* and *squabbling*.

"Melissa, you have to wait for the lawyer," Libby could hear a woman saying in a very loud voice.

"Why, Lexus? He's dead."

"It doesn't matter, Melissa. You can't take things that don't belong to you."

"But this painting does belong to me, Lexus. Dad promised me this Potter. It's in his will."

"No, Melissa, it isn't."

"Lexus, he showed me the will. I saw it."

"That was before he changed it."

"He didn't change it."

Libby could hear the alarm in Melissa's voice.

"He most certainly did."

"I don't believe you, Lexus." Now the alarm was turning to anger.

"Believe what you want, Melissa. It's true."

"You're a liar and a slut."

"At least, I'm not a compulsive gambler, Melissa."

"I most certainly am not."

"That's what I would call a person that loses ten thousand dollars in the casino in one night."

"I never did that," Melissa huffed.

Lexus waved her hand. "Fine," she amended. "Nine thousand five hundred."

"I'm not going to be distracted by your accusations, Lexus. The bottom line is, you can't take what belongs to me."

"It doesn't belong to you, Melissa," Lexus screamed. "Nothing belongs to you. Your father wrote you out of his will."

"I spoke to Dad last week and he said I was in it."

"Well, your father changed it two days ago."

"Show it to me. I want to see it."

"I can't right now."

"That's because there isn't one."

"No. That's because your father put it in a safe place."

"Ladies," said a voice, which Bernie recognized as belonging to Perceval, "you need to stop this. My brother wouldn't have wanted you fighting like this."

"Oh, please, Perceval," said a woman whose voice Libby couldn't place. "Your brother liked seeing everyone fight over the money. He fostered it."

"That's not true, Greta," Perceval protested.

The woman who was Greta laughed. "Of course it is. The only reason you're here now is that you were afraid your brother would disinherit you if you didn't show up for Thanksgiving. Do us all a favor and stop trying to play the good guy. It's annoying."

"I'm not playing at anything, Greta," Perceval said. "I'm just trying to get people to calm down. This wrangling . . ."

"Wrangling?" Greta said.

"Arguing, for those of us with a limited vocabulary, and what do you mean, 'stop trying to play the good guy,' Greta?"

"Exactly what I said, Perceval. You're certainly not one to point the finger. You and Ralph were rifling through Monty's desk drawers when the rest of us came in."

"I wasn't rifling through anything, as you so crassly put it. I was looking for important papers that we are going to need."

"Like Monty's will, Perceval?" Greta said.

"Among other things."

"You were looking to steal it."

"That is a totally unwarranted accusation," he said.

Bernie could hear indignation in Perceval's voice.

"Is it? Monty was supposed to be turning the company over to me and Bob and Audie today."

"That's absurd."

"Is it?" Greta asked.

"Yes. I would have heard if that were true," Perceval said. His voice went up an octave.

"So would I," Lexus said.

"Me too," Melissa added.

"Well," Greta said, "I think one of you did find out about that, and I think one of you killed Monty before the papers could be signed."

"What a horrible thing to say," Perceval countered, his voice quavering with indignation.

Bernie and Libby could hear Greta's laugh. They decided that she seemed to be enjoying herself.

"You and Ralph were the ones that arranged this meal, weren't you?" Greta said.

"At everyone's request," Perceval said.

"Not mine."

"That's because you invited yourself, Greta. We didn't even know you were coming until you called and told us you were arriving this morning."

"I didn't invite myself, Perceval. Your brother invited me and my cousins."

Libby and Bernie could hear Perceval sniff.

"He never told me, and I'm sure he would have. We just have your word on that."

"Maybe he didn't want you to know until the last minute. Maybe he had an announcement to make that he was saving up till dinner."

"And maybe you're making it all up, Greta. As per usual."

"Aren't you interested in what he was going to say?" Greta asked.

Lexus reentered the conversation. "You've already told us multiple times," she said. "None of us are interested in listening to your lies, and since my husband is dead now, it doesn't really matter, anyway."

"How convenient for you," Greta retorted.

"You're just full of insinuations, aren't you?" Lexus replied. "Insinuations which I don't plan on dignifying."

"Well, you did know that he would tap on the turkey pop-up button," Greta answered. "You can't deny that."

"Everyone knew that he would tap on the turkey pop-up button, and that includes you, Greta," Perceval said. "That's what he did. That's what he always did every Thanksgiving. Repeatedly. It was a family joke."

"Yes, Perceval, but all of you had a motive to kill him, which I did not."

"Sure you did, Greta," a new voice said.

"Ralph, are you accusing me?" Greta asked.

"Yes, Greta I am. You hated him as much as everyone else."

"I most certainly did not," Greta protested.

"You must have," Ralph retorted. "After all, you and your henchmen wrung every last cent you could out of my brother. That's not my definition of caring for someone."

"He was generous to me, Ralph, because I was nice to him. Unlike you."

"You weren't nice to him, Greta. You were scamming him."

"If that was true, Ralph, which it wasn't, why would I have killed him, then? Why kill the goose that lays the golden egg? Tell me that," Greta demanded.

"Maybe he finally got wise to your scams," Ralph told her. "Maybe he was going to have you arrested for embezzlement. Maybe that was the announcement he was going to make. In fact, the more I think of it, the surer I get that that was the case."

"Trying to dodge the bullet as per usual, Greta," Perceval observed.

"Meaning what, Perceval?" Greta demanded.

"Meaning exactly what I said, Greta," Perceval replied.

Chapter 11

Bernie and Libby stood beside the door. No one saw them, everyone still being engrossed in their conversations. The sisters took a moment to study the room and the people in it. Bernie estimated that the study was twelve feet by fourteen feet at most.

Crowded with mismatched sofas, chairs, and coffee tables, the room was a study in disharmony. The bookshelves looked as if they'd been bought at a deep, deep, deep discount store, probably, Bernie decided, because there wasn't much of a call for lilac bookshelves. In fact, she couldn't think of any reason why anyone would want to own something of that hue. Of course, the orange shag rug the bookshelves were standing on didn't bring out the best in the lilac, and the cheap dry-mounted reproductions hanging on the walls fought with the color scheme.

Lexus was by the window, and Bernie thought that judging from her appearance, it looked as if she'd recovered enough from the trauma of finding her husband's body to have reapplied her make-up and put her hair into an updo. Ralph and Perceval were situated a short distance away. They were standing next to a large oak desk, whose top was piled high with what Bernie presumed to be the contents of the drawers that had been pulled out.

Meanwhile, Melissa was leaning against the far wall, hugging a picture to her chest—*Must be the Potter,* Bernie thought—while Greta and Greta's two companions were sitting on the sagging sofa that was backed up against the near wall. Geoff was sitting off from everyone, with his head buried in his hands, inhabiting a cracked red leather chair that Bernie would have consigned to the rubbish pile.

It was almost a minute before the Field family became aware of Bernie's and Libby's presence, and it probably would have been longer still if Libby hadn't sneezed.

"Don't worry, folks," Libby said as everyone turned to look at her. "I'm not contagious."

Bernie plastered a big smile on her face and waved. "Hi, everyone. How's it going?" she said.

No one answered.

So much for the amenities, Bernie thought. "It's still snowing out," she announced.

"So we noticed," Ralph replied.

"It appears as if we're stuck here for the night," Bernie continued. *Nothing like stating the obvious,* she thought. If she expected anyone to offer her and Libby a room to sleep in, she was mistaken. "Are the sofas comfortable to bed down on?" she asked.

"I couldn't tell you," Melissa said. "I've never had the pleasure."

"I guess we'll find out," Libby said into the ensuing silence. "I mean, it's not as if we can go anywhere."

"Clearly," Perceval said, although the expression on his face, as well as the ones on everyone else's, said that they wished otherwise.

"I can't believe it," Geoff moaned, evidently oblivious to the hostilities swirling around him.

Either that or he was doing a really good job of acting, Libby thought. In any case, up until now he'd had nothing to contribute to the conversation, at least nothing that Libby had heard.

"You already said that," Lexus told Geoff. She'd added an expensive-looking white fur scarf to her outfit since she'd seen Monty's body.

Obviously not a PETA member, Bernie thought as she studied the scarf. She thought it was ermine, although she wasn't sure, since she'd never seen any outside of photos in fashion mags.

"In fact," Lexus continued, stroking her scarf, "you've said it multiple times. Everyone seems to be repeating themselves today."

Libby decided that she'd never seen a less grief-stricken individual than Lexus. Actually, that observation pretty much went for all of the Field clan.

"This is terrible," Geoff said, ignoring Lexus's rebuff. "Who would do something like this?"

"Obviously, someone who wanted Dad dead," Melissa replied.

Geoff let out another moan.

"Don't you think you're being a little overdramatic here?" Perceval asked.

Geoff gave him a stricken look. "How can you say something like that?" he demanded.

"Simple, Geoff. Admit it. You hated him just as much as the rest of us."

"No, Perceval. I didn't."

"You said to Melissa that you'd like to kill him."

"That was a figure of speech," Geoff cried. "Whatever he was, he was my father."

"Obviously," Melissa said.

Lexus rolled her eyes. "Well, someone here murdered Monty."

"It wasn't me," Geoff said.

"Hmmm." Lexus adjusted her fur scarf. She tapped her fingernails on her chin, then, after pausing for dramatic effect, raised one perfectly manicured hand and pointed to Bernie and Libby. "Maybe you're right, Geoff. Maybe it wasn't you. Maybe it was them."

"Or maybe it's the aliens," Bernie shot back. "Yes. I think I vote for them."

"You're absurd," Lexus replied.

"So are you," Bernie snapped. "In fact, the more you insist that Libby and I are responsible, the more it makes me think that you're responsible for Monty's death." Lexus opened her mouth to speak, but Bernie steamrollered over her. "Think about it. Why would Libby and I kill your husband, especially like that? That's not exactly good advertising for our business, is it? Of course it isn't," she replied when no one answered. "People would be afraid to buy anything we made." She turned to Lexus. "You should think before you make accusations."

Lexus shrugged. "I didn't accuse you. I was merely thinking out loud. And remember, I wasn't the one that called and told the police you killed Monty. Perceval was."

Perceval glared at Lexus before turning to Libby and Bernie. "It was an impulsive action. I was in shock when I called the police and spoke without thinking," he told them. "I've already explained that to you."

Libby stifled a cough. She hoped she wasn't coming down with a cold from the chill she'd gotten standing in the snow. "Well, I want to thank you for calling them back and retracting that statement," she said, being one of those people that believed in complimenting a person when they'd done something praiseworthy. Her dad called it her kindergarten mode.

Ralph frowned. "To be honest with you, I'm regretting that my brother did take his statement back."

"Regretting?" Bernie echoed. "How can you be regretting that?"

"Because," Ralph said as he buttoned up his sweater, "the more I think about it, the more I can't get around the fact that you were the people that stuffed the turkey."

"But we didn't stuff it with a bomb," Bernie said. "We used oyster stuffing, which someone took out and replaced with an explosive device, something, I might add, neither Libby nor I have any experience with, unlike all of you."

"So you say," Lexus said.

"Yes, we do," Libby shot back.

"Oyster stuffing doesn't explode," Bernie pointed out.

"Maybe you put some chemicals in it that made it do that," Melissa said. "I mean, we don't know what was in the stuffing, do we?"

"Celery, onions, garlic, cubed bread, oysters, salt and pepper were what was in the stuffing," Libby promptly replied. "Gunpowder was not one of the ingredients. And in any case, I have to ask you once again, why would we want to kill your father? You keep saying that, and you still haven't answered the question."

Melissa shrugged. "Lexus was the person who originally made that statement, not me. You should keep your facts straight."

"I don't care who made it. That's not the point at issue," Bernie said. Despite her best efforts, she could hear her voice getting louder. Talking with the Fields was like mud wrestling. Every time she thought she had hold of someone, they slithered away. "We have no motive."

Greta raised an eyebrow. "Let's be honest," she said, chiming in. "Monty was not a well-loved man."

"I'll take your word for that," Libby said, "because we've just seen him. He never came in our shop."

"But your father did," Ralph said.

"How is that relevant?" Libby demanded, remembering what Monty had said about her mother's cooking and wondering if that tied in with anything in some tenuous way.

Ralph snickered and turned to Perceval. "She wants to know how it's relevant," he said to him.

"Yes, I do," Bernie countered. "My father had contact with pretty much everyone in Longely. He was the chief of police."

"That's not what I was talking about," Ralph said.

"What are you suggesting?" Libby demanded, not liking the way the conversation was going.

Ralph smiled. "I'm not suggesting anything," he said. "I'm stating a fact. Ask your father what he did to my brother."

"Don't worry, Ralph. I will," Bernie replied, putting a good face on Ralph's comment, but inside she was confused. "But even if he did, so what? Whatever happened then has absolutely nothing to do with what happened today. I think you should spend a little more time looking a little closer to home."

Chapter 12

Bernie tried not to bite her lip while she thought. Was this why her dad hadn't wanted her and Libby to take the job? What was going on here? Why hadn't he said anything? Or was Ralph making this whole thing up as a way to distract her from the obvious? That was always a possibility, too. She decided to call her dad as soon as possible and find out what the story was.

Bernie took a deep breath to calm herself down. "I hate to tell you this," she said, going on the attack, "but when the police get here, they're going to realize it was one of you who killed Monty."

Ralph put his hands on his hips. "And why is that?" he demanded.

"Because from listening to the conversation all of you were having, it's clear to me that every single one of you has a motive for doing him in," Libby said.

"You were spying on us?" Ralph spluttered, indignation oozing out of every pore.

"Coming from you, that's pretty funny," Libby replied. "And we weren't spying. You were shouting at each other. We couldn't help hearing what you were saying."

"We weren't shouting," Lexus replied. "We were discussing, but even if we had been arguing with each other, that doesn't mean we killed Monty."

"One of you did," Libby told her. "After all, contrary to what you were implying, the turkey didn't explode on its own. Someone jerry-rigged it."

"Ah, now, there's a term I haven't heard in a long time," Ralph said, stroking his chin.

"I don't care what you've heard," Geoff yelled at Ralph as he jumped up from the chair he'd been sitting in and strode into the middle of the room. Everyone stopped what they were doing and looked at him. "This conversation is ridiculous."

Ralph raised an eyebrow. "Ridiculous? Would you care to elucidate?" Ralph asked Geoff.

Geoff waved his arms in front of Ralph's face. "Yes, I would. We should be focusing on Dad's body."

Perceval gave Geoff a puzzled look. "What do you want us to do with it?"

Geoff turned to face him. "We have to move it, obviously," he said.

"Unfortunately, we can't," Bernie informed Geoff. "It's a crime scene. We can't tamper with the evidence."

Geoff glared at her. "Well, we just can't leave my father lying halfway in the oven," he said. "It's not right."

"I agree," said Melissa.

"I sympathize," Bernie said. "But we really have to wait for the police to come."

Geoff pointed out the window at the falling snow. "That could be days."

Bernie privately agreed that could be the case. "We still have to wait," she said.

Lexus's eyes narrowed. "What do you mean, we can't move him?" she demanded. "How dare you say that? You aren't in charge. You can't tell anyone what to do. This is my house now. I give the orders here."

"So you say," Ralph said.

Lexus put her hands on her hips. "Yes, I do. And let me tell you there are going to be a lot of changes around here."

"The only change around here is going to be your leaving," Perceval told her.

Lexus laughed, cackled, really. "Don't you wish."

Please get me out of here, Bernie thought as she watched Lexus's nostrils twitch. Dealing with an exploding turkey and a dead guy was bad, but dealing with this family was worse.

"I'm not trying to tell anyone what to do. It's just a matter of preserving the evidence," Bernie explained to Lexus in as even a tone as possible. This, she decided, was going to be a very long night.

Lexus tossed her head. "I don't care. It's disgusting, and I don't want it where I have to see it. We're going to have to go in there, after all."

"Now your husband is an *it?*" Bernie commented. "That's certainly an interesting turn of phrase."

Lexus adjusted the neck of her white cashmere sweater. "Well, he certainly isn't a person anymore, is he?"

Bernie was about to reply when Perceval jumped into the conversation.

"Do whatever you want with my brother's body. I don't care. But, I'll tell you what I'm going to do," he said, facing everyone. "I'm going to turn up the heat. Now that my brother has passed on to that great place in the sky . . ."

"Hardly," Ralph murmured.

Perceval glared at him.

"Well, it's true," Ralph insisted. "He'd be in the other place. That is, if you believe in that kind of thing. Which I don't."

Perceval shot him another dirty look. "Let's leave theology out of this for the moment, if you don't mind. Now, as I was saying, there's no reason why we have to freeze to death anymore now that Monty isn't around."

"Good point," Melissa said. "I'll get the key. . . ."

"From his body?" Greta squeaked.

"Would you rather freeze to death?" Melissa asked her. "No, I thought not," she said when Greta didn't reply. "Fine then. I'll get the key and turn up the thermostat. Perceval, you help Geoff and Ralph with Dad."

Bernie sighed. What was the expression she was looking for? Something along the lines of being outnumbered and outgunned. "Fine," she said. "You do that and I'm calling the Longely police."

"Don't bother. I will," Lexus shot back as she whipped her cell off the side table.

Bernie had a bad feeling as she watched Lexus punch in the numbers. When Lexus got someone on the line, she asked to speak to Lucas Broadbent, chief of police, and Bernie's bad feeling grew worse.

"He wants to talk to you," Lexus said to Bernie once she had explained the situation to him, her smile leaving no doubt as to the outcome of the conversation.

Bernie took the phone reluctantly. Lucas Broadbent, known as Lucy to his detractors—which were legion—was not a big fan of her father or, by extension, of her and Libby.

"Yes," she said to him.

"How many times have I talked to you about interfering?" he bellowed in her ear.

Bernie held the phone back. "By that you mean solving cases, right?" she countered. "Or is it because Libby and I make you look bad?"

"You're just like your father," Broadbent yelled. "You never know when enough is enough, do you? I'm telling you to stay out of this."

" 'This' meaning Monty Field's murder?"

"What else am I talking about?"

"Just clarifying. I'd love to, but I don't think I can," Bernie told him.

"You'd better," Broadbent warned.

"Or you'll do what?" Bernie asked.

"I don't have time for this nonsense," Broadbent blustered. "I have people stranded all over the place. We'll take care of this Field thing when we can get up there."

"So it's okay for the family to move the body and tamper with the evidence?" Bernie persisted.

Broadbent muttered something Bernie couldn't catch. She thought he said, "Unbelievable," or words to that effect, before he hung up.

"See?" Lexus said as she took the phone out of Bernie's hand. "I told you."

"Don't you care about who killed your husband?" Bernie asked her.

Lexus took a hefty slug of the wine in her glass. "Of course I do," she said.

Her tone, Bernie decided, was anything but convincing.

"You certainly don't act that way," Bernie told her.

Lexus picked an invisible piece of lint off her sweater. "Ask me if I care what you think," she said.

"Obviously you don't."

"Obviously, you're correct."

"I guess we've reached a stalemate."

"I guess so."

Bernie repinned her hair, something she always did when she was thinking, and veered off to another topic. "I didn't know you were a friend of Lucy's," she told Lexus.

Lexus smirked. "I have lots of friends," she purred.

Bernie looked her up and down. "I just bet you do."

"What's that supposed to mean?" Lexus demanded.

"What you think it does," Bernie told her. Then she nodded to Libby. "Come on, sis, let's get out of here." And the two of them walked out of the room.

Chapter 13

Sean took a deep breath and listened to Bernie's voice mail for a second time. Suddenly he wasn't sitting by the pool in Martha's complex, soaking up the sun and trying to figure out how to politely decline going to a karaoke bar with Martha and her cronies that evening. He'd been running through his list of possible ailments he could suddenly develop without having to go to the hospital when he'd heard his phone ring.

But by the time he'd extracted the dratted thing from his jacket, it had stopped, a fact that irritated him no end. At least the old phones didn't move. They had substance. You knew where they were. Now you always had to go looking for them. Usually by the time he found it, the person on the other end of the line had hung up.

I mean, how was he supposed to remember where he put the phone? It was too small, anyway. The thing was made for a twelve-year-old girl. Just hitting those buttons was a chore. And it was light blue! What was Bernie thinking when she'd bought it for him? Imagine him liking the color. Phones were clearly meant to be black or silver. Then he'd listened to Bernie's voice mail and his irritation had been replaced by what? Alarm. Anger. Puzzlement. Shame. An emotional mess he couldn't sort out.

The question Bernie had posed in her voice mail immediately took him back to the last time he'd lost it. Sean sighed. He'd never discussed what had happened, not even with his wife. Especially not with her. What had happened was plain and simple. The facts weren't in dispute and never had been.

Sean took a sip of his water and put the bottle back down on the table. The sun was shining, it was a pleasant seventy degrees, and he was the only person at the pool. It hadn't been sunny back when it happened. He remembered the weather had been cold and raw. In the forties, with a cold rain falling.

It had been an unusually gray autumn, which hadn't offered much opportunity for leaf peeping. But that hadn't mattered to him. He'd been flying because he and Rose had bought the building on Main Street that the shop and the flat he and the girls now occupied were in. Rose had opened A Little Taste of Heaven three weeks after they'd moved in. She'd been so proud of it. Watching her bustle around the shop had made him smile. He'd loved sitting on a stool, sipping a cup of coffee, and watching her work.

Monty Field had walked into the shop on a Friday. No, it was a Tuesday, not that it really mattered, and he'd ordered $165.30 worth of fried chicken, coleslaw, green bean salad, mashed potatoes, brownies, and chocolate chip cookies.

Sean remembered the amount exactly. In those days $165.30 was a lot of money, and Rose was very excited. It was the first large order she'd gotten, and she'd worked very hard on it. Sean smiled as he remembered coming home after his shift and helping Rose mix up the chocolate chip cookies.

Monty had come back the next day and picked up the food. Unfortunately, after he put the order in the car, he realized that he didn't have his wallet with him, but he told Rose he'd be right back with the cash. And Rose had let him go. It was her second month in business, and she trusted everyone.

Only Monty Field didn't come back. He didn't come back that day or the next one or the one after that. He didn't answer Rose's calls or come to the door when she went up there. A month later Rose had come to Sean and asked him what she should do. And he said he'd take care of it. Rose had told him not to. In fact, she'd begged him to leave it alone, but he'd gone off, anyway. No one was going to treat his wife that way.

He was still in uniform when he'd jumped into his squad car and sped out to Monty Field's place. At that time Field lived a little farther up the road. It was late in the day, and he caught Field as he was coming out of his workshop. No one else was around when Sean had demanded Rose's money, which was a good thing, because the incident turned into one of those he said/he said deals.

Monty had told him he wasn't paying for inferior goods, or words to that effect. He'd told Sean that the chicken had been undercooked or burnt, that the coleslaw had made people sick, and that not only wasn't he going to pay Rose, but he was thinking of suing Rose for damages. Well, if there was one thing that Sean knew, it was that Rose's food was good. Her fried chicken was always perfect, and she was fanatical about keeping things at the proper temperature. So he'd lost his temper—he had quite a temper in those days—and he'd roughed up Monty Field. It wasn't anything that bad. Monty ended up with a few bruises and a cut lip. No broken bones. No concussion. Nothing like that.

But still it wasn't the kind of thing a sheriff should be doing. Even though Monty couldn't prove that Sean had done it—he denied it up and down—on some level the council knew that Sean was guilty as charged. So the politicians did what they were good at. They shushed things up and made a deal.

They gave Field a contract for the July Fourth fireworks on the town square and let him move his establishment to a noncommercial zone. After all, they didn't want to admit that their sheriff had beaten up a townsman. Understandably, because that would have opened them up to all sorts of liability charges. But Sean was sure it was one of the things—not *the* thing, but one of the things—that had gotten him dismissed from his job when he'd arrested the mayor's stepson for playing mailbox baseball.

Sean took a sip of his drink. However, all this had happened a long time ago—it felt like a different lifetime, when he'd been someone else—and he couldn't see any connection between him and Monty Field and Monty Field's murder. Lamebrains that they were, Monty's brothers, always a pair of winners, were probably just looking to deflect suspicion onto his girls.

God, he wished he could be up there now. But he couldn't. No flights were going in or out of any of the New York City airports. He'd checked multiple times, and nothing was flying into or out of the tristate area.

The Weather Channel announcer had reported that the storm wouldn't be tapering off until tomorrow and the cleanup would probably take a day or two. Realistically speaking, he wasn't going anywhere anytime soon. And really, he told himself, the truth was that even if he had stayed in Longely, he couldn't have gotten to his daughters, anyway. He'd be at the flat and they'd be at the Field house. The situation would have been the same. But it still didn't make him feel any better.

Not that that was the issue at the moment. His issue was, what should he tell Bernie and Libby? He mulled that over for a few minutes, and after going through several variations of the events that had transpired, he decided that he'd better tell them the truth. All of it. When he thought about it now, he realized that although he'd gone about dealing with Field in the wrong way, his instincts had been good.

He had nothing to be ashamed of. Even though he'd acted unprofessionally, his offense had been committed for a good cause. When he'd gotten that settled in his mind, he punched in the numbers to Bernie's cell and told her what had happened between him and Monty Field all those years ago.

As it turned out, he was glad he called, because the Field brothers had already hinted at the incident and this gave him a chance to set the record straight. Sean thought the conversation went well, and he was just about to hang up when Martha and her cronies came marching out of the condo complex and surrounded him, making him feel around two.

"Who are you talking to?" Martha asked, nodding at Sean's cell phone. When he said, "Bernie," she grabbed the phone out of his hand without so much as a by-your-leave. "I just want to tell you your dad is doing fine," she blared. "We're taking him to play mah-jongg."

"Mah-jongg," Bernie repeated incredulously.

"Yes. And then we're all going to a tai chi class. You'll love it," she said to Sean, catching the look on his face. "Good-bye," she said to Bernie.

Sean grabbed for the phone, but it was too late. Martha had already hung up.

"I wasn't done," he protested.

"Sorry," Martha told him as she returned the phone. "You can call her back later."

"I can call her back now," he snapped as he punched in Bernie's number again. His call went straight to voice mail. He tried again.

Martha looked at her watch. "We're going to be late for the game."

"It can wait," Sean told his sister as he tried Bernie's number for the third time. Still nothing.

"There's a storm there, right?" Martha said.

Sean allowed as how that was correct.

"So the network is probably down."

"Possibly," Sean reluctantly agreed.

"Call someone else who uses that network and see."

Even though it pained Sean to follow one of Martha's suggestions, he called Ines's cell and got the same result.

Martha gave him the smug smile she had had when they were kids. "I'm right," she said triumphantly. "Maybe the network will come back up in a half an hour or so. You can try it at the game."

"I'm not going to the game."

"Of course you are. Joan will be disappointed if you don't come. She's been looking forward to it."

"But I don't play mah-jongg," Sean pointed out. He realized he was whining.

"You'll learn," Martha said as she yanked him out of his beach chair. "It'll be fun." Martha emphasized the word *fun*, which was when Sean recollected that his sister used to teach preschool.

"No, it won't be," Sean protested.

"You never did like learning new things," Martha observed as she handed Sean his cane. Then she added, "I'm not taking no for an answer."

"You never have," Sean mumbled.

Martha turned to face him. "What did you say?"

"Nothing."

"I heard you."

"Then why did you ask me what I'd said?"

Martha sighed. "You're right. Some things never change. How about gin rummy? You used to like that."

Seam smiled. "I did, didn't I?"

Martha clapped her hands. "At last, a positive response."

Then she changed the topic. "What were you talking about with Bernie and Libby, anyway?"

"Monty Field's death." And he told Martha what had happened.

"Joan will be interested to hear that," Martha said when he was through.

"Why?"

Martha gave him an incredulous look. "Because she lived next to him."

"Joan Adams? So you're in contact with her?"

"Of course I'm in contact with her. Who do you think we were going to be playing mah-jongg with?"

"You're kidding."

"Why do you think I told you she was looking forward to seeing you?"

Sean didn't say anything.

"You haven't been listening to a thing I've been saying, have you?"

"Sure I have."

"No, you haven't."

"Does she live around here?"

Martha pointed to the entrance of a five-story building. "She's waiting for us in there."

Sean started walking again. For the first time since he'd arrived, he was glad that he'd come down.

Chapter 14

"At least now we know why Monty told us what he did," Bernie said, thinking of the conversation they'd had about her mother's chicken.

"Dad should have told us," Libby said.

"I can see why he didn't want to."

"I can see, too. Poor Dad."

The sisters were on the other side of the kitchen, conversing in a low voice as they watched Perceval, Geoff, and Ralph pull Monty's body out of the oven and wrap him in an old quilt Lexus had given them. It was a quilt, Bernie couldn't help reflecting, that looked like something you'd wrap around furniture when you were moving.

"Dad will survive," Bernie told her.

"But not happily," Libby said.

"That's true," Bernie replied.

Libby didn't comment. She was wondering where the three men were going to store Monty Field's body.

"I bet he'd rather be here," Bernie continued.

"Dad? Without a doubt," Libby replied, refocusing on what her sister was saying. "I think he'd rather be in the middle of a firefight than there, given what you told me."

Bernie grinned. It was a well-known fact that her dad

hated playing dominoes and checkers, but he reserved his special scorn for mah-jongg. Bernie remembered him saying, "A game for rich, spoiled old ladies who have nothing better to do." Talk about karma. The idea of her dad playing that made her laugh out loud. "If my cell were working, I'd love to call and tell him I told him he shouldn't go down there," she told Libby.

"Which would be cruel," Libby said.

"But satisfying." Bernie gave her cell another glance. It was still a no-go. She made a face. "Unfortunately, it's not an option."

Her reception had gone out right after Martha had hung up her dad's phone, so she and Libby hadn't been in touch with their dad since then. Not being able to talk to him made her nervous. Which was ridiculous. She wasn't two. But since there was nothing she could do about it, she turned her attention back to the drama at hand.

"So where are you taking him?" Bernie asked Geoff as she watched Geoff, Perceval, and Ralph trot by with Monty Field's body wrapped in the quilt.

"To the garage, of course," Geoff replied. "Where did you think we were going to put him?"

Bernie shrugged her shoulders. "I guess I thought you'd have him lying in state in his bedroom."

"Maybe we should do that," Geoff said to Ralph, having missed the sarcasm in Bernie's comment.

"Hardly," Ralph replied. "Lexus would have a fit."

"One of the other bedrooms?" Geoff said.

"No. They're all occupied. The garage is the only available space."

"Somehow it doesn't seem very respectful."

"Well, it's better than having your dad lying around the kitchen," Perceval pointed out to Geoff.

Geoff waffled. "I don't know," he said.

Ralph snorted. "Come on," he said to Geoff. "Let's go. Monty's getting heavy."

"That's because he's deadweight," Perceval rejoined. "Don't you get it," Perceval said when no one laughed. "Deadweight. Ha. Ha. Ha."

Geoff scowled. "That's not funny, Perceval," he said as he shifted his grip so he could get a better grasp on his father's body.

"You never did have a sense of humor, not even when you were a kid," Perceval told him as the three men started walking again.

"I laugh when something's funny," Geoff retorted. "And you're not. Dad didn't think you were, either."

"Your dad wouldn't have recognized a joke if it came with a laugh track attached to it," Perceval told Geoff as the men neared the door.

"Just because he didn't think that blowing up Lexus's van with a bottle rocket was funny," Geoff said.

"Oh, please. Let's not exaggerate. The van was just damaged a little. And, anyway, Geoff, it was your rocket."

"Yes, it was, but I wasn't going to set it off."

"That's not what you told Melissa," Perceval replied.

Bernie could see the color rising in Geoff's cheeks.

"By all means, take her word for it," Geoff said. "She wouldn't know the truth if it hit her in the head."

Ralph spoke before Perceval could answer. "Please, gentlemen," he said, addressing both men. "Could you stop bickering and show a little respect."

"For Monty?" Perceval's tone was incredulous. "Why? He never had any respect for me or for you, either, for that matter."

"I wouldn't go that far," Geoff said.

"I would," Perceval replied. "Look what he did to us. If that doesn't show a lack of respect, I don't know what does."

"I have to agree," said Ralph. "Treating us like we were kids. Making us account for every cent we spent. That was just wrong."

"Maybe he had a reason for doing that," Geoff protested.

"You can't be serious," Perceval retorted.

"I am."

"Sure. The same way he made Alma account for every penny she spent," Ralph observed.

Geoff rubbed his hands together. "Money doesn't grow on trees, you know."

"Oh my God," Perceval said. "Now you're sounding just like him. Why are you defending him when he treated you like dirt, too?"

But Bernie couldn't hear Geoff's reply, because by now the three men and the corpse were out in the hallway.

"Ah, that's what I love about the holidays," Bernie said. "They always bring out the best in everyone."

"So it would seem," her sister said. "So it would seem."

Chapter 15

Libby took a tissue out of her shirt pocket and blew her nose.

"I hope you're not getting sick," Bernie said. "Because if you are, please stay away from me."

"Lovely," Libby replied when she was done blowing.

"Well, you'd say the same thing," Bernie countered.

"No, I wouldn't."

"Fine, but you'd think it."

"That's different from saying it."

"How so?"

"It's not as rude."

Bernie shook her head. "Let's agree to disagree on this one," she said. "Good," Bernie said when Libby nodded. Then she said, "I wonder if Perceval and Ralph really overspent or if Monty was just being incredibly cheap."

"Well," Libby replied, "we know that Monty was a skinflint. Look at this house. There are the public areas and the private areas, and he spent no money in the private areas. At all."

"Agreed," Bernie said, studying at the kitchen again. "If what they said is true, it had to be difficult for Perceval and Ralph to live like that," she mused. "Having to account to your brother for every cent you spent."

"I certainly would find it demeaning," Libby said.

"But demeaning enough to murder someone?"

"Absolutely," Libby said. "People have killed people for a lot less, as you know. Things build up and up, especially if you work with someone day after day. And you have that whole family history going on. That never helps."

"What do you think about trying to put the blame on us?" Bernie asked Libby.

"I think it's a really lame move," Libby said. "I think it's the move of someone who is not well grounded in reality."

"And yet the whole family seems to be falling in with it."

"And why not?" Libby said. "It's convenient. If it flies, fine, and if it doesn't, they haven't lost anything. It's a distraction."

"True." Bernie checked her reception again. There was still no service. Something occurred to her. "Have you seen a regular phone around here?" she asked Libby. If there was, she could use that to call her dad.

Libby thought for a moment. "Now that you mention it, no."

"So we're really on our own," Bernie observed.

"Apparently so. See?" Libby said. "Sometimes new technology isn't the best."

Bernie opened her mouth and closed it again. This wasn't the time to get into an argument about the need for a new, computerized cash register. They could do that back at the shop. For a moment both sisters were silent while they thought about their predicament.

"It could be days before we get out of here," Libby said, breaking the silence.

"Well, a day," Bernie, always the more optimistic of the two, replied. "At least we have food and a place to sleep."

Libby rebuttoned her sweater. "And a corpse in the garage."

"Nothing is perfect."

"Very funny, Bernie."

"But it's true. I hate to say this, but I'm kinda glad Monty's out of the kitchen," Bernie said.

"Actually, I am, too," Libby admitted. "The thought of looking at him whenever I had to go in here was freaking me out."

"Not that we should be going in here and contaminating the crime scene," Bernie said.

Libby chewed on the inside of her lip. "It's already contaminated, what with everyone trooping in and out of here."

Bernie took another look around the kitchen. It was truly beyond bleak. She was willing to bet that Monty's first wife had never set foot in the place, and she was certain that Lexus never had.

"I would hate to work here," Libby said, echoing Bernie's thoughts.

"Me too," Bernie agreed. "Some pictures on the walls would help."

"And a paint job."

"And new counters and a backsplash."

"In fact," Libby said, "ripping the whole thing out and starting over would help." She nodded toward a lower cabinet drawer. "I wonder why Monty never followed the plans he had drawn up that we found."

"Probably cost too much money," Bernie said.

"Probably," Libby echoed. "So, now what?"

"Now we find out who killed Monty."

"Do you have a plan?"

"No. I'm figuring we'll just shake things up and see what happens."

"I'd feel better with a plan."

"I know you would, but this is the best I can come up with at the moment. Or we could just sit around by the fire and toast some marshmallows and wait for enlightenment," Bernie said.

"That's what we would be doing if we were home," Libby said.

"Waiting for enlightenment?"

"Toasting marshmallows. If we were home, we could even make the marshmallows."

Bernie laughed. "Now, that's going a little overboard."

"But they *are* better," Libby insisted. She had made a couple of batches last winter and was thinking of making some again. They really were a different animal from the store-bought ones. They were different enough that she thought she might have a market for them. "I tell you one thing," she continued. "I certainly wouldn't want to sit around the fire with the Field clan."

Bernie laughed again. "Why? Because they're such lovely, warm people?"

"Yup. They're just a delightful group," Libby said. "So who do you think is the guilty party?"

"It could be anyone, although Geoff seemed pretty upset about his father's death. Maybe too upset," Bernie observed.

"True," Libby said, thinking back. "He was a little over the top, especially considering the way his dad spoke to him about our van. And he was really pissed at him about that."

"He doesn't conceal his emotions well, does he?" Bernie noted.

"Not at all," Libby agreed. "On the other hand, I keep coming back to the fact that Ralph and Perceval were the ones that ordered the turkey. . . ."

"Yes, but everyone knew that. And everyone knew about Monty's habit of tapping on the pop-up button," Bernie replied.

"And the fact that he insisted on having one of those frozen, battery-raised turkeys for Thanksgiving. I thought they were awful before," Libby said. "But I'll never be able to pass them in the meat department again without thinking of Monty."

"Yeah," Bernie said. "If you or I were going to kill someone with one of those, we'd hit them over the head."

"That's because we don't know about explosives." Libby bit at her cuticle. "But everyone here does."

"I'm not sure about Lexus. I can't see her getting her hands dirty."

"Maybe she got someone to help her."

"That's a distinct possibility." Bernie rubbed her hands together. If the heat was on, she wasn't feeling it in the kitchen. "After all, Geoff, Perceval, and Ralph have all had experience with explosives. But you know, when I think about it, that device would be extremely simple to rig. All you'd need is some black powder, which you can get at any sporting goods store, a nine-volt battery, and a couple of leads, and you're in business. You or I could do it."

"Not me," Libby said.

"Well, maybe you're right about that," Bernie conceded. "You don't do explosives."

"Or windows. How do you know so much about building bombs, anyway?" Libby demanded.

Bernie grinned. "Last year of high school. Rian Sutter."

"Mom liked him."

"That's because she didn't know we were out at Luell Park, blowing up tree stumps. He used to let me help."

"How exciting," Libby said.

"I thought so."

"How come you never told me?"

"Because you would have run straight to Mom."

Which was a fact Libby didn't even try to deny. "Whatever happened to him, anyway?" she said instead.

"Last I heard, he was working as a ski instructor somewhere in Vermont. I will say it was fun."

"What?"

"Blowing things up. It gave me a real sense of power." Bernie was silent for a moment. Then she said, "Let's not forget about Melissa. She didn't seem real happy with her dad."

"No, she didn't," Libby agreed. "But remember how she bragged that she was better than Geoff with explosives?"

"Yeah. So?"

"So why would you want to brag about something like that if you'd rigged the turkey? It seems to me as if you'd be trying to make yourself out to be incompetent."

"Maybe she doesn't care. Maybe she figures she'll never get caught. Maybe she's got an ego thing going."

"Maybe," Libby agreed, even though she wasn't convinced. She stamped her feet to keep the circulation going. "What about the three cousins?" she said suddenly.

"What about them?" Bernie asked. As her mother would say, the cold was settling in her bones.

"Well, from the conversation we overheard, it sounds as if they were getting something from Monty, which would rule them out motivewise."

"That doesn't necessarily have to be true," Bernie said. "Maybe they were lying to everyone. Maybe as Perceval . . ."

"Ralph . . ."

". . . whoever said, they found out that Monty was about to cut them off and they decided to dispose of him before he could."

Libby sucked in her breath and let it out. "We don't know that."

"We don't know anything," Bernie replied. "Really, when you come down to it, we have eight people who in varying degrees had the motive and the means and the opportunity to kill Monty," she said to her sister.

"This is true," Libby replied, "but Perceval and Ralph are still at the top of my list."

"Mine, too, if it comes down to it," Bernie said. "At least Alma isn't here. We can eliminate her."

"If Alma was here, we wouldn't be," Libby pointed out. "The bottom line is we don't know anything that will help us sort this out."

"We don't know anything *yet*," Bernie corrected. "The operative word here being *yet*. But we will before the police arrive."

"You have an idea."

Bernie beamed. "I thought you'd never ask."

"I was afraid of that."

"You're going to like this."

"No, I'm not."

"Okay, you're not, but it's something I think we have to do."

"And that is?"

"Look in the bunker."

"You're kidding me, right?"

"Not at all."

"And we should do that, why?" Libby asked. The idea of going to a place where there was lots of explosive material definitely did not appeal to her.

Bernie shrugged. "Well, Monty was killed by an explosive device. I'm betting that's where it was probably made. And there might be business files that we can take a gander at. Plus, no one is there right now, so now is the time to take a look."

"No one with any smarts is out anywhere right now," Libby said.

Bernie smiled. "Exactly," she said. "Which leaves the field to us."

Libby nodded reluctantly. Much as she hated to admit it, what Bernie said made sense. Although maybe not. After all, whoever rigged the turkey probably hadn't left a note saying, *Hey, guys, I've done it. Come and get me. I'm in the study.* On the other hand, the files might contain some useful information. They wouldn't know that until they looked. It was a way to get started, or as her mom would have said, it was something to do, and doing something was better than doing nothing, because if you did nothing, then nothing was ever going to happen.

"If we can get in there," Libby said, making one last excuse to postpone the inevitable. "The door is probably locked."

"It might be, but we won't know if we don't try," Bernie answered. She looked out of the window at what was going on outside. "It's going to be a fun walk," she said. "Don't you want to get out there and test yourself against the elements?"

Libby turned and studied the snow. "I can't imagine anything I'd rather not do," she replied. Bernie liked storms and extreme weather, whereas she did not.

Bernie laughed. "The bunker really isn't that far from the house."

Libby noted that her sister's tone was dubious. "It's far enough," she said, "especially considering that we don't have the right gear. Like decent boots. Or goggles."

"Oh, pooh," Bernie said. "Who needs boots, anyway? And as for goggles—give me a break! It's not as if we're taking a walk across Antarctica and are going to come down with snow blindness. What are you, anyway? A woman or a wimp?"

"A wimp."

Bernie didn't argue the point. Instead she said, "Let's suit up and get going."

"I don't think this is such a good idea," Libby persisted. The storm. Going into a place that housed explosives. Everything about this little venture spelled trouble to her.

Bernie shrugged. "If you don't want to go, that's okay with me."

"I'm not saying that. I'm saying I don't think it's safe."

"Don't be silly. It's a three-minute walk. At most. And I promise nothing is going to explode when we're in there. Listen, seriously, if you don't want to come, you don't have to. I'll go by myself. It'll be fine."

"No. I'll come," Libby said. After all, she couldn't let her sister go off in that storm by herself. What would her dad say? He'd never forgive her if something bad happened.

"You're sure?"

Libby sighed the sigh of the long-suffering. "I just said I was, didn't I?" she answered as she followed Bernie out of the kitchen, down the hallway, and to the front door.

Chapter 16

Libby and Bernie didn't encounter any of the Field clan on their trip to the front hallway, which Bernie decided was a good thing. The fewer excuses and evasions she had to come up with, the better.

"Where do you think they all are?" Libby asked Bernie while her sister turned the latch on the front door lock to the open position. Bernie wanted to make sure they could get in when they returned.

Bernie glanced up and shook her head. "Not a clue." It was quiet in the house, she thought. Too quiet, really. Where was everyone? There were eight people in here, after all. But she couldn't hear anyone moving around. She couldn't hear the television going. She couldn't hear any music. The phrase *snow-shrouded silence* came to mind.

"Maybe they're all in the garage, saying a prayer over Monty's body," she suggested as she opened the door a fraction of an inch. She quickly closed it again to make sure the lock was disengaged, but she didn't close it quick enough. A fingerling of wind managed to push its way through the crack and deposit a small pile of snow onto the hallway floor.

Libby looked at the snow and wished she was in Florida with her dad. "Spitting on it would be more likely," she said as she zipped up her parka and flipped her hood up in preparation for going outside.

She hunted for her gloves in the pockets of her parka, but they weren't there. She realized she must have dropped them when she and Bernie tried digging out the van. Terrific. By now they were probably buried under another six inches of snow. Oh well, she'd just have to go with cold hands.

"Ready?" Bernie asked.

"Not really," Libby replied.

And truth to tell, she never would be. She didn't like cold weather, which Bernie knew, and storms like this made her nervous, which Bernie also knew. For a moment Libby felt a flash of resentment against her sister for making her do this, never mind that her sister wasn't really making her, her own sense of guilt was, and that she could have said no but hadn't.

Bernie pulled the front door open. She had to hang on to it tightly because otherwise the force of the wind would have sent it smashing up against the wall.

"Here we go," she said.

"This is horrible," Libby cried as she and her sister stepped out in the maelstrom.

Bernie shut the door behind them.

The figure lurking behind the column that divided the living room and the hallway watched Bernie and Libby leave. El Huron had listened to Libby and Bernie talking among themselves as they made their preparations for their exit. Their conversation had amused El Huron. The sisters were resourceful, El Huron thought. El Huron, as the figure had come to name itself, would give them that.

But they were careless, careless the way people who had

been protected and coddled all their lives tended to be, careless in the way that people to whom nothing truly bad had happened were. They should be more careful. They should check to see who was around before talking about their plans in a voice that could be heard by strangers. Their father had probably warned them about this sort of foolishness, but they hadn't listened, and now they would pay the penalty.

El Huron always checked everything. Twice. Or more. One could never be too careful. That was the lesson El Huron's mother had taught. El Huron smiled again, thinking about the name. "Ferret." That's what *el hurón* meant. At first the figure had thought about calling itself "the fox," but "the fox" was clichéd. And, anyway, the movie *El Zorro* had ruined the name. Then the figure had considered "the lion," but the lion hunted in prides and tigers were dying out. Soon they'd exist only in cages.

No. Ferrets were good. Ferrets were survivors. They endured no matter what. Both the males and the females were equally ferocious. They'd attack and win against an adversary five times, even ten times, their size. And they were smart. They could figure things out. They learned from observation. And most importantly, they could slip in and out of places most other animals couldn't get into. They could flatten themselves down until they were almost invisible. No one noticed them. Not when they didn't want to be seen.

El Huron had practiced the art of invisibility since being a small child and had accumulated lots and lots of information in that manner. People constantly underestimated El Huron, and that was a mistake. As Libby and Bernie would find out shortly. They should have left well enough alone.

Now, however, they were making extra work for El Huron. So El Huron would be forced to teach them a lesson. And that would be easy. Too easy, really. Just like Monty's turkey was easy. A little of this. A little of that. A fuse. And bang. There you were. El Huron had tried to talk with him. To reason with him. To give him chances. But he hadn't listened. He'd never listened. Neither did the family, for that matter. Everyone was too busy trying to get everything they could for themselves.

The figure cocked its head and thought. Maybe El Huron would give Libby and Bernie a break. El Huron didn't dislike them. Not really. If anything, El Huron felt pity for them. They could have been anybody. They were merely a means to an end. Or maybe El Huron wouldn't give them a break. Maybe their time had come. Still, the skinny one with the dark hair had given El Huron a cookie once. El Huron remembered when people were nice. No, El Huron would decide when the time came by flipping a coin. Leaving things in the hands of fate pleased El Huron. El Huron smiled. The smile grew into a grin as El Huron reviewed the plan for what must have been the hundredth time. El Huron believed in preparation.

The wind was gusting at forty miles an hour, driving the snow in horizontal lines, as Bernie and Libby moved away from the house. Snowflakes pelted their cheeks, stung their eyes, and melted on their lips. Bernie stuck out her tongue. The snowflakes left a slight taste of salt.

Both women found it difficult to see anything. The entire world had turned white. The earth and the sky had merged into one mass. For a moment, Libby couldn't tell up from down or left from right. She felt dizzy and had to take a deep breath to steady herself.

Maybe Libby was right about being out here, Bernie thought as she pulled the turtleneck of her sweater over her mouth and secured her hood under her chin. This was worse than she thought it would be. Maybe they should have waited to go outside, not that Bernie would tell her sister that.

"I'm not even sure where the bunker is," Libby shouted to her sister as she wrapped her scarf around her mouth and her nose to make breathing easier. "I'm not sure where anything is." She couldn't see more than a couple of inches in front of her.

"I think I know," Bernie shouted back. "I think it's straight ahead and then we take a jog to the right."

"You think?"

"I know," Bernie lied. "Trust me."

Those were the kinds of words that sent shivers down Libby's spine. The last time Bernie had said that, she and Libby had ended up in an oak tree—literally—sitting on a branch and waiting for a night watchman to leave. Her idea of risk and Bernie's idea of risk were not the same.

"I guess I'm going to have to," Libby said in spite of that, "because I don't have a clue where we should be going." And much as she wanted to, she wasn't going back, either, because she needed to stick with her sister, whom she'd dearly love to strangle at the moment.

Actually, Libby could picture missing the bunker entirely and staggering around and around until she and her sister froze to death. No one would miss them until it was too late. Okay, she knew the freezing-to-death part was a bit melodramatic, that she and Bernie were in Westchester, not the Arctic, but the vision persisted, anyway. After all, people had died inches from their tents because they couldn't see them. They'd walked by them. Of course, that was on Everest and this was in Westchester County. There was a difference. She knew that. Still, the vision persisted.

For a moment, she thought of sharing her concerns with Bernie, but then she thought better of it. She would only mock her out. Libby decided her dad was right as she sunk into snow over her knees. She *was* watching too much Discovery Channel. She could feel the cold white stuff working its way into her boots. Terrific. Now she could get pneumonia on top of everything else. She looked down to keep the snow out of her eyes as she slogged along, looking up once in a while to make sure that Bernie was in front of her.

Walking was hard work, and Libby's legs and feet got colder with every step she took. She contemplated returning to the Field house once again. This time she turned around to see if she could see the house, but she couldn't. All she saw was a vague gray shape that seemed to move, and then it was lost to view.

Well, that wasn't the house. It was too small. And, anyway, houses didn't move. Or maybe it was a corner of the Field house and her eyes were playing tricks on her, though when she thought about it again, the shape did look somewhat personlike, if that was a word.

Libby squinted, hoping to see the gray shape again to better identify it, but now nothing was visible except the snow. There probably wasn't anything there, anyway, she concluded. *It's probably my imagination,* she thought as she turned back. But something about the shape bothered her enough to make her feel as if she should tell Bernie. Libby put her hand on her sister's shoulder. Bernie stopped and turned around. Her scarf and the front of her jacket were white.

"I thought I saw something moving in back of us," Libby blurted out.

"You mean a person?" Bernie asked.

"Something," Libby said, unable to be more accurate.

"It's just your mind playing tricks," Bernie told her, and she turned and started walking again before Libby could say anything else.

"I just hope you know where you're going," Libby said to Bernie's back.

Bernie didn't reply. *She probably can't hear me,* Libby reflected. Her feet were getting colder and colder with every step she took. They were starting to burn, and she couldn't feel her fingers anymore, even though she had them jammed in the pockets of her parka. And then there was the fact that her nose was running and her eyes were tearing from the cold. She was definitely not a thing of beauty at this moment. A few minutes later she saw another gray shape looming up in front of them. *Please let this be the bunker,* she prayed. She just hoped that the door to it was open, because she was turning into a Popsicle.

With the way her luck was going recently, the door would probably be locked, just as she predicted it would be, she thought glumly. Why she let Bernie talk her into things like this, she didn't know. After all, she was the oldest. She should be the one in charge. She took another step forward. Five more steps and she had come to the bunker. Now that she was closer, she could see it was the actual building.

Bernie was struggling with the door.

"Let me help," Libby said. She grasped the handle with Bernie, and they both yanked. They heard a pop, and the door went flying open, throwing them both into the snow.

"Guess it wasn't locked," Bernie said as she picked herself up and brushed herself off.

"Guess not," Libby agreed as she shook the snow off the back of her scarf as the door blew shut.

"Shall we try again?" Bernie asked, nodding toward the door.

Libby nodded back. At this moment she didn't care if there was enough nitro in there to blow herself and everyone else up. She just wanted to get in out of the storm.

"Here we go," Bernie said.

She and Libby braced themselves. They grabbed the

handle and pulled. This time they both managed to remain upright as the door swung open. Libby loosened her grip and edged her way inside. Bernie followed. The door shut with a thud. It was pitch black inside. The sisters couldn't see anything.

Chapter 17

"Wonderful," Bernie said as she fumbled around the walls, searching for the light switch. "We should have brought a flashlight with us."

"We don't have a flashlight," Libby reminded her.

Bernie was too busy cursing to reply. Actually, it didn't take her long to find the light switch, though as Libby would later tell her father, it seemed like an eternity, what with the wind making strange whistling noises outside.

"Got it," Bernie said and flicked the switch.

There was a whoosh and a fan turned on. *Must be the venting system,* Bernie thought as her fingers found the switch next to it and turned that one on as well. Suddenly the room was bathed in light. Pink, green, and blue auras danced in front of the sisters' eyes.

Libby blinked and looked around. She didn't know what she'd expected, but this was not it. "The place looks bigger from the outside," was the first thing she said as she took a step out of the small entrance foyer she and Bernie were standing in.

Bernie put her hood down and unzipped her jacket. "It does, doesn't it?"

"How on earth do they manufacture things here?"

"They don't." Bernie wiped the snow off of her cheeks with the back of her hand, then wiped that on the back of her jacket. "Remember, you told me this is where Monty and his family come up with new ideas for fireworks. It's not where they manufacture them. I think I remember reading that their plant is somewhere in Pennsylvania, which would make sense. Since it's illegal to sell fireworks in New York State, it might be illegal to make them here as well."

"And set them off," Libby added as she stamped the snow off her shoes. It made a little wet pile on the gray concrete floor.

"That's what I just said."

"I was thinking of Dad."

Bernie smiled. "Yeah, it used to piss Mom off no end when Dad lit them off on the Fourth of July."

"It certainly did."

Bernie laughed at the memory. "She used to get so angry."

"It never stopped Dad, though," Libby noted.

"No, it didn't, did it?" Bernie replied as she looked around. "In fact, it egged him on."

The room she was standing in was twelve feet by twenty feet and was lined with shelves on two sides. A bulletin board was affixed to the third side, which was the wall opposite the door. Two long metal tables, the kind one found in restaurants, ran the length of the shelving. Four office chairs on wheels were pushed under them. One of the tables had scales, measuring cups, mixing bowls, and retorts, as well as a box of Kleenex and a yellow legal pad.

"Just like home," Bernie said, indicating the bowls. "A pinch of this, half a cup of that, and voilà. You have an explosion."

"As in the turkey."

"Exactly," Bernie said.

Libby lightly touched the bowls and the scales with the tips of her fingers. "Really, if you put it that way, it's not that different from what we do. After all," she added, thinking of one of her earlier cooking mishaps, "if you add enough baking soda to cake batter, the cake explodes."

Bernie chuckled. "I'd forgotten about that."

"I haven't," Libby said, thinking back to how long it had taken her to clean the oven with her mother standing over her.

She looked at the pad. Someone had jotted down two numbers and a word. The first number was 899.92. That was followed by a question mark. The second number was spelled out. It was one million and was underlined three times. A little farther down the page was the word *Africa* and the word *GAB* spelled out in capital letters. At the bottom of the page the same person had written the word *explanation*. They'd underlined the word several times and followed it with five exclamation points.

Libby handed the pad to Bernie. "What do you make of this?" she asked.

Bernie studied the page for a little while. Then she said, "Well, for openers, look at the way *explanation* is written. The underlining, the exclamation points, the amount of pressure the person used bearing down on the pen. I'd say whoever wrote the word *explanation* was extremely upset. As in he wanted one and it had better be good."

Libby nodded. That was her feeling as well.

"My guess is that these notes refer to something that's happening in Africa," Bernie continued. "Maybe the company is sending fireworks to Africa. A lot of fireworks. A million dollars' worth is a lot of fireworks. So is eight hundred ninety-nine dollars and ninety-two cents, for that matter."

Libby sniffed. Her nose was still running and her throat felt tickly. Maybe her nose was running not because she was cold; maybe it was running because she was getting sick. She'd been fighting off something for a week now, and she was sure the little trek she'd taken hadn't helped.

Libby sniffed again. "Those numbers seem a little improbable," she replied. "Why wouldn't they make their own fireworks in Africa, instead of spending money to have them imported?"

Bernie shrugged. "Well, they send wallboard here from China, don't they?" she asked. "And I know they were sending bricks from there to here. I mean, these days who knows."

"That doesn't say a lot of good things about our economy," Libby said as she hugged her parka to her. It was cold enough in here so that she could see her breath. But she reminded herself it was still better than being outside. Hopefully, by the time they were done, the storm would have subsided somewhat.

"No. It doesn't. At least what we do can't be outsourced," Bernie said.

"That's true," Libby agreed.

Both sisters were quiet while they thought about that. After a minute or so had elapsed, Bernie went back to thinking about the matter at hand.

"Or maybe," she ruminated, "I'm wrong and there were two different sales, which would mean almost two million dollars' worth of fireworks. Wow. That's a lot of gunpowder."

"It certainly is." Libby didn't want to think about how much. "But what about the word *GAB*? That doesn't fit in anywhere."

"No, it doesn't, does it?" Bernie agreed. She studied the notepad some more. A moment later she had the beginnings of an idea. "What if the letters aren't a word?" she said slowly. "What if they're initials?"

"So?" Libby said. "I'm not sure what you're getting at."

"Well, what if the initials stand for Greta, Audie, and Bob? That would fit in with the rest of the page."

Libby grinned. "Yes, it would. And they did say they were here to see Monty about a business deal."

"Exactly. But maybe it's not a deal that's pending, but one that's already been completed."

"And the two numbers written on the page aren't two different deals, but the differential between what Monty expected and what he got."

Bernie nodded. "Hence the word *explanation*. As in he's demanding an explanation for the discrepancy."

"The only problem with that scenario," Libby countered, "is that Monty didn't seem upset when he was talking to them out front after we arrived. Quite the opposite, in fact."

"That's true." Bernie tapped the edge of the pad against her front teeth. "But maybe Monty was just acting. He strikes me as the kind of man who lulls someone into a sense of security and then pounces."

"He'd have them arrested if they were embezzling money, that's for sure," Libby said. "Look at what he did to Alma."

"Without a doubt. Maybe he was planning to have them arrested here and the storm interfered and Greta, Audie, and Bob found out and killed him first."

"How did they find out?"

"One of the other family members told them. Had to be," Bernie said.

"Why would they do that?"

"Because they wanted a share of the cash."

Libby nodded. "I can see that. But could they have jerry-rigged the turkey that fast?" she wondered out loud.

"If they knew what was going to happen, then they would have come prepared. But even if they didn't, even if they found out when they got here, it wouldn't take them that long to rig the turkey if they knew what they were doing."

"And you think they could have?"

"Absolutely. I bet if we talked to them, we'd find that they've been playing around with this stuff all their lives. It's a family business, after all."

Libby clicked her tongue against her teeth. "I guess now they've got a motive. If what we're postulating is true."

"Nice word."

"I think so."

"Hopefully, we can find something in the company files that will back this up."

"Facts are always good," Libby observed.

"So I've been told," Bernie said. Not that she necessarily agreed with that statement when the facts proved to be inconvenient.

She put the pad back down on the table and studied the shelves lining the bunker walls. On the far wall were containers of chemicals. Most of the containers were plastic. All of them had pasted-on white labels with the names of their contents carefully spelled out in big black block letters.

"Do you know what any of this stuff is?" Libby asked as she gave the wall a brief once-over.

Bernie shook her head. "Well, it's not used for making apple pies, that's for sure."

"I should have taken chemistry in college," Libby lamented.

Bernie laughed. "I doubt if that would help you with this," she said as she turned to study the contents of the shelves on the opposite wall. Those shelves were full of cartons with names like Fire, Black Cat, Big Shot, Ass Kickin' Mule, and Sundance written on them. "Fireworks," Bernie said, and she walked over and opened one called Great Bear. "I wonder what this is like when it goes off."

"Don't know. Don't care," Libby replied, her attention drawn to the bulletin board on the wall opposite the door.

She and Bernie moved toward it. The bulletin board was covered with news clips and photos of fireworks displays. Under each one, someone had written the location, date, and time of the event. Bernie noted that all the displays shown were on the East Coast. Then she noted that the handwriting under the displays was the same as the handwriting on the legal pad. Bernie wondered if it was Monty's. She thought it probably was.

"Nice displays," Bernie said, studying the pictures. "They look very professional." She indicated the room with a sweep of her hand. "So is this setup. Everything here is immaculate." She knocked on the wall the bulletin board was attached to. "I wondered if this wall is the weak one," she mused.

Libby looked at her sister. "Weak what?"

"Weak wall."

"What are you talking about?" Libby asked.

"Nothing. I just read somewhere that every building where they store fireworks in has one weak wall so that if there's an explosion, the entire place isn't leveled."

Libby crossed her arms over her chest. "This is not a piece of information I need to know."

"I thought you'd find it reassuring."

Libby gave her sister an incredulous glance. "Sometimes you amaze me."

"That's what Brandon says," Bernie replied.

"And he doesn't mean in a good way."

"Ha. Ha. Ha. I am a paragon of virtue."

Libby choked on her cough.

"Well, almost," Bernie conceded and she pointed to the next room. "That has to be the office. Maybe we'll find something that'll help us in there."

"I certainly hope so," Libby groused. "I'd hate to think that we took that walk for nothing."

"It wasn't that bad," Bernie said as she and Libby moved toward the office.

"You're just saying that to annoy me," Libby said.

"No, it's true," Bernie replied. "You know, testing your mettle against the outdoors and all that."

Libby rolled her eyes. "This from the woman who has

told her boyfriend the only camping she'd do is at a motel with a pool."

"That's different."

"How is it different?"

"Peeing."

"Peeing?"

"Yeah, the whole peeing and pooping thing. I'm not a big fan of doing it outdoors. The thought of wiping myself with leaves that could turn out to be poison ivy gives me the heebie-jeebies."

"That's what would happen to me," Libby said.

Bernie sniggered. "It did happen to you at Camp Wassatanga."

"I prefer not to talk about that," Libby said with as much dignity as she could manage.

By now both women were at the doorway to the office. They looked inside.

Their hearts sank.

Chapter 18

The place was a mess. There was no other word for it. Whereas the room outside was totally organized, the office was chaos. Papers were strewn all over the desk and the floor. They spilled out of the two file cabinets and onto shopping bags filled with what looked like unopened junk mail.

"Obviously, Monty's secretary quit," Bernie said.

"Yeah. About five years ago. If he ever had one." Libby massaged her forehead with her fingers. She was getting a headache.

"Or," Bernie continued, "someone could have gone through the papers already. That would be my thought."

"Not a happy one."

"No, it's not," Bernie agreed.

"Then we might be going through all these papers for nothing," Libby said, thinking once again of the walk they'd taken.

"Yeah, but we won't know until we do."

Libby groaned. She knew her sister was right.

"And we should do what we're going to do quickly, because the family is going to start wondering where we are pretty soon."

"Let them," Libby said, even though she didn't mean it. It would just make more trouble for them, which was the last thing she needed right now. She looked around, trying to come up with a battle plan, and that was when it hit her. "Do you see what's missing?" she asked Bernie.

"Order?" Bernie responded.

"Ha-ha. No. A computer. There is no computer."

"Maybe Monty didn't use one," Bernie suggested.

Libby pooh-poohed Bernie's statement. "Even I use a computer," she said. "I don't think you can be in business without one these days." She pointed to the power strip on the floor and the printer attached to it. "And if he didn't use one, then why would that be there?"

"Good point." Bernie sighed. "So someone took it, probably the same someone who went through the papers in the office."

"Or someone could have brought the computer back to the house to use. Or it could be in the shop, being fixed. Maybe the hard drive crashed."

Bernie went around the desk, opened a desk drawer, and rummaged around. A moment later she held up a pamphlet. "Well, at least we know the machine is a Dell laptop," she said. "Not that that helps a heap, since lots of people have them."

"Well, any information is better than no information."

"That's Dad talking."

Libby grinned. "When you hear something a thousand times, you tend to remember it."

"It wouldn't hurt to ask everyone at the house what happened to the computer," Bernie said as she continued to go through the desk drawers.

"It never hurts to ask. It's getting the answers that's the problem."

"Especially from that lot."

Bernie kept looking through the desk. She didn't find

much—just disks for old programs, wadded-up Kleenex, stubs of pencils, and bags of empty Snickers wrappers. What she didn't find was more significant. There was no address book, no directory of any kind, no appointment book, and no check ledger or deposit slips.

"Well, that's interesting," Bernie said as she closed the left-hand desk drawer, which had been empty except for a ball of rubber bands and a box of paper clips.

"Maybe Monty kept all of his numbers in his phone," Libby replied. "And his accountant writes his checks and files all his information."

"I'll give you his accountant, but not the phone book or the appointment calendar."

"Why?"

"Because smart phones are expensive, and pen and paper are cheap."

"Or he could have been one of those guys that keeps everything in his head."

"True. But there still have to be records somewhere," Bernie said. "The question is, where?"

"At his accountant's."

"Maybe."

"Most probably."

"Which we don't have a name for."

"Even if we did, he wouldn't tell us anything."

Bernie pulled the collar of her jacket up around her neck. "And there's something else."

Libby waited.

"Geoff and Melissa were in here when we arrived. Remember how they came running out of the bunker . . ."

"After they set off those fireworks." Libby grimaced. "How could I forget?"

"Which introduces a whole different set of dynamics. It means they either noticed the state of affairs in here and chose to say nothing—"

"Which is a possibility." Libby indicated the mess in front of her and Bernie with a wave of her hand. "Or they were responsible for this. . . ."

"Or this is how the place usually looks, so it wasn't worthy of comment."

Libby nodded her head emphatically. "Exactly."

"I find it hard to believe the latter," Bernie said.

"Me too," Libby agreed. "On the other hand, they weren't acting"—she paused to find the word she was looking for and finally settled on—"as if they'd done anything wrong."

"Well, they could have gone through the office earlier. They could have taken the computer then. In which case, they wouldn't be shocked or upset about what they found in there."

"But then why go back in?"

"True."

"Or the person who did this might have told them already," Libby pointed out. "And they might be covering for him or her."

"Also a possibility," Bernie conceded. "Or someone else could have snuck in here."

Libby sighed. "You realize we're just going around in circles."

"I know." Bernie refastened her hair. "It may come down to being a question of what's not here, rather than what is," she mused. "And that wouldn't be good for us, because a positive is always easier to deal with than a negative."

Libby just looked at her. "You realize I have no idea what you're talking about."

Bernie laughed. "I'm not sure that I have any idea what I'm talking about, either."

She tapped her teeth with her fingernails while she thought of the crew back in the house. She could easily see everyone there scamming money. She thought of Geoff and his father and what she'd overheard Ralph and Perceval say, not to mention Lexus, the loving wife.

Was there passion there or love? Probably not. But hate or revenge, on the other hand . . . Bernie could see that for sure. Family and business could be a bad combo under the best of circumstances, and this wasn't the best of circumstances.

"Okay," Bernie said. "On a practical level, I think we need to find everything that we can pertaining to Africa first. At least we know there should be files on that. And if they're not here, that will tell us something as well."

Libby nodded. "And then we should look at the other accounts and see who was handling them. That is, if anyone other than Monty Field was. I get the feeling the man was a total control freak. . . ."

"You mean jerk," Bernie said, thinking back to her dad's story about Field and her mom.

Libby nodded. "That too. And jerks make enemies. Serious enemies."

"Yes, they do." Bernie thought again about Field's family and about how little love seemed to be lost between its members, and felt a sudden rush of gratitude that her family wasn't like that.

Libby went over and looked through the three paper bags leaning up against the far side of the desk. They were filled with old newspapers and flyers. She sighed. "Nothing of use here. Maybe we'll turn something up in the files that will give us a hint on what direction we should be going in."

"And even if nothing turns up," Bernie said, "we'll get some background information on the operation, and that can't be a bad thing."

Libby stamped her feet to get her circulation going. Her feet were cold and wet, and the fact that she didn't have another pair of shoes or socks to change into filled her with dismay.

"How about you take the filing cabinets to the right and I'll take the rest of the paper bags and the file drawer on the left?" she suggested to Bernie.

"Works for me," Bernie said.

For the next ten minutes or so, aside from a muttered comment, Bernie and Libby worked silently. The only sounds were the howl of the wind and the rattle of the metal roof. Most of the papers in the file cabinet on the left-hand side of the room proved to be old orders, supply lists, receipts, and bills that needed to be paid, none of which were past due.

"Monty seems to have kept current with his expenses," Libby noted as she went through them.

"Always a good thing businesswise," Bernie shot back as she lifted a set of file folders out of the drawer and began looking through them. They proved to be bank statements from five years ago. "The business was definitely making money at that time," she commented as she perused them. Nothing leaped out at her. "I wonder where the current statements are."

Libby looked up. "Good question. If we had the accountant's name, we could call him up and ask him."

"But we don't have his name, so we can't."

"We should ask Ralph. Or Perceval."

"It would be interesting to see what they say . . . or don't say."

"I'm betting on the *don't say* myself." Libby closed the file drawer and started looking through some of the other bags full of papers. "Well, Monty definitely never met a piece of paper he didn't like, that's for sure. Most of this stuff is just junk," she said after a couple of minutes.

Bernie looked up. "So is this. I mean, why file articles on weight loss and termite control?"

"Because he wanted to lose weight and he had a termite problem."

"These are business files." Bernie shook her head. "There's nothing here about Africa. In fact, there's nothing here that's current. Just old water bills. Old utility bills. Old bills of lading." And Bernie shut the first drawer and opened the second one. It, too, was chock-full of files. "Maybe there's something about Africa in here." She bent down and quickly thumbed through the files. "Nope. Just more crap." She closed the second drawer and opened the third. It was empty. She cursed under her breath.

"What?" Libby asked.

"There's nothing here. I bet this is where the information we want to see was kept."

"Or not."

"Or not." Bernie wound her scarf more tightly around her neck. "Or maybe it was Greta or Bob or Audie who took the files."

"Or Ralph and Perceval."

"Or Lexus. Or Geoff and Melissa."

"Well, at least we know someone who hasn't taken the files."

"Who?"

"Monty."

"Not necessarily true. Maybe he hid them somewhere."

"Why would he do that?"

"Because he was stealing money and he didn't want anyone to know."

"Another motive for killing him."

"Without a doubt."

"Well, we are fairly certain of one thing at least," Libby said.

"What's that?"

"That that's Monty's handwriting on the pad."

Bernie nodded.

"So I guess we've made some progress," Libby said.

"A smidgen," Bernie said.

"What's our next step?" Libby asked her sister.

Bernie thought for a moment. "I think the question we have to answer is, what can we do with what we've got?"

"Meaning?"

"Well, we can't call on outside help."

"Correct."

"And no one wants to talk to us."

"Well, they'll talk. They just won't tell us the truth."

"Correct again. We're in a static situation."

"Agreed."

"So therefore we need to do something to make something happen."

"Why do I so think that's a bad idea?"

"Then what would you suggest, Libby?" Bernie asked.

"Look for the files. Look for the computer."

"We can do that as well."

"So how are we going to shake things up?"

"I don't know," Bernie confessed. "I haven't gotten that far yet. We should have gotten to the bunker earlier."

"I don't think it would have made a difference."

Libby was probably right, Bernie thought. The files and the computer had been taken before she and Libby got here. The likelihood was that they'd been taken before Monty was killed, although they could have been taken afterward, as well. Bernie tried to think back to everyone's movements and figure out where everyone was chronologically, but she couldn't. She'd been more focused on other things—like getting the van out of the snowdrift, bringing in the supplies, and trying to figure out where everything that they were going to need in the kitchen was.

She glanced at her watch. Although it seemed like a lot longer, she and Libby had been in the bunker for a little over half an hour now. It was probably time to head back. She was about to tell Libby that when she caught sight of a square black box standing upright next to the file cabinet. She hadn't seen it before, because it had been pushed into the space between the wall and the file cabinet.

"I think I found something," she said as she reached in and took the box out.

"Is that what I think it is?" Libby asked excitedly as she caught sight of it.

"I hope so." Bernie opened the box up. "Yup. It's a corporate kit."

"Sweet," Libby said. She went and looked over Bernie's shoulder as her sister started going through the pages.

"The company's official name is Fortuitous Fireworks," Bernie said.

"That doesn't sound like the kind of name Monty would come up with," Libby observed.

"Maybe his wife did. Remember, it was her dad's company to begin with."

"True. I wonder what she was like."

"Another question to ask Dad when we can get hold of him."

"I just can't imagine being married to someone like Monty."

"Me either. Or staying married to him."

"There must have been something there."

"Perhaps she was an old-fashioned gal. You know, one of those 'married till death do us part' kinda women."

Libby shuddered. "That's probably why she was so fat."

"Drowning one's sorrows in food—a well-known remedy," Bernie observed.

"Well, I suppose it's better than alcohol."

"Not when you get up to four hundred pounds," Bernie said, briefly looking up before she turned another page. "The company is an LLC," she informed Libby.

"I would expect nothing less," Libby said.

Bernie continued leafing through the pages. "Now, this is interesting," she commented as she came to the stock certificates. "Monty had a sixty percent ownership in the company. All the other family members make up the remaining forty percent."

She handed the certificates to Libby, who looked at them and handed them back. Then Bernie handed Libby another page.

"Look at this," she commanded.

"So," Libby said, scanning it, "according to this, Perceval is the treasurer, and Ralph is the secretary, and Geoff and Melissa are on the board of the LLC."

"But note that Greta, Bob, and Audie have no official positions."

"But if Monty gave them his stock . . ."

"Then they'd control the business."

"But why would he do that?"

"He wouldn't. He'd just tell everyone he was going to."

"And play everyone off against everyone else."

"But if, let's say, Ralph and Perceval . . ."

"Or Melissa and Geoff . . ."

"Believed that . . ."

"Then they'd have a reason to kill Monty . . ."

"Because they'd be out on their asses."

"No wonder everyone wanted Monty dead."

"Yes indeed."

Libby was about to ask what that meant in terms of the Africa deal when she heard a noise.

Chapter 19

El Huron cursed as the door to the bunker slammed against the wall. The wind had gotten the better of El Huron, wrenching the door out of El Huron's hand. No matter. The women probably hadn't heard anything, anyway, between the wind and the fan. Actually, it didn't really matter if they had. It just meant that El Huron had to act with even more dispatch, more coolness than usual. And if the women had heard and came out of the office into the large room, that would not matter, either. All they would see was a gloved figure wearing a ski parka and mask. Impossible to identify. El Huron had taken precautions to make sure of that. No. El Huron's identity would remain a secret, as it had all these years.

El Huron would have loved to take the ski mask off, because it itched terribly—El Huron was allergic to wool—but this was not a possibility. El Huron could not take the chance and jeopardize everything, especially not at this stage of the game. Instead, El Huron slid a gloved hand underneath the wool mask and scratched El Huron's cheek.

Then El Huron unzipped the parka and took out the fireworks El Huron had placed there for safekeeping so they would not get wet. Most people who did not know about these things would consider that to be a dangerous thing to do, but El Huron had been raised with them, had played with them as a child, had felt the sting of the dragon, and knew that was not the case.

There was one Dragon Egg, one Eagle, and one Crazy Gator. They should do the trick. The fuse on the Dragon Egg was short, while the one on the Eagle was longer, and the one on the Crazy Gator was the longest of all. Baby Bear, Mama Bear, and Papa Bear. That was how El Huron thought of them. Each one with a job to do, each one complementary to the other, as was the case in any well-run family. El Huron took a lighter out of the inside pocket of El Huron's parka. El Huron flicked it. A small flame danced out. El Huron watched it for a brief moment before El Huron's thumb released the top. The flame died.

The fireworks were timed to go off one after the other. El Huron carefully laid the fireworks on the floor about a foot away from the door and looked up. El Huron half expected to see the women coming out of the room, but El Huron did not. He just saw the empty corridor between the rows of shelving. El Huron smiled in relief. El Huron would admit that El Huron had been slightly concerned. But not anymore. The plan would work. The plan would work perfectly. El Huron took a deep breath and set the timers on the delay-action fuses. When El Huron was sure everything was as it should be, El Huron shut off the fan and jammed the switch. Then El Huron turned and left the bunker, carefully shutting the door. El Huron wasn't positive but thought one of the women said something.

"Good luck to you," El Huron murmured.

Whatever happened now was in the hands of God. El Huron was simply the instrument of vengeance and chaos.

El Huron paused for a second, then turned and started back to the house. El Huron walked briskly, pushing against the wind, and in a matter of moments El Huron had arrived. Before entering, El Huron took off the ski mask and stuffed it in the parka pocket. Then El Huron turned the doorknob and walked inside, being careful to close the front door as quietly as possible. El Huron did not make the same mistake twice.

El Huron quickly balled up the parka El Huron had been wearing, walked into the hallway that led to the utility closet, opened the closet door, and stuffed the parka in the corner, under the tarps. El Huron smiled again, feeling certain that El Huron's mother would approve of El Huron's actions had she known. She would do more than approve. She would be proud.

The noise had startled Libby. She'd jumped, and the papers she was holding had slipped out of her hand.

"Relax. That's the outside door blowing open and shut," Bernie told her sister.

"But we closed it," Libby protested.

"Evidently, not tight enough." Bernie pointed to the ceiling. "Listen to the wind," she said. "It sounds as if it's going to blow the roof off."

It's true, the wind is howling, Libby thought, but she distinctly remembered Bernie slamming the door to the bunker shut. It had made a heavy thud, and Libby had had the irrational feeling that they'd never be able to open the door again and that they'd be stuck in the bunker, in the dark, forever.

"No," Libby said. "I'm sure we did close the door all the way."

"Then the noise was something blowing up against the bunker," Bernie told her.

Libby thought that over for a moment. She wanted to believe it, but she couldn't. "Like what?"

"I don't know. A garbage can, part of a tree limb."

"But there are no trees around here."

"Then, it was something else, Libby."

"It really did sound like a door slamming."

"Maybe it did, but it's not." Bernie stamped her feet impatiently. She hated when her sister got this way.

"But you don't know that for a fact," Libby argued.

"Yeah. I do. And even if you're right—and I'm not saying you are—what difference does it make? I'll tell you—none."

"It does make a difference because then that would mean someone came in."

Bernie snorted. "That's absurd."

Libby narrowed her eyes. Now she was getting mad. "It most certainly is not."

"It is! Think about it for a second."

Libby folded her arms over her chest. "I already have."

"Obviously you haven't."

"And what makes you say that?"

"Because if someone came in, they would know we were here. They'd have to. The lights are on. It's obvious someone is inside. And they would have said hello or come in to see what we're doing."

"Maybe they don't want us to know they're here."

"And why is that?"

"Because they don't wish us well."

"If they didn't wish us well, we'd know that already. They'd have shot us or thrown some exploding something in here." Bernie moved closer to the door. "Hello," she called out. "Anyone here?"

No one answered.

"Hello," Bernie yelled.

Again, there was no reply.

Bernie turned to her sister. "Satisfied?" she asked.

"No."

"Now you're being really paranoid."

"I'm not. What if the person that killed Monty is trying to kill us?"

"We've already gone through that."

"Yeah. But what if?"

"And they'd be doing that why?"

"Because then we can't prove that we didn't do it."

"Do what?"

"Kill Monty."

"That is so not the issue."

"But it could be."

Bernie looked at her sister. "I think you're going into chocolate withdrawal."

"No. Seriously. Think about what I said."

"I have. And I repeat. We need to find you some chocolate."

"You don't think that what I just said is possible?"

"I find it possible, but highly improbable. Killing us seems overly complicated."

Libby sighed. Maybe Bernie was right. Maybe this place was getting to her. Maybe she did need something to eat. She was just about to tell her sister that when she heard an explosion.

Chapter 20

There was a series of pops and hisses, followed by a loud boom. Thirty seconds later there was another loud boom, followed by another one sixty seconds after that. The noise ricocheted off the walls, increasing in volume until it was deafening. Libby and Bernie could smell the gunpowder. The air outside the office turned red and purple. Libby and Bernie started coughing as the smoke started drifting to where they were standing. Bernie ran and slammed the door shut.

"Okay, you were right," Bernie told Libby.

Despite the circumstances, Libby allowed herself a moment to feel smug. "Told you," she said.

"And whoever did this must have set the fuses on a delayed timer, otherwise they would have gone off immediately."

"Great," Libby said. "That makes me feel so much better."

"It'll be fine," Bernie lied, because she wasn't sure it would be.

She closed her eyes as she thought of all those shelves of chemicals in their plastic containers. They were probably okay. They probably wouldn't go off. Unless they were hit with a piece of flying debris. And even then they'd be okay. After all, Melissa and Geoff had made it out all right. The plastic the containers were made out of had seemed pretty thick. But if the containers did rupture . . . Well, it would be adios, muchachas.

Libby coughed again. The smoke was getting to her. She looked around and grabbed a handful of circulars and newspapers and crammed them in the space between the floor and the door.

"There, that should help a little," she said.

"They should have a sprinkler system in here," Bernie said.

"Well, now's the time for it to come on," Libby commented.

Only it didn't and the room continued to fill with smoke.

"Isn't there a venting system?" Libby asked her sister.

"Yeah. Remember, I turned it on when we first walked in here."

"So then why isn't it sucking the smoke out?"

"Someone must have turned it off," Bernie said, realizing that she hadn't heard the whir of the fan for the last couple of minutes. "When we get out of here, I'm going to kill whoever did this."

"If we get out of here."

"No, Libby. When."

"We might be better off staying put," Libby suggested.

"Here?" Bernie asked incredulously.

"Yes. Here. We could cover our mouths with our jackets and go underneath the desk and wait it out."

"If everything blows, that's not going to help."

Libby stemmed another coughing fit. "But what if whoever did this locked the bunker from the outside? Then we're better off under the desk."

"We don't know that."

"We didn't know someone was going to set off explosives in the bunker, either."

"That's true, Libby, but we still have to try. Remember what Dad always says, 'Action is always better than inaction.' "

"I don't know."

"I do. We can always come back if the door is locked. We've got to get out of here."

"I suppose."

"Look, the longer we wait, the more chance there is that one of those containers out there will go off."

Libby started coughing again. "I hate fireworks," she said when she'd stopped.

"I know you do." Bernie zipped up her jacket and put up her hood. "And I have a feeling I'm going to feel the same way by the time we're out of here."

Libby suited up as well. The fabric would offer some protection from the flying sparks.

"Ready?" Bernie asked her sister.

"No."

"Okay," Bernie told her, ignoring Libby's last comment. "I'm going to open the office door, and we're going to make a dash for the outside door."

Libby crossed her fingers.

Bernie put her hand on the doorknob. "On the count of three," she said.

"Wait." Libby blew her nose. "Okay."

"One. Two. Three." And Bernie yanked the door open and took Libby's hand.

They ran. Little hot pellets burned their cheeks and foreheads. The fireworks boomed around them. The noise was deafening as the sound waves bounced off the sides of the bunker. Lights pulsed. They were like strobes and were so bright that Bernie and Libby couldn't look into them.

Libby ran with her eyes focused on the floor. Bernie, who was in the lead, did the same, but she ran with her hand out, because she didn't want to hit the door face-first. It seemed like forever, but it was less than ten seconds before her hand came in contact with the door. She pushed. Nothing happened. Her heart fell.

"Is it locked?" Libby said between coughing spasms.

"I hope not," Bernie croaked back.

By now her eyes were tearing from the smoke. She backed up and rammed the door with her shoulder. It gave a little. She wiped her eyes with the back of her hand. Why had she worn mascara? Her eyes felt as if they were on fire. Then she tried again. The door gave.

"Thank God," Bernie said as she and Libby stumbled outside.

They stood there, taking deep breaths. Snow fluttered down around them. Bernie wiped at her eyes with the back of her hand and brushed at an ember on her jacket. She was just glad that she hadn't worn her new puffy coat, the one she'd gotten on sale at Barneys for an embarrassingly large sum of money. Then she and Libby both looked at each other and started laughing hysterically.

"You don't look so great," Libby said to Bernie, once they'd stopped.

"Well, you're not exactly a vision of loveliness yourself," Bernie replied, which set them off into another gale of laughter.

Libby wiped the tears from her eyes. "Yeah. But at least I don't have mascara smeared all over my face."

"This is true. I guess the ads lied. I guess it wasn't waterproof."

Libby giggled. For some reason she thought Bernie's statement was hysterically funny. "You should demand a refund."

"Maybe so." And Bernie reached down, grabbed a handful of snow, and washed her cheeks with it. It numbed her face.

"Better," Libby said. "Now you just look like a street urchin, instead of someone who slept in a coal bin."

"Thanks."

"What are sisters for? Well, I guess this proves one thing," Libby said, changing the subject.

"What?" Bernie asked. The snow was swirling around her, but she didn't care. She was happy to be outside and to be able to breathe again.

"That whoever did this wants to kill us."

Bernie stuck her hands in her pockets to warm them. "No. It proves that whoever did this doesn't care if we live or die."

"How can you say that?"

"Because if they wanted to kill us, they would have set off something larger and blown the whole place up." Bernie gestured to the bunker. "But it's still standing."

"That might have been an accident on their part."

"Also, they could have locked us in there and left us to suffocate, then claimed it was an accident. Who would be the wiser?"

"Now, there's an attractive thought."

"No. I think that whoever did this knew exactly the right amount of explosives to use."

"The same way they knew what they were doing with the turkey," Libby said, thinking aloud. "They used just enough to kill Monty, but not enough to injure anyone else in the vicinity."

Bernie nodded. "Exactly. Maybe they wanted to teach us a lesson."

"God," Libby said. "I really hate these people."

"Me too." A trail of footprints leading back in the direction of the house caught Bernie's eye. They were faint and growing fainter. She pointed. "I'm willing to bet that given the rate that it's snowing, those must belong to the person that set off the fireworks in the bunker."

Libby went over and put her foot in one of the rapidly filling footprints. "Well, whoever these belong to has bigger feet than I do."

"That's not hard, considering you're a size six. Everyone has bigger feet than you do. When we get back to the house, we should check everyone's boots and see if they're wet."

"Good idea." As Libby turned back to Bernie, her stomach started to rumble. Suddenly she realized she was ravenous. If she'd thought about it at all, she would have expected that she'd be too upset to eat.

"Hungry?" Bernie asked.

"Surprisingly, yes."

"Me too," Bernie admitted. "Although what I could really use is a nice stiff drink. Like a Scotch. Single malt. Straight up with no ice. Then maybe a strip steak with some fries and a tossed salad with a good olive oil and lemon juice."

"And a tarte tatin for dessert."

"Naturally," Bernie said.

Libby sighed wistfully. "Personally, I'd settle for some chocolate. Seventy percent dark. Lindt. Or even some Hershey's Kisses. No. Definitely Hershey's Kisses. They're comfort food."

Bernie wiped the snowflakes off her face. "Tea with rum in it wouldn't be bad, either. Or maybe hot brandy with apple cider and cloves."

"And a nice hot bath."

"And a fire."

"And Marvin."

"Ditto Brandon." Bernie chewed on the inside of her cheek. "I mean, it's one thing to investigate a murder and another thing to be stuck in the same house with the murderer, a murderer with a flair for the dramatic."

"Agreed," Libby said. "Most people just shoot people they want to kill."

"Maybe Monty's death was designed to send a message."

"Like don't eat commercially raised turkeys. Support your local poultry farmers."

Bernie laughed. "Not quite."

"So whom was the message intended for?"

Bernie shook her head. "Don't know. If we knew that, we could figure out who the killer is." She hugged herself. The euphoria from having escaped the bunker was fading, and she was noticing the cold creeping up her legs again. Then she realized she was shivering.

"Of course," Libby said, "there's always the possibility that we're overthinking this and our murderer just made do with the materials they had at hand."

"There is that," Bernie allowed. "Well, there's one thing I am sure of."

"What's that?"

"That we need to get something to eat."

"Definitely," Libby said.

Bernie and Libby stopped talking and concentrated on walking. It seemed to be harder to do that than it was when she and Libby had come out to the bunker, maybe because this time they were walking into the wind, or maybe it was because she was even colder and wearier and hungrier than she had been.

"I'll tell you one thing," Libby said as they got closer to the front door of the Field house.

"What's that?"

"Whoever did this is going to be surprised to see us."

Bernie grinned at the thought. "And how." She was really going to enjoy seeing the look on their faces.

Chapter 21

Sean looked at Joan. He wouldn't have recognized her if she had passed her in the street. Her hair, what there was of it, was now a bright shade of orange, instead of a pale blond. She'd gone from skinny to barrel shaped, having, in Sean's estimation, gained at least fifty pounds in the intervening years. But it was her face that really gave him pause. Her nose, which Sean had always thought belonged on a Roman warrior, was now a peanut-sized nub of a thing, while her eyes seemed to be frozen wide open.

"You look wonderful," he lied. "You haven't changed a bit."

"Neither have you," Joan said.

At that they both looked at each other and burst out laughing.

"Sorry to hear about Rose," Joan said.

"Likewise Edward," Sean replied, having been filled in as to the fate of Joan's husband by Martha on the way over.

Joan pursed her lips. They seemed to be the only part of her face that could move. "Actually, it was a mercy. By the end, he couldn't find his way out of bed by himself. It was hard." For a moment Joan seemed to fold in on herself; then she rallied. "But thanks to your sister, I've made a new start here. New place. New face. Of course, I might have overdone it in the plastic surgery department."

"Not at all," Sean lied for the second time in five minutes. "You look exactly the way I remember you—perfect."

Joan playfully hit him with the heel of her hand. "You always were a flirt."

Sean just laughed because it was true. Then Martha went into the kitchen to make everyone some tea, while he and Joan took seats around the dining room table. *I bet it's going to be decaf,* Sean thought gloomily as he watched Joan put the kettle on to boil. The fact that the plates and the cups on the table were Styrofoam, the spoons were plastic, the cookies were store-bought, and there was Nutrasweet on the table did not augur well for what was to come. His daughters always used tea leaves and steeped the tea in a china pot after having first warmed the pot to the proper temperature. Then they served the tea in bone china cups. The word *Styrofoam* did not pass their lips, let alone enter their house.

"Tell Joan about Monty," Martha called from the kitchen.

Sean did. Joan listened, and then she started talking about Penny, Monty Field's wife.

Joan shook her head. "Her and Monty were quite the pair. They really deserved each other. They were horrible neighbors. I know I shouldn't speak ill of the dead. . . ."

"Oh, go ahead," Sean said.

Joan giggled. "I don't know what Penny did with her time except eat." Joan made a disapproving sucking noise. "She didn't take care of her boys. She didn't take care of her house. It was always a mess."

Martha tsked-tsked her disapproval.

"It's true," Joan asserted, giving Sean a combative stare.

Sean put up his hands in a gesture of surrender. "I remember."

Joan gathered the cards together and began shuffling. "You know how I always thought it was Monty that killed her?"

Sean nodded. "I do."

"Now I think maybe I was wrong. Now I think maybe it was one of the brothers."

Joan started dealing. Sean noticed that her moves were fast and practiced.

"What made you change your mind?"

"It's stupid, really. Something one of the children said. Only, I can't get it out of my mind."

Sean leaned forward. "Tell me."

Joan thought for a moment. "I'm trying to remember the exact wording. I'm sorry, but I don't think I can," she said after another moment had gone by.

"It's okay," Sean said. "Just tell me what you do remember."

"The boy . . ."

"Geoff?"

Joan nodded. "Had just finished mowing my lawn—incidentally, he'd done a crummy job—and he'd come in to get paid. As I was getting my wallet, I asked him how things were going. . . ."

"This was after Penny died."

"That's right," Joan said. "Anyway, he said, 'Not so good,' and I asked him why and he said because his dad was going to send him and his sister up to his brother's camp. . . ."

"Which brother?"

"I'm not sure."

"I think both brothers owned a camp somewhere in Sandy Pond," Martha said, interrupting.

Sean nodded his thanks to his sister, then told Joan to go on.

"So," Joan said, taking up her story where she'd left off, "I said to Geoff that I could see that it was probably pretty boring being up there, and he said no. That wasn't the problem. He was scared to go up there, especially after what had happened to his mother. Then he clapped his hand over his mouth, like he had said something he shouldn't have, and ran out the door. He left his money behind, so I went over to give it to him, but he wouldn't come to the door. I went over a couple of times after that, but he was never there."

"Did he go up there?"

Joan shook her head. "I don't know."

"What happened to the money you owed him?" Sean asked just to have something to say.

Joan shrugged. "I gave it to his dad."

"Interesting," Sean said. He really didn't know what to make of what Joan had just told him.

"I never spoke to him again. I guess I should have called you," Joan said. "But," she continued, "I wasn't sure, and you couldn't find any proof that Penny hadn't died of a heart attack. It seemed better to let the matter rest and not stir things up. So I told myself that I might have been mistaken in what I had heard. That maybe the kid was upset about something else. You know how teenage boys are."

Sean nodded again, waiting for Joan to continue talking.

"But deep down in my heart I always felt that there was something wrong, that I should have reported what I heard to you."

Sean took a sip of his tea and put his cup back down. The tea had grown cold. He wasn't a big fan of tea in general and green tea in particular, and cold green tea just wasn't a possibility, especially when he was drinking it out of a Styrofoam cup, which felt awful on his lips.

"You know," he said, "my dad always used to say that hindsight is twenty-twenty, and he was right."

"No," Martha said. "It was Mom who used to say that hindsight is twenty-twenty, and Dad who used to say, 'Tell me the past and I'll tell you the future.' "

"It comes down to the same thing," Sean said impatiently. "The more pressing question is, why would one of the brothers kill Penny—if that's what they did? What would their motive be? Most of the time it's the husband who kills the wife."

"Or vice versa," Martha threw in.

Joan shook her head. "I don't know."

"I do," Martha said. "It had to be something to do with money. It always has something to do with money."

Sean thought for a moment. Then he said, "As in one or both of the brothers were stealing money from her and Penny was going to have them arrested."

"Maybe Monty was in it, as well," Martha suggested.

"The stealing or the murder?" Sean asked.

"Both," Martha said.

"The only problem with that scenario," Sean said, "is that Penny Field's death was never judged a homicide."

"A minor point," Martha said, drinking the last of her tea.

Joan reached over, took a vanilla wafer out of the package on the table, and conveyed it to her mouth. "Money really is the root of all evil," she observed after she'd chewed and swallowed.

"No," Sean replied. "People are." And he took out his cell and tried to dial Bernie.

Unfortunately, the network was still down.

Chapter 22

Everyone sitting around the dining room table did a double take when Bernie and Libby straggled into the dining room.

"Surprised to see us?" Bernie asked the assembled population.

The Field clan quickly averted their eyes and resumed doing what they had been doing when Bernie and Libby walked in, which was eating. Bernie glanced around. This was not going as planned. She'd hoped someone would clutch their chest and practically fall off the seat at the sight of them. Obviously, that wasn't happening. Maybe they shouldn't have cleaned up first.

"Should we be surprised to see you?" Lexus asked, speaking for the group.

"You guys looked as if you were surprised," Bernie told them.

"Well, we were wondering where you two had gotten yourselves off to," Perceval allowed. "That's true."

Melissa looked up, then went back to eating. Libby noticed her plate was stacked high with food.

"It looks as if you two were someplace not very pleasant," Geoff observed. He seemed to have developed a tic in his right eye since Bernie had seen him last. Maybe it was their presence. Bernie certainly hoped so.

Lexus cut into a piece of turkey. "Yes, where did you two run off to? To coin one of my mother's expressions, you both look like something that the cat dragged in."

"That's rather rude." Bernie thought that she and Libby had done a pretty good job of cleaning themselves up under the circumstances.

"But true."

Bernie was about to explain why they looked the way they did, but before she could, Lexus continued talking.

"And what, may I ask, are you doing with those?" Lexus pointed to the pair of duck boots Bernie was carrying. "I know there must be a reason you're carrying them. I just can't think of what it could be."

Bernie lifted them up. "I want to know who these belong to."

"They're mine," Geoff said. "What the hell are you doing with them?"

"They're wet," Bernie said.

"Of course they're wet," Geoff said. "I was outside smoking a cigarette."

"In this weather?" Libby said.

"Nicotine is a powerful drug," Geoff replied. "Or at least that's what I read."

"I didn't know you smoked," Bernie said.

"Why should you?" Geoff said. "I'm trying to quit, so I smoke two cigarettes a day. Not that that's any of your business."

"It most certainly is," Bernie told him.

Geoff cocked his head. "And how do you figure that, pray tell?"

"Because it ties in with you being outside," Bernie told him.

"Believe me, I would smoke inside if I could, but my stepmother," Geoff said, emphasizing the word *stepmother*, "won't allow it in the house."

Lexus nodded. "He's quite right. I won't."

"That isn't the issue," Bernie said.

"Then what is?" Lexus demanded. "Make your point and get on with it."

"Her point," Libby replied, "is that someone tried to kill us."

There. Finally. It was said, Bernie thought. She looked around the table. No one seemed terribly concerned. In fact, she'd seen more of a reaction at the train station when the announcer came on and told everyone that the Metro-North was going to be late.

Lexus raised an eyebrow. "How horrible for you."

"It doesn't look as if that particularly upsets you," Bernie noted.

Lexus reflexively touched her diamond studs with the tips of her fingers. "Well, you and your sister are standing here now. As Monty used to say, 'No harm, no foul.' Or something along those lines."

"I find that an odd attitude," Bernie told her. "I also find it odd that you haven't asked us what happened."

"You are free to think whatever you like, dear." Lexus dabbed at the corner of her mouth with her napkin. "What's what happened to you have to do with Geoff's boots, anyway?"

"What do you think?" Bernie told her.

"I don't have the vaguest idea."

"The person that tried to kill us followed us out to the bunker. Hence his boots would be wet."

"That's very clever," Melissa observed. "How CSI of you."

Libby was about to comment when Lexus put her hand

to her heart and took a deep breath. "Are you saying what I think you're saying?"

"I don't know," Bernie said. "You tell me."

"You're implying that Geoff tried to kill you," Ralph said.

"We're saying that he was outside at the right time," Libby said, ever cautious. "And that he might be involved in the incident."

Incident, Bernie thought. Definitely not the word she would have used.

"That's ridiculous," Lexus protested. "Absolutely ridiculous. Geoff has always had a bad temper, but he'd never do anything like that," she said, her face a mask of innocence.

"Lexus!" Geoff cried.

Lexus turned toward him. "Yes, sweetie pie?"

"Be quiet."

"I was only trying to help you out," Lexus replied, an angelic smile still on her face.

Geoff's cheeks had gone blotchy with anger. "Well, don't," he told her.

"I don't see why you're so angry," Lexus cooed.

"You think you're going to throw this off on me so you can get everything, you've got another thing coming."

"Why, Geoff, I don't know what you're talking about."

Geoff started to get up from the table, but Ralph put a restraining hand on his shoulder. "Don't let her get to you like that."

"But," Geoff spluttered.

"Geoff, sit down," Ralph ordered.

Bernie could see all the fight going out of Geoff. A moment later he complied.

Ralph patted him on the back; then he turned to Libby. "What happened to you two, anyway?" Ralph asked her.

"Didn't you hear the explosion?" Libby asked.

Melissa set her knife and fork down on her plate. "Explosion?" she repeated.

"Yes, explosion," Bernie said.

"What explosion?" Perceval asked.

"The one in the bunker," Bernie said. "The one that just happened."

"Well, we wouldn't hear anything that happened in the bunker," Perceval said. "Monty designed this house to be soundproof and flame resistant, as well. So there was an explosion in there?"

"I don't believe you didn't hear it," Bernie told him.

"Why would we lie?" Perceval asked.

"Why would one of you try to kill us?" Bernie countered.

"You're probably just making this all up," Lexus told her.

"Someone set off fireworks in the bunker," Bernie said.

"That's not such a big deal," Perceval said. "I thought you said there was an explosion."

Bernie gritted her teeth. "There was. The fireworks exploded."

Greta laughed. "We've had that happen to us lots of times, isn't that right, Audie?"

Audie smiled. "Oh, definitely. Look at yesterday. Nothing to make a fuss about."

Bernie smiled. "How's Africa going?" she asked, interested to see Audie's reaction.

The technique of slipping a non sequitur in was something she'd learned from her father. But once again she didn't get the reaction she'd hoped for, because Audie said, "Politically? Economically? Socially? I mean, I really wouldn't know, would I? It's not my field."

"What is your field?" Bernie asked.

Audie waved a hand around in the air. "Oh, a little of this and a little of that. You know how it goes."

"Not really. I'm asking because you and your cousins have had business dealings in Africa."

"And that is your business how?" Greta asked Bernie.

"I think it's my business because I think you and your cousins were selling fireworks in Africa, and I think you cheated Monty out of a substantial sum of money, and he was going to go to the police, so you killed him."

Greta dabbed at her mouth with the hem of her napkin, placed it next to her plate, and pushed her chair away from the table. "How fascinating. I do enjoy fiction. Tell me, do you have any proof of that?"

Bernie thought back to the yellow pad, which was probably covered with soot by now, and the records that she couldn't find, and the computer that wasn't there, and did the only thing possible under the circumstances. She lied.

"Yes," she said.

"I don't believe you," Greta replied.

"I think we're missing the salient point here, anyway," Perceval said.

"And what would that be?" Libby asked.

"You had no right being in the bunker."

"Good point, Perceval," Ralph said as he rested his knife and fork on his plate. "What were you doing in there?"

"You were investigating, weren't you?" Geoff asked.

"What do you think?" Libby said.

"You were warned not to," Perceval said. "The police told you to leave everything alone."

"So report us," Bernie told him.

"I intend to," Perceval said, "not to mention charging you for trespassing."

"Yes," Geoff commented as he reached for the cranberry sauce. "You should have listened. The bunker is a dangerous place to be."

Bernie wanted to wipe the smirk he was wearing right off his face. "Not if someone doesn't throw lit fireworks in it, it's not."

"Who would do something like that?" Greta asked.

"Who indeed?" Libby echoed.

"But rest assured that we'll find out," Bernie said.

Lexus stifled a yawn. "I like your cranberry sauce. Do you use orange peels in it?" she asked Libby.

"Yes, we do," Libby said.

"I thought so," Lexus said. "It gives everything a nice flavor."

"Bad accidents happen all the time," Geoff said. "You could have been killed."

"We almost were," Libby informed him.

Audie tsked-tsked. "What a shame that would have been," he said.

"Yes, indeed," Bob agreed.

"In the prime of one's life," Melissa said, taking a break from eating.

"My sentiments exactly," Libby replied.

Everyone at the table looked up at her and smiled. The smiles were not nice.

"Of course," Lexus said thoughtfully, "you might have staged this thing by yourself. After all, there's only your word for it that someone threw fireworks into the bunker."

"And why would we have done something like that?" Libby asked.

Melissa shrugged. "To make us look bad. To make people feel sorry for you."

"Right. What I find amazing is that you seem to be so calm about the fact that your bunker was damaged," Bernie observed.

"Accidents have happened before and they'll happen again," Lexus told her.

"And we never keep anything of importance in there, anyway," Geoff said.

"We?" Bernie repeated.

"We," Geoff said. "We're a family business. Always were. Always will be."

"What about your computer?" Bernie asked. "And your files?"

Perceval laughed.

"So you use a computer?" Libby asked him.

Ralph answered instead. "Of course we use a computer. After all, this is the twenty-first century."

"Because I couldn't help noticing that it wasn't there," Libby continued.

"That's because it's in the trash. The hard drive blew," Ralph said. "I just haven't gotten around to getting a new one yet. Good thing, too, considering."

"I hope you had everything backed up," Bernie said.

"I have one word for you," Ralph said. "The Ethernet."

"Yes," Perceval continued. "We've had explosions before, so we'd be fools to do otherwise."

"Lots of explosions," Geoff said.

Lexus conveyed her piece of turkey to her mouth and chewed.

"It won't take very long to put the bunker back together," Melissa said. "A couple of days at the most."

Bernie looked at Libby to get her reaction to the conversation, but Libby wasn't looking or listening to the people. Her attention was focused on everyone's plates.

"What are you eating?" she asked Lexus, even though she already knew. Libby just couldn't believe her eyes.

"Your turkey, obviously," Lexus said. "After all, it is Thanksgiving."

Chapter 23

For once, Bernie was struck dumb. She simply was having a hard time believing what she was seeing.

"I have to say the turkey is really very good," Perceval commented to no one in particular. "Even if it is a little on the dry side."

"Personally, I think Alma's was better," Ralph said. "Although this one is passable."

"I'm sure Monty would have enjoyed it," Greta said. "You know how he felt about turkey."

"Too bad he didn't get a chance," Perceval said. "Thanksgiving was his favorite time of the year."

"Wait a minute," Libby interrupted. "Where did you get that turkey?"

"In the garage of course," Ralph said. "How clever of you to bring two."

"We didn't," Bernie said.

Perceval looked down at his plate. "I don't get it."

Bernie gritted her teeth. "You most certainly do," she managed to get out. In truth, she could hardly contain her fury at herself. While she and Libby had been out in the bunker, almost getting themselves blown up, everyone here had been eating the evidence. So far the score was two to zero in favor of the Field family. "That's the turkey we originally brought. Someone took it out of the oven and substituted the one that blew up for ours."

"I don't think so," Perceval said. He looked at Geoff. "Do you think that's the case?"

"It's very diabolical if it is," Geoff replied.

"Of course it's the case," Bernie practically screamed. "You're eating evidence."

"Good grief," Lexus said, taking another bite. "Who knew?"

"Who indeed?" Geoff's sister said.

"What did you think the turkey was doing out there?" Bernie demanded.

"Resting," Lexus said. "Turkeys have to rest before you carve them. Everyone knows that. Like Ralph said, we thought you brought two. You know, like a backup in case something went wrong with the first one."

"Which, considering the circumstances, was very wise." Ralph put his hand to his mouth. "Oh dear. I've just had a thought. How did you know we were going to need two turkeys unless you knew one of them was going to blow up?"

"I didn't, but you did," Bernie said. "You and your brother were the ones that ordered the turkey in the first place. 'Make sure,' you said, 'to get the frozen kind with the pop-up button. That's the kind our brother likes.' "

Perceval put his knife and fork down. "I resent that accusation."

"I'm not accusing. I'm stating a fact."

"Everyone knew that my dad liked that kind of turkey. It was the only kind he would let Alma buy," Geoff said.

"Where is the rest of the turkey now?" Bernie demanded.

"In the kitchen of course," Greta said. "Where else would it be? Go see if you don't believe me."

"I intend to," Bernie said.

"What are you going to do?" Lexus asked her. "Impound the turkey as evidence?"

Lexus's laugh followed Bernie into the hallway.

"That went well," Libby said once they were out in the hallway.

"We'll just have to go to Plan B," Bernie snapped.

"Which is?" Libby asked.

Bernie remained silent.

"That's what I thought," Libby said as she and Bernie neared the kitchen. "We don't have a Plan B, do we?"

"Not yet," her sister told her. "But we will."

Libby wasn't sure if this was good news or not. At times her sister's plans—witness what had just happened—left a good deal to be desired.

"We shouldn't do this," Libby said as Bernie took a knife and cut several slivers of meat off the turkey and put them on a plate, next to the corn-bread stuffing and Brussels sprouts with chestnuts.

"Of course we should," Bernie said as she added a smidgen of sweet potato to her plate. "At least I am."

"This is your Plan B? Eating the evidence?"

"Continuing to eat the evidence. The turkey is already more than half gone."

"We should save the remainder for forensics."

"Go ahead if you want, but I'm going to have some more before you do."

Libby thought about that. Her stomach was rumbling, and the turkey was looking very good. "Maybe I'll do that after I have a little."

Bernie took a taste of the corn-bread stuffing. It wasn't bad. Even cold. In fact, it was pretty darn good. There was just enough black pepper in there to give it a little bite. And the pepper contrasted nicely with the sweetness of the corn bread and the onions. In addition, the celery offered just the right amount of crunch.

"I was just thinking what Dad would say," Libby said.

"He would say, 'Preserve the evidence at all costs.' But there is no evidence. Not anymore. Except, of course, for the turkey carcass and some of the meat."

"He'd have a fit if he was here," Libby said.

"If he were here, we wouldn't be having this discussion."

"I suppose you're right," Libby conceded.

"I know I am. He'd eat his shoe leather before he ate the turkey, simply as a matter of principle," Bernie said.

"But we should probably save the remains of the turkey that blew up, even though there's not much to save."

Bernie took another bite of turkey. "No. There isn't."

"So what do you think?"

"About the turkey?"

"What else?"

Bernie chewed and swallowed before replying. "Perceval is right. It's dry. It needs something else." She looked around the kitchen. "Like cranberry sauce. Or butter."

"They're on the dining room table."

"I know that. Do you feel like going out to the dining room to get it?"

"Ha. Ha. Ha. Do you?"

"Not hardly," Bernie said.

"Well, neither do I." Libby poured herself a glass of cider and took a sip. "Turkey really is a hard thing to cook well."

"Unless you deep-fry it," Bernie noted. "That locks everything in."

"Which we can't do, because we have no place to put the deep fryer."

"I still think Mom's way of cooking the turkey breast side down works best," Bernie said.

Libby broke down and cut herself some turkey. What the hell. Everyone else was. "You know what I'd really like to do," she said after she'd spread some stuffing on the turkey, "is cook a wild turkey and see what they're like."

"I'm guessing dry and stringy," Bernie said. "There is a flock of them in the park. We could catch one and find out if you like."

Libby shook her head. "Thanks, but no thanks. I'm not into killing what I eat."

"That's the latest trend."

"Count me out," Libby said. She took another bite of turkey. Bernie was right. It was dry. She sampled the dark meat. It was moister, but then it always was. She looked around the kitchen as she chewed. She and Bernie were standing well away from the oven. Aside from the lack of Monty, everything was pretty much the way they'd left it when Monty had died—except, of course, that now most of the food they'd brought was out on the dining room table.

"So what do you think?" Libby said as she helped herself to the stuffing that was in the Tupperware container. She took a taste. It had come out pretty well, if she had to say so herself. Maybe, a little more Tabasco sauce, but otherwise it was perfect.

"Think about what?" Bernie asked, cutting herself another piece of turkey. After all, a girl had to eat. And this was Thanksgiving, even though it was shaping up to be the worst one she'd experienced.

"About the Fields. Who do you think did it?"

"Murdered Monty or threw the fireworks into the bunker?"

"They're one and the same."

"Are they? We don't know that for a fact."

"I think we can assume that."

"You know what Dad says."

"I know." Libby paused to place some braised Brussels sprouts and chestnuts on her plate. They were, in her estimation, a particularly felicitous combination. Most people didn't like Brussels sprouts at all, but if you sautéed them quickly, instead of boiling them, or braised them in a little chicken stock, they were really quite pleasant. "*Assume* means 'making an ass out of you and me.' "

"Exactly," Bernie said as she cut off a heel from the semolina bread she'd made yesterday. She couldn't understand why people left the heel when it was the best part of the loaf.

"I still think it's a safe bet," Libby said as she conveyed a piece of Brussels sprout to her mouth.

Chairs scraped in the dining room.

"I wonder if they're ready for dessert," Libby said after she'd chewed and swallowed.

"Do you want to go out and see?"

"Not really. Do you?"

"No. They can come and get it if they want. I'm not serving it to them."

"Me either," Libby said, "I think they've managed quite well without us so far."

"In fact," Bernie said, "I'm going to cut us a couple of slices of the pumpkin and apple pies before they disappear into the dining room."

Libby nodded her approval. The thought of eating dessert cheered her immensely. "Pie is always a good thing."

"Yes, it is. Especially for breakfast."

"I wonder if Alma ever made pies," Libby mused.

"I doubt it," Bernie said.

"If she had, it might have been a happier household."

"Much as I like pie, I think that might be imbuing it with too much power," Bernie said as she came back with two generous slices of pie for each of them. "Monty strikes me as a mean man. Actually, given the way he looked, he struck me as someone who didn't like to eat. . . . Except for turkey."

"Yes. Except for turkey. I don't trust people who don't like food," Libby said.

"Me either," Bernie agreed. "But getting back to the matter at hand, what do we know about everyone that we didn't know before?"

"Well, we know that Lexus didn't have an interest in the company," Libby said.

Bernie nodded.

"And we know about the structure of the company, and we know that someone followed us out there and showed us that they were not happy with our being there." Libby finished off the last of her Brussels sprouts and set to work on the sweet potato dish she'd made, the one without the marshmallows. "We also know that Geoff's boots were wet, so he might have followed us to the bunker."

"Or someone else might have, only they hid their boots."

Libby tasted the sweet potatoes. The bit of fresh, grated ginger she'd used set them off to perfection. Maybe when they got back home, she'd make a sweet potato pie or one combining sweet potatoes, parsnips, orange marmalade, cream, and eggs. Parsnips were definitely an underutilized winter vegetable. In fact, she rarely saw them anymore, which was a pity. They were great in soups or by themselves, and they married well with potatoes.

"Libby, are you listening to me?" Bernie demanded.

"Definitely," Libby said, bringing her attention back to the matter at hand.

"So aside from the fact that Geoff may or may not have been outside smoking a cigarette, what else do we know?"

Libby thought for a moment. "We know that no one seemed terribly concerned about the fireworks going off in the bunker."

"Or surprised. In fact, they were very casual about the whole thing. It seems to me," Bernie said, "that given the timeline, it would be impossible for everyone not to know what was happening."

"So we're talking about an Orient Express situation?" Libby asked. The prospect did not make her happy.

"I'm not so sure about everyone having a literal hand in what happened to us and Monty, but yes, I think that there's a good possibility that everyone knew that someone went out to the bunker to teach us a lesson."

"Or kill us."

"Or kill us," Bernie conceded.

"That you agree with me makes me feel so much better," Libby said.

Bernie grinned. "I thought it would. It could be worse, though."

"Really. How?"

"At least it's getting a little warmer in here. Soon we'll even be able to take off our coats."

Libby started to laugh, but her laugh was cut off by a bloodcurdling shriek.

Chapter 24

Libby and Bernie followed the Field family up the stairs to the second floor. All the members of the Field family were present except for Lexus. Therefore, Bernie brilliantly deduced, she had to be the screamer. This was why she was a great detective—not.

The Fields were as per usual bickering among themselves. As Bernie listened to them, she reflected that while their pace wasn't glacial, it wasn't as rapid as it should have been given the circumstances.

"My heavens," Ralph said as he panted up the stairs. "I hope it's nothing dreadful. I don't think I could take anything else." And he clutched his chest, something he'd been doing since he'd had two stents put in last year. Just in case anyone forgot.

"Everything is not always about you," Greta snapped. "Can you please go a little faster?"

"I'm going as fast as I can, given my heart," Ralph said.

"There's nothing wrong with your heart that losing twenty pounds and exercising a little wouldn't cure," Bob noted.

"Now you're an expert on that, too," Ralph snapped.

"It's a well-known fact," Bob told him. Bob was a go-to kind of guy, who went to the gym three times a week to lift and do the treadmill, and had little patience with sluggards and excuse makers, two categories he put the rest of the Field family in.

"Is there any area your expertise does not apply to?" Ralph, who found it hard to talk and walk at the same time and had consequently slowed down to a crawl, asked him.

"There's no need to run," Perceval said, interrupting Ralph and Bob's tiff. "I'm sure it's just Lexus, having another one of her fits."

"Lexus has fits, but she doesn't scream like that," Greta said.

"How would you know?" Perceval threw over his shoulder. "You're never here."

"I'm here often enough," Greta shot back.

"Lexus is probably just pretending," Ralph grumbled as he climbed another stair.

There was a second scream, but no one increased his or her pace. If anything, they slowed down fractionally. Like they knew what they'd find up there, Libby couldn't help thinking.

"And she would do that why?" Melissa asked.

"Because her highness likes the idea of us all being at her beck and call, obviously," Ralph replied.

"I hope it's not something terrible," Geoff said as everyone hit the second-floor landing.

"I already said that," Ralph told him as the Field family turned right.

Again, Libby was struck at how everyone seemed to know where to go. Bernie, on the other hand, was struck by how Geoff was clenching and unclenching his fists. But he didn't say anything.

Everyone continued down the hall and turned left at the

third door. There was a slight bottleneck as everyone pushed through to get inside. Libby and Bernie were the last to make it.

"Good God," Audie said as Bernie and Libby elbowed their way to the front of the crowd.

They were standing in Lexus's bedroom, which Bernie quickly noted was furnished all in white, white evidently being Lexus's signature color, as the design magazines that Bernie read liked to say. Two Prendergast watercolors and a small Turner landscape hung on the walls.

Lexus was standing by her bed, an ornate canopy-type affair. "Who did this?" she screamed, pointing at her late, unlamented husband, who was now lying peacefully, sans the old quilt he'd been wrapped in, on Lexus's snowy white linen bedspread, or as peacefully as you could with half your head blown away. Monty's hands were clasped together, a firecracker had been laid on his chest, and his face was tactfully covered with a Hermès scarf. "I want to know who did this."

No one said anything.

Melissa put her hand over her mouth to stifle her giggle.

Lexus rounded on her. "You think it's funny?" she yelled at Melissa. "Well, do you?"

"No," Melissa said, choking back the laughter.

"Obviously you do. I want to know why."

"It's just you'd never let Dad in here, and now he's lying here, getting yucky stuff all over your precious comforter." Melissa started laughing again. "I'm sorry. I just can't help it."

"You can help it, and you're not one bit sorry."

"I am," Melissa insisted, but Bernie didn't think she looked very repentant.

Evidently neither did Lexus, because the next thing she said was, "Not sorry enough, fat girl. You'll pay for this."

"Fat girl?" Melissa squeaked. "At least I'm not throwing up everything I eat. You're not going to look so great when all your teeth rot out of your mouth."

Lexus looked her up and down, then said, "At least I don't have to empty bedpans for a living."

Melissa started toward Lexus, but Geoff touched Melissa on her shoulder. "It's not worth it," he told her when his sister turned toward him.

"You're right," Melissa said. "It isn't."

Lexus ignored both Melissa and Geoff and pointed at Monty. "I want him out of here. I want him out of here now."

Ralph cleared his throat. "Where do you want him?" he asked.

"Where do you think, you moron?" Lexus shrieked. "I want him back in the garage, where he belongs."

"Actually, he looks kind of peaceful here," Geoff observed.

Lexus whirled around and faced him. "You and your sister did this, didn't you?" she hissed.

Geoff took an involuntary step back in the face of Lexus's wrath. "Why would we do something like that?"

"Because you both think it's funny," Lexus snarled. "Look at your sister. She's still laughing. You've both always hated me since the day your dad married me. You and your sister are nothing more than leeches. You and she sucked your father dry with your demands. You and your sister just couldn't get enough. Enough money. Enough food. Enough stuff. That goes for all of you."

"Us want things?" Greta cried. "Coming from you, that's hilarious. You're the original gimme girl."

"I loved him," Lexus said.

Greta rolled her eyes. "How can you say that with a straight face? You're just bad news. What happened to Alma was your fault."

"How do you get that?" Ralph asked her.

Greta turned to him. "You mean, you don't know?" she asked, her eyes wide open in amazement.

"Know what?" Ralph asked.

"That she was screwing around with Alma's son."

Lexus snorted. "What a load of crap," she said at the same time that Ralph said, "You're kidding."

"No. I'm not," Greta said to Ralph. "That's why Monty fired Alma after all those years. He thought she knew."

"At least," Lexus told Greta, "if you're going to tell a lie, tell a believable one."

"Monty told me."

Lexus raised her eyebrows. The corners of her mouth twitched. "And I'm supposed to believe that?"

"He did," Greta insisted.

Lexus snorted. "This is beyond ridiculous."

Greta leaned forward. "I don't hear you denying it."

Lexus took a deep breath. Then she addressed Bernie and Libby. "Now you can see what I've had to put up with." She waved her hands in the air before adjusting her white fur scarf. "The lies. The deceit. The moment I set foot in here, everyone has been trying to turn Monty against me. Why? you may ask. Because they're jealous of me. They're jealous of my looks and my style. They're jealous that Monty loved me."

"That's a laugh," Melissa told her. "My dad said you were the biggest mistake he ever made. He was going to divorce you."

Lexus shook her finger at her. "Another lie. Well, just you wait. And that goes for everyone else here, as well."

Bernie noted that the Field family did not seem particularly perturbed by Lexus's warning.

"Because let me tell you," Lexus said, continuing her diatribe, "when I run the company, things are going to be different. All of you are going to be out on the street so fast, it's going to make your heads spin. And I, for one, will enjoy watching you actually having to work for a change."

Perceval crossed his arms over his chest and leaned against the wall. "You're not running the company," he said. "You're not in the company in any way, shape, or form. Monty wasn't that stupid. He wasn't going to mess up a perfectly good business because of some dumb bimbo."

Lexus wrinkled her nose. "Bimbo?"

Bernie helpfully supplied the translation. "Floozy. Loose woman."

Lexus's expression hardened. She thrust out her jaw. "It's in the will," she said.

Ralph snorted. "Oh, that will. The will you keep telling us about. The will Monty supposedly just made. The one that supersedes all the others. The will that you won't allow us to see. The imaginary will. Is that, perchance, the one you're talking about?"

"I want you all out of my bedroom," Lexus screamed. "I want you to take Monty and go. Except for you two." She pointed at Libby and Bernie. "I want you two to stay."

"Where should we put him?" Geoff asked.

Lexus's face turned red with anger. "I already told you. In the garage. In a snowbank. Anywhere you want, as long as it's not in my house."

"This is not your house," Melissa noted.

Lexus's face turned even redder, if that was possible. "It will be."

"Over my dead body," Melissa replied.

"That can be arranged," Lexus told her.

Melissa gasped and put a hand to her heart. "You heard how she threatened me," she said to the rest of the family.

"Out," Lexus screeched. She gestured toward the door. "I want all of you out now. And take Monty with you. And by the way, that scarf that's covering his face, that's one thousand dollars."

"We'll wash it and return it to you," Melissa said. "How's that?"

"You are such a piece of trailer park trash," Lexus spit out.

"That's pretty funny coming from the woman who used to work in a strip club," Melissa said.

"At least," Lexus said, "they paid me to take off my clothes. They'd pay you to keep them on."

Melissa flushed and hurried out of the room.

"So," Lexus said to Bernie and Libby when everyone from the Field family, both living and dead, had vacated her room, "you see what I'm up against."

"It's a shame about your scarf," Bernie said.

Lexus brightened. "Yes, isn't it? See, I knew you'd understand. That's why I want to hire you."

"Hire us to do what?" Bernie asked as she watched Lexus strip her bed and roll everything up in a ball.

"Obviously, to find Monty's killer."

"Correct me if I'm wrong, but I thought you thought that we were the guilty party." Bernie said.

"Not really."

"But you said that," Libby pointed out.

"I know I did and I'm sorry, but that was just because I didn't want anyone else to think I suspected them. I hope you'll forgive me."

Bernie put her hands on her hips. "Is anything that comes out of your mouth the truth?"

"But this is," Lexus insisted. "Please. I'm scared. You have to help me." Then she took the bed linens and threw them out in the hallway.

"What are you going to do with those?" Libby asked.

Lexus shuddered. "Throw them out, of course. Would you sleep on them again?" she asked Libby.

"Probably not," Libby allowed.

"Exactly," Lexus said. "Every time I looked at them, I would see Monty, with half of his head gone, lying there."

Libby was interested to see that Lexus actually had dabbed at her eyes when she'd said that. She didn't think that women did stuff like that anymore—at least not since the 1930s.

"Why the change of heart?" Bernie asked.

"I haven't had, as you put it, a change of heart."

"Okay. Why are you asking for our help now?"

"It's simple. Because whoever was targeting Monty is targeting me, and by the time the police get here, it'll be too late and I'll be dead."

"You think that was what leaving Monty on your bed meant?" Libby inquired.

Lexus gave her a scornful look. "What else could it mean?"

"It could be someone's idea of a practical joke," Bernie said.

"Mean-spirited practical joke," Libby added.

"Or it could be a sign that someone thinks you're guilty of Monty's death," Bernie noted.

"How do you get that?" Lexus asked.

"You know, putting the victim on the murderer's doorstep, or in this case on her bed," Bernie said.

"Don't be ridiculous," Lexus scoffed. "It was a clear message to me that I'm going to be next."

Bernie coughed and Lexus turned toward her. "Are you planning on paying us?" Bernie asked.

Lexus looked offended. "Of course."

"How much?"

Lexus favored Bernie with a radiant smile. "We'll talk about that later. And, of course, I'll put in a good word with the chief for you."

"Oh, goody," Bernie said. "I was hoping you would."

"Because Lucas is a very"—Lexus emphasized the word *very*—"very good friend of mine." And then she wiggled her way out the door. Or tried to. It was something that was hard to do when there was nothing back there to wag.

"Nice lady," Libby said when she was gone.

"She's very sure of herself, isn't she?" Bernie observed.

"Well, she's blond and skinny."

Bernie raised an eyebrow.

Libby explained. "I've just noticed that women like that think the world revolves around them."

"Unlike women like us?"

Libby got defensive. "You know what I mean," she said.

Bernie conceded that she did.

"Okay," Libby said. "Let's start again. Do you think Lexus is for real?"

Bernie rubbed her nose while she thought. Finally she said, "I think she's for real about wanting everything for herself. I think she's for real about being upset about finding Monty's body in her bed. As for the rest, I don't know."

Libby paused for a moment, then said, "I didn't think old Lucas had it in him."

"Think Viagra," Bernie said. "But Lexus is probably lying about that, anyway. She didn't say she'd screwed Lucy. She intimated it, which is different."

Libby wrinkled her nose at the thought. "True. Why would she do anything with him?"

Bernie put a finger to her cheek. "Hmm. Let me think about that for a moment. Certainly not for his looks or his charm. I'll bet even Mrs. Lucas doesn't do anything with him. Maybe Lexus needed to have a parking ticket fixed."

"No. It would have to be something more serious than that," Libby said.

Bernie laughed. "Like murder two, and even that wouldn't be worth it. No. I think she's flat-out lying."

"Why do you think that?"

"Woman's intuition."

"Dad thinks that's an overrated commodity."

"That's just because he doesn't have any."

"This is true. So," Libby said, "are we going to help Lexus out or not?"

"No. We're going to help us out. If our interests and Lexus's interests coincide, good. And if not, oh well."

"Makes sense to me," Libby said. "So as long as we're up here and the Field family is downstairs, maybe we should start by searching everyone's bedrooms."

"Works for me," Bernie said. "Something interesting might turn up."

And it did, although not in the way Bernie and Libby expected.

Chapter 25

Bernie and Libby were walking down the hallway. They were trying to do this as quietly as possible, which was proving difficult, because the floorboards kept creaking at random intervals, which, Bernie reflected, was what old floorboards did. Even walking on the edges of the threadbare runner didn't seem to help much. The sequence went: step, step, creak, step, step, step, squeak.

The hallway itself was a dark, dim place. The walls were papered over with wallpaper that seemed to make the space even narrower than it already was. There were no pictures or photos on the walls. Ropes of cobwebs hung from the ceiling, attesting to the house's robust spider population.

"Very cheery," Libby said.

"Yes, isn't it?" Bernie replied. "I think the word you want is *Dickensian*."

Libby thought of their flat, with its large windows, cheerful jonquil-colored walls, and happy hodgepodge of family photos. "I can't imagine growing up here," she said.

"Me either. It would have been beyond depressing," Bernie said, also thinking of their flat, with its comfy sofa and leather chairs and the morning light that streamed in the windows. "Monty really knew how to spread the cheer around. I can see why he's someone who will not be missed."

"He probably hadn't touched anything since his wife died."

"Probably," Bernie agreed.

"Even some brighter lights might help," Libby observed.

"That would run up the electric bill."

Libby pointed at the ceiling light fixture. "I bet those bulbs are fifteen watts each," she said. "How are we supposed to see where we're going?"

"In this case, maybe it's better that we can't," Bernie replied.

"One thing is clear, though," Libby continued.

"What's that?"

"Lexus got special treatment from Monty."

"You're saying that because of the way her room looked?" Bernie asked.

Libby nodded. "Exactamundo. It's clean, it's freshly painted, and it's got thick wall-to-wall carpet." She pointed to the hallway floor covering. "Unlike this stuff . . ."

"Which is threadbare . . ."

"And has no color at all. Plus the furniture is new. She has that big, comfortable bed and a matching bedroom set. . . ."

"It looks high-end," Bernie noted. "Maybe Stickley or Harden. And she has art on the walls. Originals, not prints. That's a biggie. No wonder no one else in the family likes her. I bet their rooms aren't furnished like that. Not even remotely."

"I bet you're right," Geoff said as he popped out of the bathroom in back of Libby and Bernie and tapped both of them on their shoulders.

Bernie jumped. Libby shrieked. It occurred to Libby as she whirled around that she'd been doing lots of shrieking since she'd come to the Field house and that Geoff was responsible for at least half of those shrieks.

Geoff looked at her and put a finger to his lips. "Sssh," he said.

"Sssh yourself," Libby told him. She was furious. She hated being frightened, and her heart hadn't slowed down yet. What happened if she had a heart attack? "You shouldn't go jumping out at people and scaring them like that."

"I wasn't jumping. I was stepping," Geoff said.

Libby waved a hand in the air. "Don't go semantic on me. The results are the same."

"Then I apologize."

"You don't look apologetic to me," Libby snapped. "Not one single bit."

Geoff attempted to look downcast. "Well, I am."

Libby was unconvinced and undeterred. "Do you like scaring people?" she asked Geoff, taking a step toward him. "Do you get off on it? Does it make you feel powerful? Is that why you put Monty's body in Lexus's bed? So you could hear Lexus scream?"

Geoff drew himself up. "I had nothing to do with that," he replied.

"Well, you certainly weren't knocking yourself out to get up there."

"Neither was anyone else," Geoff protested.

Which was true, but Libby decided to ignore that minor detail. "Is that why you threw the firecrackers in the bunker?" she said instead. "So you could scare us? Or maybe you wanted to kill us, like you did Monty?"

"I didn't do any of those things," Geoff protested. "I already told you so."

"I don't believe you."

"Well, it's true," Geoff insisted.

"What did Lexus say about your temper?"

"She's a liar," Geoff cried. "She wouldn't know the truth if it bit her in the ass."

Libby watched Geoff. He seemed different somehow. More jittery. Or maybe *impatient* was a better word. He kept on tapping his fingers against his legs. And he had a rocking motion going on. Back and forth. On the balls of his feet to his heels and back again. It was barely noticeable, but it was there. And there was something with his eyes. She just couldn't pinpoint what it was, especially in the bad light.

"Then why did you jump out at us?" she demanded.

"I didn't jump out," Geoff cried. "We already went through that. I just wanted to talk to you."

"You waited for us in the bathroom."

"And your point is?"

"That's a strange place to wait."

Geoff wiped his nose with the back of his knuckles. "Got an itch," he explained. "There's something in this house I'm allergic to."

"About the bathroom," Libby said.

Geoff's rocking motion increased. "For heaven's sake, if you must know, I had to pee. Is that all right with you?"

"It's fine," Libby said, grudgingly.

"I have to talk to you, to both of you," Geoff said. "It's a matter of life and death."

"Yours or ours?" Bernie said. She had barely managed to keep herself from rolling her eyes during the course of Geoff and Libby's conversation.

Instead of answering, Geoff took Libby and Bernie by their arms and propelled them into a room farther down the hall. Then he shut the door behind them.

Libby looked around. As Bernie had predicted, Geoff's room was the opposite of Lexus's. It was small and shabby looking. Narrow and long, it reminded Libby of a jail cell or maybe a cell in a monastery. There were old-style thick-slatted venetian blinds on the windows. The windows themselves looked as if they hadn't been washed in twenty years, which pretty much went along with the paint job. The only decoration on the grayish brown walls was an elaborately decorated samurai sword hanging over the desk.

"Nice," Bernie said, nodding to it. "Is it real?" she asked.

"What do you think?" Geoff sounded insulted.

"I don't know," Bernie told him as she took in the rest of the room. "That's why I'm asking."

"Of course it's real," Geoff told her.

"Aren't those things expensive?" Libby asked.

"I wouldn't know," Geoff told her. His tone was haughty. "It was a present."

"Nice present," Bernie commented.

Geoff flicked a piece of dust from his coverlet. "I thought so."

"From whom?" Bernie asked.

Geoff hesitated for a moment, then said, "From myself. I deserved it."

"I didn't say you didn't," Bernie replied.

Libby decided that if she had to come up with a name for the room, she'd call it Arrested Development, because it appeared to be frozen in time. The bed over in the corner looked as if it would be fine for a ten-year-old boy but uncomfortably cramped for a teenager, let alone an adult male, to sleep in. Libby wagered that Geoff had had the football-themed coverlet that was on his bed since junior high school. Ditto the pillow, which seemed thin and uncomfortable.

The four-drawer dresser and the desk along the far wall looked as if they were both made out of particleboard. The goosenecked lamp sitting on the desk was the kind you could get in any drugstore for $9.99. A canvas-backed chair was butted up to the desk, while a faded rag rug lay on the floor next to the bed. There was a cinder-block-

and-board bookshelf under the window filled with old high school textbooks and a few comics. Bernie thought that the room was the kind of place where you went only to sleep.

The desktop was bare except for a Mac laptop and a couple of candles that sat toward the back. One was of a wizard in blue robes and a pointed hat. He had a beard and was carrying a staff in one hand and a crystal ball in the other. The second candle was another wizard, only this one didn't look as friendly. He was wearing black robes and a black hat and had a frown on his face, and instead of a staff and a crystal ball, he was carrying a wand and a skull.

"I was younger," Geoff explained as he saw Libby looking at the candles. "I thought they were pretty cool."

Libby nodded in an absentminded way. "Were you interested in magic?"

"If you're talking about the game, yes, I was."

That wasn't what Libby had meant, but she didn't say that. Instead she said, "Do you like your Mac?" It stood out in the room like a beacon of light. Besides the sword, it was the only thing of value in there.

Geoff smiled for the first time. "I love it. Absolutely love it."

"Another present to yourself?" Libby asked.

"Absolutely. PCs aren't good for graphics."

"Do you do the computer stuff for the business?" Bernie asked.

Geoff nodded. "What there is of it. I wanted to do a Web site. It could have been way cool, but Dad nixed it. But at least he listened to me about backing up. Otherwise we'd really be screwed."

"How come you didn't get the hard drive replaced on the business computer?" Bernie asked.

"We did. No point in doing it again," Geoff said.

"You're right," Libby said. "There isn't."

"Nope. Just gotta trash it."

"Okay," Bernie said, changing the subject. "So why do you want to talk to us?"

Geoff shifted his weight from one foot to the other. They were all standing, because outside of the bed there wasn't anywhere to sit down, except on the canvas chair, and that sagged so badly in the middle that Libby was afraid if she sat down in it, she wouldn't be able to get out of it again.

"I want you to find out where Lexus hid my father's real will," Geoff said.

"Real will?" Bernie asked.

"The one my father actually wrote."

"So the one Lexus is talking about is a forgery?" Libby asked.

Geoff nodded. "She did it. I've seen her practicing his signature."

"If that's the case, why hasn't she presented it by now?" Bernie demanded.

"She will," Geoff said. "She's just waiting for the cops to get here."

"Won't the family attorney be able to tell the difference?" Bernie asked.

"I'm not sure. Lexus is pretty good with the whole handwriting thing, and my dad changed his will a lot. Whenever he got mad at us, he'd write one of us out."

Somehow Libby wasn't surprised. "So how do you know that Lexus's version isn't the current one?" she asked.

"Because he told me he was going to divorce Lexus."

"And why was that?" Libby asked.

"Because he found out she was sleeping with someone."

"So we heard in Lexus's room," Bernie said.

"Alma's son," Libby added.

"It's true," Geoff said. "What?" he asked as he looked at Libby's and Bernie's faces. "You don't believe me?"

"No, I don't," Bernie said. "What I do believe is that you or Greta or Melissa might have told your dad that. Maybe your stepmother was sleeping with someone else, but it wasn't the maid's son. I don't think that Lexus is into sex unless it gets her something. She's strictly a quid pro quo kinda gal."

"That's a horrible thing to say," Geoff cried.

"What? That you lied to your dad or that Lexus uses sex to get what she wants?" Libby asked.

Geoff's eyes flitted all over the room.

"That's what I thought," Libby said. "And while we're on the subject of honesty, I also don't believe that your dad confided in you. He was a control freak, and control freaks by definition like to keep things to themselves. After all, information is power."

"Are you calling me a liar?" Geoff demanded, his glance finally coming to rest on Libby.

"How about a wishful thinker?" Bernie threw in.

"Well, he did tell me," Geoff insisted.

Libby thought he sounded like a five-year-old caught taking money out of his dad's wallet. "It's just that from what Bernie and I observed," she told him, "you don't seem to have had that kind of relationship with your dad."

Geoff relaxed a little. "I know it doesn't seem like it, but we were very close. I was his favorite."

Bernie raised an eyebrow.

"Really," Geoff said. "It's true."

Libby shifted her position slightly. She was getting tired of standing. "Let's say that is true," she said. "How does that tie in with your telling us that you had to speak to us because it's a matter of life and death?"

Geoff moved a half a step closer to her. Libby noticed that the tic under his eye was getting worse.

"She knows that I know what she did."

"You mean Lexus?" Libby asked.

Geoff nodded.

"How do you know that she knows?" Bernie asked.

Geoff dismissed her question with a wave of his hand. "I do. I feel it here." He pointed to his stomach. "In my gut. It's like a cold shadow every time she walks by."

"That's quite a metaphor, isn't it, Libby?" Bernie said.

"Mctaphor?" Geoff looked puzzled.

"Forget it," Bernie said.

"Forget what?" Geoff asked.

Libby jumped back into the conversation. "Okay. Let's grant what you said is true," Libby told him.

"It is true," Geoff insisted. "Why would I lie?"

Libby decided not to respond to that. If she did, they'd be there all night. Instead she said, "So, I repeat, how is this a matter of life and death?"

"Because Lexus is going to kill me so I can't talk."

"What are you going to talk about?" Bernie asked.

Geoff favored her with a "how stupid can you be" look. "The will. I'm going to tell the authorities about the will."

"Fine. What's your proof?" Libby asked.

"I don't have to tell you," Geoff said.

"Probably because you don't have any," Bernie told him.

Geoff stamped his foot. "I certainly do. And, anyway, she's done other stuff."

"Like what?" Bernie asked.

Geoff didn't answer.

"That's what I thought," Bernie said. "I find it odd that your stepmother just asked us to find Monty's murderer and now you're asking us to protect you from her, don't you, Libby?"

"Absolutely, Bernie. Do you think there's a correlation?"

"Without a doubt, Libby."

"I know what she asked," Geoff said. His voice had taken on a whiny undertone. "I was there, remember?"

"Why don't you tell Libby and me what's really going

on?" Bernie told him. "We can't help you if you don't know."

"What's going on," Geoff said, "is that Lexus is trying to pin Monty's death on me. Obviously."

"It's not obvious to me," Libby said.

"Or me," said Bernie. "In fact, I'm totally confused. I thought everyone thought that Bernie and I killed your father."

Geoff jerked his head from side to side. "No. Perceval just said that."

"So did Lexus," Libby reminded him.

"But she was just using that as a ploy to take suspicion away from her," Geoff said.

"It seems a little convoluted to me," Libby said. "What do you think, Bernie?"

Bernie leaned her back against the wall. "Seems a little convoluted to me, too."

"I mean," Libby continued, "you just told us, she wants to throw suspicion onto you."

"No," Geoff said. He got a crafty look on his face. "What she wants to do is kill me."

"And I suppose Lexus brought Monty up from the garage and put him in her bed so she could blame you," Bernie said.

Geoff beamed.

"Never mind that I don't think she'd be able to carry him up," Bernie observed.

"She had help," Geoff told her.

"You're sure of that?" Libby said.

"Yes," Geoff said. "I am."

"You want to tell me who that person was?" Bernie asked.

"It's none of your business."

"Now we're supposed to protect you from two people. Wow. That's a pretty tall order. I mean two is a lot, but when we don't know who the second one is . . ." Bernie allowed her voice to trail off. "Well, even you can see that's a lot to ask of us."

"Forget the other person," Geoff told her. "They're of no consequence. I need you to concentrate on Lexus."

Libby glared at Geoff, trying to scare him into telling her the truth. After a moment she was forced to conclude that this was not going to work. Geoff seemed unimpressed. But then, Libby reflected, she couldn't remember anyone she'd ever scared. It was too bad, but there it was.

She sighed and said, "No doubt Lexus rigged the turkey, too."

Geoff nodded his head vigorously.

"And then," Libby continued, "she blamed us so we would then be forced to investigate and come up with you as the perpetrator of said deeds."

"See?" Geoff said. "I knew you were smart."

"And the reason for this is?" Bernie asked.

"I already told you."

"Tell me again," Bernie instructed.

"The reason is that if I'm out of the way, she gets to inherit everything."

"But why should Lexus pick on you?" Bernie asked. "Why not someone else in your family? Why not Perceval or Ralph?"

The tic under Geoff's eye got faster. Bernie thought it was like watching a live electric wire sparking.

"That's simple," Geoff said. "I'm the primary heir."

"What about your sister and your uncles and your cousins?" Bernie asked.

Geoff snorted. "They're total losers."

"I bet they'd say the same about you," Bernie noted.

Geoff's expression turned sullen. His foot tapping increased. "No. It's true."

"That you're a total loss?" Bernie asked in her sweetest tone of voice.

"No," Geoff yelled. Then he got his voice back under

control. "Melissa is a compulsive gambler. She'd sell the business in a heartbeat and gamble the proceeds away. My uncles are just stupid. That's why my dad makes—made —them run every penny that they spend by him, and as to my cousins . . ." Geoff paused to take a breath. "My dad just found out that that whole Africa scheme they were supposed to be doing was a gigantic scam."

Bernie nodded. That fit in with what she and Libby had found written on the yellow pad in the bunker.

"But you're perfect," Libby said.

Geoff sniffed and rubbed his nose with the back of his hand. "I never said I'm perfect. I make mistakes. But I do work and I am reliable. I'm the only one my dad liked."

"It didn't sound that way when he came out and asked why you hadn't shoveled a path to the kitchen. Did it sound that way to you, Libby?" Bernie asked.

Libby shook her head. "Not even a little bit."

"That's just the way he talked," Geoff said. "He didn't mean anything by it."

"Well, you seemed pretty upset," Libby observed.

"I wasn't really," Geoff said.

"You looked as if you were going to punch him out," Bernie said.

"No," Geoff said. "You're mistaken."

"Your fists were clenched," Bernie said.

"You're wrong," Geoff said.

Bernie backed up and tried a different route. "So what you're saying is that your dad had bad people skills?" Bernie asked.

Geoff smiled. "That's exactly what I'm saying," he replied. He sounded relieved.

"I see," Libby said as she absentmindedly picked up the wizard with the blue robes off the desk and ran her finger along the edges of his pointed hat. The candle felt surprisingly heavy for what it was supposed to be. As if something was hidden inside the wax.

"Don't touch that!" Geoff cried. "That's very fragile. Put it back."

But it was too late. Libby had already turned the wizard upside down.

"Interesting," she said when she saw what was inside.

Chapter 26

Libby looked at Geoff's face. It was beaded with sweat. "That's my medicine," he cried.

"I always hide my medicine somewhere, don't you, Bernie?" Libby said.

"Oh, absolutely," Bernie replied. "That's why I put my socks in the medicine cabinet and my medicine in my sock drawer. Safer that way."

"Actually, I put mine in the oven," Libby said. "I like to be one hundred percent secure."

Bernie nodded. "You can never be too careful. That's my motto."

"Dad's too," Libby said.

Bernie smiled. "That's where I got it from."

"It *is* my medicine," Geoff cried. "I never know when I'm going to need some."

"I bet you don't," Libby said.

"I have a condition," Geoff whined.

"How about issues?" Bernie said. "Do you have them, too?"

"I have a condition," Geoff repeated.

Bernie tapped her cheek with her finger. "Let me think.

Hmmm. I'm guessing your condition has something to do with your nose."

Geoff folded his arms across his chest. "I have a sinus condition. A serious sinus condition. Okay?"

This time Bernie did roll her eyes. "No. It's not okay."

"Well, I do," Geoff said.

"Aren't you embarrassed that you can't come up with anything better than that?" Bernie asked him. "Seriously. I'd be embarrassed if I was you. A little creativity goes a long way."

Geoff pressed his lips together and looked down at the floor.

Libby held up the package she'd taken out of the hollowed-out wizard. "That's a lot of medicine. How many ounces would you say?"

Geoff didn't say anything.

Bernie took the clear ziplock bag from her sister and weighed it in the palm of her hand. "I'd say it's at least one to one and one-half ounces. No wonder those are magic candles. Tell me, did your father know about this?"

Geoff continued looking down at the floor.

"Did someone tell him?" Bernie asked.

"No one told Monty anything," Geoff snapped back.

"Aha." Bernie pointed a finger at Geoff's chest. "That implies that there's something to tell."

Geoff glared at her. "You think you're smart, don't you?"

Bernie smiled. "Actually, I do."

"Well, I think you're an idiot."

Bernie looked at Libby. "Don't you think it sounded as if someone told Geoff's dad that he was using coke?"

"It sounded that way to me," Libby agreed.

Geoff looked everywhere but at Libby and Bernie. "Well, they didn't."

"So you say," Libby observed.

"Yes, I do."

"Maybe it was the same people that told Monty about Lexus," Libby observed.

"They have quite a little rumor mill going around here, don't you think?" Bernie asked Libby.

"I do indeed." Libby looked at Geoff again. "You know, even if no one told Monty, which I don't believe, I bet he did know about your"—she hesitated for a moment—"condition, as you put it. Or he suspected as much. That kind of thing is hard to hide. Especially since your . . . medicine . . . is so expensive. Were you taking money out of the business to buy it?" She nodded toward the coke. "Most people end up doing that."

Geoff scowled. "Of course I wasn't."

"I don't believe you," Bernie said. "I bet your dad caught you stealing and he was going to turn you in to the police."

"Dad didn't know anything," Geoff insisted.

"Is that why he wasn't very happy with you?" Bernie asked, disregarding Geoff's last statement.

"Not happy at all," Libby chimed in. "I know our dad wouldn't be."

Geoff looked up. "It's not what you think," he said.

"Really," Bernie said. "Then what is it?"

"I lied before," Geoff told her. His face was scrunched, as if he was trying to concentrate.

"No kidding," Libby said.

"I'm holding this for someone."

"Wow," Bernie said. "Now, there's a shock."

"I am," Geoff insisted.

"How kind of you. And who might that someone be?" Libby asked.

"I can't tell you."

Libby shifted her position. "Of course you can't," she sneered. "Mostly because there is no one."

Geoff flushed again. "Yes, there is. They told me it was dish detergent. I didn't know what it was."

Bernie laughed. "Is that what they're calling coke these days? How much did this cost? I bet it wasn't cheap."

"I told you it isn't mine," Geoff answered.

"And we don't believe you, do we, Bernie?" Libby said.

"No, we don't," Bernie replied. "My understanding is that your dad kept you on a pretty tight leash. That you were maxed out on your credit cards." It was a guess, but judging from the expression on Geoff's face, it was a pretty good one.

"Where did you hear that?" Geoff demanded.

Bernie shrugged. "You just told me."

"I did no such thing."

"Your reaction told me," Bernie said as she handed the ziplock bag back to Libby.

"You don't know anything," Geoff cried.

"Maybe I don't," Bernie said. "Or maybe I know that you're the person that killed your dad, after all," she said.

"And why would I do that?"

"I just told you. He was going to call the cops on you. Or maybe he was going to kick you out. Or disinherit you and you'd be left with nothing. That would be pretty hard for someone like you to handle, wouldn't it?"

Geoff jerked his head in the direction of the ziplock bag Libby was holding. "I told you that stuff isn't mine."

"Right," Libby said. "Only you won't tell us whose it is."

"I can't," Geoff said.

"Why ever not?" Libby asked.

"Because I don't know. Someone put it in the wizard when I wasn't here."

"So you're changing your story again?" Libby asked.

"This time I'm telling the truth," Geoff insisted.

Bernie clicked her tongue against her teeth. "So why didn't you tell us that before?" she asked.

"Because I didn't think you'd believe me," Geoff said.

"And you're right," Libby said. "We don't. I don't think I've ever met such a bad liar, have you, Bernie?"

"Nope," Bernie said as she looked at her phone. There was still no service. She slipped it back in her pocket and looked up at Geoff. "It's kind of insulting how little effort you put into your lying. It makes me think that you think that we're not worth the effort, and that hurts my feelings. Maybe we should tell your uncles what we found. And your cousins. And your sister. Maybe we should ask them if they put the coke in the wizard. It would be interesting to hear what they have to say. I'm sure they would be pleased by your accusations, don't you, Libby?"

"Oh, absolutely. I can hardly wait to hear their comments."

"Screw you," Geoff said.

"That's so rude," Bernie said.

"No need for name-calling," Libby said as she started to put the bag of coke in her pocket.

"What are you doing with that?" Geoff cried.

"I'm going to use it to wash the dishes," Libby said.

"You can't," Geoff wailed.

"You're right," Bernie said. "All that money down the drain. That would be a shame. No, instead we're going to keep it to show to the police when they turn up. Which they most assuredly will do sooner or later."

"You can't do that," Geoff repeated.

"And why not?" Libby said. "Are you going to stop me?"

Geoff looked at Bernie and Libby for a moment. His eyes widened. Bernie could see what he was thinking. She began to shout a warning to Libby to move away from him, but she had gotten only as far as "Watch the . . ." when Geoff reached over, grabbed the bag of coke, and dashed out of the room.

"Maybe I shouldn't have said that," Libby said as she and Bernie ran after Geoff.

"You mean the 'are you going to stop me' thing?" Bernie replied.

"Yeah. That."

"You think?"

It was a matter of seconds before Libby and Bernie reached the hallway, but by that time Geoff was gone.

"Where did he go?" Bernie asked as she listened for his footsteps.

There weren't any. Not only that, there were no tell-a-tale creaks, groans, or squeaks from the floorboards, either.

Libby shook her head. "It's like he disappeared."

"Well, he has to be somewhere," Bernie said. "People don't just vanish. At least not in real life they don't."

"I guess we should start looking," Libby said.

"I guess so," Bernie agreed.

"And we're going to do what when we find him?"

Bernie clicked her tongue against the roof of her mouth. "We're going to ask him some more questions."

"And if he won't answer?" Libby persisted.

"Then we'll ask again."

"And if he still won't answer?"

Bernie let out an annoyed grunt. "Then we can at least say we tried. And, anyway," Bernie added, "looking for him will give us a chance to finish going through all the rooms on this floor."

"So what are we waiting for?" Libby asked.

Bernie held out her hand. "After you, Alfonse."

Libby bowed. "My pleasure."

Chapter 27

"This place creeps me out," Libby said as she started down the hallway.

"It must be the wallpaper," Bernie said.

It was a faded yellow with thin brown stripes spaced about three inches apart. In between the stripes were representations of tiny pineapples interspersed with cherries, both of which were rendered in minute detail. The effect of the wallpaper in the narrow space was to make the space even narrower.

"No. That gives me indigestion," Libby said. She stood there biting the cuticle of her thumb while she thought. "No, it's something else. Something's missing here."

"Like decent decor? Like the feeling that someone gives a damn?"

"Besides that." Libby was silent for another minute. Then she said, "It'll come to me sooner or later. Meanwhile, we should get started."

"Yes, we should," Bernie agreed. "There are seven bedrooms and two bathrooms. I figure one for Lexus and one for Geoff. Then I'm guessing that Melissa and Greta each have their own room, because I can't see them sharing. They'd kill each other."

"And Monty definitely does."

"So that leaves Ralph and Perceval, and Bob and Audie each sharing a room. How do you want to do this?"

"It would be faster if we separated," Libby said. "You could take three bedrooms and a bathroom and I could do the same and we both could take Monty's room."

"Yes, it would be faster," Bernie agreed.

Libby started on her cuticle. "However . . ."

"I'd feel better if we were together, too," Bernie told her.

"Thanks," Libby said. "Appreciate it. After all, there's no sense taking chances."

Bernie nodded. "You corner people and you never know what they'll do."

"And Geoff could be our murderer," Libby said. Then she pointed to the door closest to her. "I think we should start here and work our way toward the stairs. And then we can check the downstairs."

"Works for me," Bernie said. "I wish I had a cigarette."

"And I wish I had a piece of chocolate."

The women looked at each other. Bernie gave a tiny nod.

"Here we go," Libby said, and she took a deep breath, pushed the door of the nearest bedroom open, and went inside. *Spartan* was the word that came to Libby's mind as she looked around.

"Could they have made this room any smaller?" Bernie commented from behind Libby's back.

"Not by much," Libby replied. "It's even smaller than Geoff's room is."

She estimated that the room measured eight feet by ten feet at the most. Shoehorned into it was a twin bed, a nightstand, a small dresser, and a garish rose-flowered area rug, leaving just enough room to walk around. There were no curtains or blinds on the windows, and Libby could see that thick flakes of snow were still falling out of the sky.

Libby checked under the bed, while Bernie went over and opened the partially opened closet door all the way. Two pairs of slacks and a cashmere robe were hanging inside. Underneath was a twenty-inch suitcase, one of the expensive kind. Bernie bent and read the tag on the suitcase. It was Greta's.

"Some guest room," Bernie said as she moved over to the dresser and opened the top drawer. "The cells at the Longely police station are more attractive."

"At least they're brighter. Anything interesting?" Libby asked as Bernie went through the top dresser drawer.

Bernie shook her head. "Not so far. We have some very expensive lingerie, a pair of silk pajamas, three cashmere sweaters, and a cosmetic case." Bernie opened it. "Which contains some very pricey products," she announced, holding up a night cream that cost five hundred dollars an ounce. "This woman definitely has money. Not that we didn't know that before, but this confirms it."

"Which she might have got from her Africa scam," Libby said.

"And maybe she's spent it and wants more," Bernie commented as she went through the second and third drawers, both of which proved to be empty. "Maybe Greta has a serious case of the entitlements."

"Obviously, she's not a big reader," Libby said, noting the lack of reading material on the nightstand. "And she wasn't planning on staying very long," Libby added. "Either that or she is a light packer." Libby tapped her fingers on her thighs as she looked around the room.

Bernie straightened up. "I think we can say with one hundred percent certainty that Geoff's not here."

"Maybe he was and jumped out the window," Libby suggested.

"No. I don't think so." Bernie pointed to the lock on the upper window sash. "Not unless he is Harry Houdini. See that?"

"Yes."

"It's locked."

"Obviously."

"Well, these locks only lock from the inside. In order to go out the window, Geoff would have had to have had an accomplice, otherwise the window would still be unlocked. And we haven't heard anybody else up here, and given the way the floor creaks and groans, I think we would have." Bernie went over to the window and nodded toward the white expanse of snow. "And even if he did somehow manage to relock the window, if he landed in the snow, he would have left tracks. And there are none. Also, the snow on the windowsill would be messed up."

Libby went back to gnawing on her cuticle. "Still, it's odd."

"The whole thing is odd, if you ask me," Bernie said as she yanked a hank of hair off her face and repinned it. "The first thing I'm going to do when we get out of here is cut this all off," she muttered.

Libby didn't comment, since Bernie had been threatening to cut her hair off for the last ten years. "On to room number two," she said instead.

Chapter 28

As soon as Bernie opened the door to the next bedroom, she smelled tobacco smoke. She put up her hand for Libby to stop. "Oh, Geoff," she called out. "We're here."

Silence.

"Come out, come out, wherever you are," Bernie sang.

Nothing.

"If your voice doesn't make him come out, nothing will," Libby cracked.

"Ha-ha. Very funny," Bernie said as she gestured for Libby to take the closet while she looked under the bed. "I have a nice voice."

"Is that why Mrs. Marconi forbade you to sing in the school chorus?" Libby asked as she took in the room.

It was a little bit bigger than the one she and Bernie had just been in, but not by much. However, since it had two single beds in it, instead of one, it actually felt smaller. Again, there were no blinds or curtains on the windows, which meant no one could be hiding behind them. Also, all the corners in the room were clearly visible, so that took care of that problem.

Libby quickly moved toward the closet, grabbed the

doorknob, yanked it back, and peered inside. No Geoff. Just clothes, and not too many of those.

"Clear," she said.

"Ditto under the bed." Bernie got up and brushed the dust off her knees.

Libby bent down and checked the tags on the luggage. "So either Geoff was here and he's gone somewhere else, or Bob and Audie smoke."

"Probably the latter possibility," Bernie said.

Libby grunted as she went through the clothes on the hangers. There were two pairs of men's jeans, a pair of corduroys, two pressed white shirts, and two jackets hanging on the metal rod. Libby looked at the labels. She knew from Bernie that this particular brand of jeans sold for 250 dollars a pair and that the shirts on the hangers were equally expensive.

"Maybe Monty got the furniture at a big lots sale," Bernie commented, looking around. "Same dressers. Same beds. Same night tables as in Greta's room. He must have gotten a discount. This feels as if it's made of cardboard," she said as she pulled one of the nightstand drawers open.

"It could very well be," Libby said. She closed the closet door and moved on to the dresser, while Bernie checked out the nightstand.

The top of the nightstand was bare, but when Bernie opened up the drawer, she saw a pack of cigarettes and a lighter. "Bingo," she said, holding up the cigarettes. "Bob and/or Audie smoke."

"So maybe Geoff wasn't in here," Libby said. The top and middle dresser drawers contained boxers, socks, two pairs of pj's, and some sweatshirts.

"Or he was here and he left," Bernie noted. She searched the rest of the nightstand. The only thing she found was a Swiss Army knife and a couple of dollars worth of spare change. For a moment Bernie debated about taking the knife but in the end decided against it. "Two rooms down and five to go," she announced, closing the door to the room behind them.

"Don't you think it's odd," Libby said as they walked down the hall to the third room, "that all the bedroom doors are closed?"

Bernie paused for a moment. "Odd? No. Indicating a major lack of familial trust? Yes." She opened the door to the third room. "This has to be Melissa's," she said when she got a gander at what was inside.

Melissa's room, like Geoff's, was frozen in time. A happier time. Melissa's mom had probably furnished it for her daughter, Bernie decided. Certainly Bernie couldn't see Monty doing it. The room was a study in pink. There were pink drapes on the windows, a pink coverlet on the bed, and a pink area rug on the floor. The walls were painted a soft off-white, and Bernie could see the faint outline of stars on the ceiling. Two posters adorned the walls. One was of Disney's Cinderella and the other was of Snow White. The top of Melissa's dresser was covered with a collection of dolls and stuffed animals, while a large stuffed penguin sat sentinel on her bed. The top of her nightstand was littered with diet books, none of which, Bernie thought, seemed to be doing Melissa much good.

Bernie quickly opened the closet door, while Libby looked under the bed.

"I don't know where Geoff is," Libby commented as she got up, "but I have a feeling he's long gone from here."

"I do, too," Bernie said as she went through Melissa's clothes. Half of them were nurses' uniforms, and the other half were cheap jeans and sweatshirts. "She doesn't spend a lot of money on her clothes," she said.

Libby looked up from the dresser drawer. "Ditto her underwear and T-shirts. Even mine are better than these." Which was saying a lot.

Bernie looked at her sister. "Thank me for that. So either Melissa isn't interested in clothes or she doesn't have money to spend on them."

"Unlike Greta."

"Yes, unlike Greta. Who only buys the best."

Libby closed the dresser drawer and went over to the nightstand. She picked up the watch that was sitting next to the lamp. "This probably cost ten ninety-nine." She put it down and picked up a bracelet made of links. "And this probably cost less. I'm thinking dollar store."

Libby opened the nightstand drawer. It was filled to overflowing with lottery tickets. She held one up to show to Bernie. "Well, at least we know what Melissa spends her money on." Then Libby picked up a letter from Turning Stone, a casino near Syracuse, and opened it. The letter was comping Melissa for her next visit. There were several similar letters from casinos around the country.

"Casinos only send those to their good customers," Bernie said after Libby had finished reading the contents of one of the letters to her.

"And I'm sure she is that." Libby picked up the penguin, then put him down on the bed. He seemed like a sad little guy. She took another quick look around the room. If there was anything of interest there, she couldn't see it.

Libby walked out first and Bernie followed, closing the door behind her.

"So Monty's kids turn out to be a cokehead and a gambler," Bernie said to her sister. "No wonder he didn't want to leave his business to them."

"Maybe that's why they wouldn't kill him."

Bernie stopped turning the doorknob on Lexus's door. "Excuse me?" she said.

Libby explained. "Well, apparently they're getting money from their dad."

Bernie nodded. "Geoff is for sure because he works for

him, and Melissa, being on the board of directors, is entitled to a share of the profits."

"But if he dies and the business goes to someone else, then they'll be cut off."

"Interesting. I see what you're saying. I'm not sure I agree, but it's definitely something to think about." And on that note Bernie entered Lexus's room.

All the bed linen was off the bed, but other than that, things looked substantially the same since she and Libby had been there. Bernie took the closet, and Libby looked behind the curtains and under the bed.

"There's no sign of Geoff," Libby said.

"Not that I expected there would be," Bernie said. "Why hide in the room of your mortal enemy?"

"On the other hand, it would be the last place anyone would look," Libby replied as Bernie quickly went through the closet.

Unlike those of the other family members, Lexus's closet was bursting at the seams. "This is a woman who likes to shop," Bernie commented as she went through the clothes. "Lots of high-priced designer stuff. Except it's four to five years old. Then some newer, cheaper, dowdier stuff, the same kind of stuff that Melissa has in her closet. A definite disconnect."

"Meaning?" Libby said.

"My best guess," Bernie said, looking through Lexus's pocketbooks to see if anything was in them, "is that the old stuff is what Monty bought Lexus before they got married, and the new stuff is what he got her after." She held up a black sheath dress that looked big enough to cover a postage stamp and a schlumpy black skirt. "I would not be happy if I were Lexus. She's young, she's pretty, and apparently she's on a very tight budget."

"And this is how she copes," Libby said, waving a baggie that she'd found in the nightstand. It was filled with pills.

Bernie walked over and took a look. "I see Ambien, Xanax, OxyContin, and Valium. Not a bad collection."

"I guess this is what it takes to live with Monty," Libby said.

"And she's not even getting anything for it."

"But she might if he dies."

"Not if the rest of the family has anything to say about it."

"True."

Bernie looked again at the bag of pills Libby was holding. For a moment she was tempted to take some of them but decided against it. She'd learned the hard way that she and that stuff didn't mix. Instead, she looked at her watch. "We need to finish up."

"Bathrooms now or later?"

"Let's get them over with now," Bernie said.

Which was what they did. Bernie and Libby looked in the linen closets and behind the shower curtains and in the towel hampers, even though there was no possible way Geoff could have fit in there. But the bathrooms proved to be empty, and the sisters went back to the bedrooms.

"Do you really think that Geoff is hiding in one of them?" Libby asked her sister as they walked down the hallway.

"Well, I thought there was a chance before, but now I'm not so sure," Bernie admitted. She paused for a second, then said, "Actually, I don't think he's here at all."

"Why?"

"Too still."

"Too still?"

"Yeah. You know, like when you walk into an empty house, you can feel that no one is there. Well, that's the feeling I'm getting on this floor."

"Then where do you think he is?"

Bernie shrugged. "It's a big house. He could be downstairs. In the garage. In the basement. Up on the roof. Who knows?" She paused in front of the bedroom she assumed to be Ralph and Perceval's. She was about to open the door when she thought she heard a noise. "I'm taking back what I said. Maybe I'm wrong about his being here, after all. Did you hear that?"

"What?"

"I'm not sure. Something moving."

"I don't hear anything," Libby said.

Bernie put her right hand up and laid a finger on her lips. Libby stood there, listening. She could see Bernie concentrating on something, but she didn't know what. They both stood in the hallway for another moment, but all they heard were the voices of the Field family drifting up the stairs.

"I guess I was mistaken," Bernie said after another moment had elapsed.

"You? Heh. Heh. Never."

"Cute." Bernie bit her bottom lip. "I think this place is getting to me," she told Libby.

"I'm not surprised," Libby answered. "It's already gotten to me."

She pushed the door open and walked into Ralph and Perceval's room. Bernie followed. The room had the same institutional feel as Greta's, Bob's, and Audie's rooms. But unlike those of that threesome, Ralph's and Perceval's clothing was old and worn. The collars of their shirts were frayed, their sweaters were pilling and wearing out at the elbow, while the hems on their trousers had seen better days.

"Certainly not holiday wear," Bernie said as she closed the closet door.

"And speaking of holidays," Libby said as she spread out the contents of the nightstand drawer on one of the beds.

Bernie went over to take a look. There were three guidebooks to India, a slew of travel brochures, printouts of fares, and notes giving the names of hotel rooms and the names of guides.

Bernie picked up one of the brochures. "It looks as if they're planning a vacation."

Libby picked up one of the proposed itineraries. "The hotels are all first class. So are the flights. And they're going to be gone for three weeks. Sounds nice."

"Sounds spectacular."

"We could do that, too."

"Yes, we could. If we had the time and the money. Commodities that Ralph and Perceval are suddenly in possession of."

"Of course, they could have been saving up for a long time for this trip."

"They could have," Bernie agreed.

"Do you believe that?"

"No. Do you?"

"Not at all."

"Interesting that they're going off next month."

"Isn't it?" Libby replied. "The timing is very interesting, indeed." She held up a letter addressed to Perceval that had been lodged in one of the travel books and opened it. "Especially when Perceval bounced a four-thousand-dollar check a couple of weeks ago."

Bernie whistled. "Probably just a minor bookkeeping error. Maybe Ralph has the money to cover the trip."

"Why don't I think so?" Libby said.

"Funny thing, but I don't, either."

Libby smiled. "It's nice when we agree on something."

"Sometimes we do. For instance, we agree that butter is good."

"I mean besides cooking." Libby picked at one of her nails. "So I guess Perceval and Ralph are expecting to get a windfall of some kind. Like an inheritance."

"Yes," Bernie said. "Like an inheritance. Or access to a lot of spare cash."

"Funny coincidence."

"Yes. Isn't it?"

Libby gathered all the travel materials up and replaced them in the nightstand drawer. "Well, this certainly gives us something to think about," she said. "I wonder if the rest of the family knows about the trip."

Bernie grinned. "Let's ask."

"By all means," Libby said as she and Bernie went across the hall to Monty's room. "You'd expect Monty's and Lexus's rooms to at least be connected," Libby said as she opened the door and went inside.

"Think of it as a metaphor for their relationship," Bernie said, following.

Then she stopped talking. The room took her breath away. It gleamed. The furnishings were few, but everything in it was exquisite. The chest of drawers was Quaker, as were the nightstand and the bedstead. A Renoir hung on one wall, while a Cezanne and a Monet hung on another. A finely woven Oriental carpet covered the gleaming wood parquet floors, and a Tang horse sat in lone splendor on the dresser.

"You think these paintings are authentic?" Libby asked her sister.

Bernie nodded. "Yes, I do."

"They could be copies."

Bernie studied the Renoir. She studied the other furnishings, noting the care with which everything had been placed. "I don't think they are. I think everything in this room is genuine. I think Monty saved the best of his collection for himself."

Libby opened the closet door. There were four pairs of pants, three shirts, and a sports jacket hanging in the closet. "Well, he certainly didn't spend a lot of money on his clothes. Or his shoes." She picked up the one pair in the closet. They were old Docksiders worn down at the heel. Then she put them back down on the floor, which was old and grimy. "I guess when Monty had the floor re-done, he didn't bother with the closet," she commented before she closed the door.

Bernie ran her finger lightly over the back of the Tang horse. "I can't imagine what it would be like to own something like this," she murmured before going over to the nightstand and looking at the printed material stacked up on it. There were gallery catalogs, notices of impending sales from Sotheby's and other auction houses. Bernie paged through them. Judging by the check marks, it looked as if Monty was interested in bidding on an upcoming Turner and a Sargent landscape.

"I guess he lived for his art," Bernie said as she put the catalog for an upcoming sale down on the nightstand and opened the drawer. There was nothing in it but a pack of tissues and a bottle of Motrin.

"You know," Libby said, "I was thinking about how I would feel if our father spent every cent on his interests and nothing on us. Especially if the money was coming from a company that our mother's father had started."

"That would probably make it worse."

"Obviously, Monty thought that his art was a better investment than his children."

"I hate to say this, but given Melissa and Geoff, he was probably right."

And on that note, Bernie and Libby walked out of Monty's room, closing the door behind them, and headed for the stairs. They were almost there when Bernie noticed that the door to Geoff's room was half opened.

She poked Libby in the shoulder and indicated the door with her chin when Libby turned around. "We closed it all the way, didn't we?" she whispered.

"Yeah, we did. Maybe Geoff is behind the door," Libby whispered back.

Bernie nodded. Then she walked over and kicked the

door as hard as she could. The door slammed against the wall.

"Guess not," she said.

She and Libby stepped inside.

"It would be pretty funny if Geoff was here all along," Libby said.

"Not really," Bernie answered as she looked around.

Geoff wasn't.

In fact, everything was the same.

Except for one thing.

The sword on the wall was gone.

Chapter 29

The entire Field family—minus Monty and Geoff—was seated in the study, drinking coffee, when Bernie and Libby came in and told them what had happened with Geoff.

Perceval harrumphed and slapped the arm of the chair he was sitting in. "See, I knew Geoff was bent," he pontificated. "I knew he was totally unreliable. I've been telling my brother that for years. But he wouldn't listen. He didn't want to know what was right in front of his face."

"No one cares what you think, Perceval," Lexus snapped. "The key issue here is that Geoff is wandering around the house, carrying that god-awful sword with him." She turned to Bernie and Lexus. "I can't believe you let Geoff get away. How irresponsible can you be?"

"We didn't *let* him do anything," Libby said as she unbuttoned her sweater. The place was now extremely warm, almost hot, really. Melissa must have hiked the heat up to eighty. "We couldn't stop him."

"And you don't know where he is?" Lexus demanded.

"Not at the moment, no," Libby replied. "We looked everywhere we can think of, and we can't find him."

Ralph leaned forward in his chair. "Does that mean you looked in the bedrooms?"

"That's what I just said," Libby told him.

"Who gave you permission to do that?" Ralph asked.

"Why?" Bernie asked. "Is there something you don't want us to see? Like your plans for your trip to India?"

"You're going to India?" Melissa asked Ralph.

"Perceval and I were going to India on business," Ralph told her.

"Dad never told me," Melissa said.

"Melissa," Perceval replied, "my brother never told you about lots of things."

"He never told me, either," Greta said.

"Maybe," Ralph said, "that's because he didn't want you to know."

"It's an expensive trip," Bernie said. "First class all the way."

Ralph straightened up. "One can't do business looking like a beggar."

Libby raised an eyebrow. "I find the timing suggestive, don't you, Bernie?"

"Absolutely, Libby."

Perceval sniffed. "If you're suggesting what I think you're suggesting, I'm deeply offended."

Bernie put her hand to her heart. "Oh, the pain."

Perceval started to say something, but before he could answer, Lexus said, "Oh, for God's sake, Ralph, grow up. We have a real problem here with Geoff." She turned back to Bernie and Libby. "Did you look downstairs?"

"Of course we did," said Libby.

She and Bernie had searched all the rooms in the back end of the first floor without any luck. Then, thinking that Geoff could have also gone out through one of the downstairs doors, they'd checked the kitchen door. It had proved difficult to budge, because the door opened outward and there were almost two feet of snow butted up against it. And when they'd finally succeeded in opening it, they'd seen a pristine expanse of white. There were no tracks of any kind in it.

The same held true of the front door. Although it opened easily, no fresh footprints leading away from the house were visible. They could make out their old footprints, but those were already half filled in, with their direction clearly heading toward the house.

Then they'd checked the garage. She and Bernie had looked in and under the two cars parked there, had opened the cabinets and the utility bins, and had looked around the pallets that Perceval and Ralph had laid Monty out on. They'd even gone through the trash. Geoff hadn't been there, but the Dell had. Bernie had declared this to be a good thing, because at least they could cross that off their list. The last thing she and Libby had done was check the basement. It had been empty except for the hot water heater and a couple of old, broken-down bikes.

Lexus ran one of her fingers around the collar of her white turtleneck. "He's going to kill us all," she announced. "He's going to hack us to bits. I knew Monty should never have allowed Geoff to bring that sword in the house. I told him it was dangerous. But Monty wouldn't listen. He always knew everything."

"I very much doubt Geoff would do anything like that," Melissa countered.

Since Bernie had last seen Melissa, Melissa had changed into a pair of low-riding, tight-fitting jeans, a man's wife-beater T-shirt, and a fire engine red hoodie that ended two inches above her waist, exposing a large roll of fat. It was not a good look for anyone, let alone Melissa.

"How can you doubt that?" Lexus cried. She waved her hands in the air. "He's already killed his own father. A man who will do that will do anything."

Melissa snorted.

"What's that supposed to mean?" Lexus demanded.

"My God, you're such a drama queen."

Lexus pointed at herself. "Me? Hardly. Aren't you concerned for your own safety?" she asked Melissa.

"Not even a little. Why should I be? If he kills anyone, which I highly doubt, he'll kill you," Melissa told Lexus, "not me."

"What a horrible thing to say," Lexus replied.

"Well, I wasn't the one that ratted him out to my dad. I wasn't the one that told my dad Geoff was using drugs. I wasn't the one who told him he was stealing from the company."

"That's ridiculous," Lexus cried. "How can you make accusations like that?"

"Simple. I can make them because they're true."

"Monty didn't know that Geoff was using drugs," Lexus told her.

"Until you told him," Melissa said.

Lexus shook her head vigorously. "No. No. No. You were the one that told. Not me."

"What a colossal lie," Melissa cried.

"I'm not saying anything that isn't true. Monty told me you had," Lexus said. "But he already knew."

"Now, there's a laugh," Ralph said, chiming in.

"He did," Lexus insisted.

"Monty never told you anything," Ralph said. "He hardly spoke to you."

"He most certainly did," Lexus insisted. "He talked to me for hours and hours."

"Ha," Melissa said.

"Don't 'ha' me," Lexus spit back.

"He didn't talk to you. He hated you," Melissa said. "Marrying you was the biggest mistake he ever made."

Lexus drew herself up. "No, Melissa. He hated you."

"He did not."

"Yes, he did. He hated the way you were always tiptoeing around and trying to get money from him. He called you a loser and a sneak. In fact," Lexus continued, "the more I think about it, the surer I am that you were the one who told Monty that Geoff was using coke and stealing money from the company to get it, and then, when Monty kicked Geoff out, you hatched the plan with Geoff to kill your dad. That's exactly the kind of thing you'd do." Lexus touched her hands to her lips. "I'm appalled. I really am."

Melissa grew pale. Then her cheeks became mottled. "How can you live with yourself, Lexus? My father loved me. And I had no idea what Geoff was doing. Why should I? We barely even talked."

"Another lie, Melissa. Is nothing that comes out of your mouth the truth?"

"No. You're the liar," Melissa protested. "You're the one that twists everything into something that it's not."

"How stupid do you think I am?" Lexus demanded.

"You don't want me to answer that, do you?" Melissa asked.

Lexus fluffed out her hair before replying. "You can insult me all you want. That doesn't change the facts. You and Geoff were tight. You two were always together. In fact, you two were in the bunker together earlier in the day. You caused an explosion."

"That was Geoff's fault," Melissa shot back.

"Geoff's fault. Your fault. That just bears out what I was saying about you two," Lexus said.

"We weren't tight, as you like to put it. I was down in the bunker with Geoff because he had a new idea for some fireworks and he wanted to show me."

Greta twisted the gold bracelet on her wrist around. "Obviously, someone knew about Geoff and told Monty," Greta observed.

"It's not obvious to me at all," Ralph said, chiming in. "We have no proof whatsoever that Monty knew that his son was a cokehead. Or that he was taking money."

"That's true," Libby interjected.

"Of course it's true," Ralph said, annoyed at being interrupted. "And it is irrelevant on top of everything else."

"No, it's not," Audie protested. "It gives Geoff a motive for killing Monty."

"We don't know that," Ralph said.

"We don't not know it," Perceval interjected.

"You never have liked Geoff," Ralph said to his brother.

"I like him, Ralph. I just believe in looking the facts in the face, as it were."

"So do I, Perceval. So do I." Ralph banged his mug on the side table for emphasis. A trickle of coffee ran down the side. "The only thing we know for sure is that Geoff had a package of something hidden in one of those stupid candles of his. In fact, we don't even know that it is what these . . . ladies . . . say it is."

"Yeah," Bernie said, "It's probably Ivory Snow."

"Well, it might be," Ralph said.

"Don't be an idiot," Greta said to him. "Of course it's coke. Why else would Geoff be acting the way he is?"

Ralph favored her with a wintry smile. "There could be another reason."

Greta leaned forward. "Like what?" she said.

Ralph waved his hands in the air. "I don't know. Something. I'm sure he'll have an explanation."

Greta leaned back, a triumphant smile on her face. "I, for one, can hardly wait to hear it."

"We will when we find him," Ralph said.

"If we find him," Greta said. "He's probably in the next county by now."

"Oh, he's here all right. No one," Perceval pointed out, "is going anyplace in this weather."

Ralph unbuttoned his sweater. "Forgive me if I believe in the whole 'innocent until proven guilty' thing."

"How sweet," Lexus said, the sarcasm dripping from

her voice. "You probably are against capital punishment as well."

"As a matter of fact, I am," Ralph said.

"Wonderful." Lexus pulled at the collar of her white cashmere turtleneck sweater. "That makes me feel so much better. I think we should all spend the night down here. It'll be safer."

"You can do what you like," Greta replied. "I intend to spend my night in a bed."

"Aren't you afraid?" Lexus asked.

"Of Geoff? Hardly."

"But he killed Monty. And we're going to be next."

Greta fixed Lexus with a gimlet look. "You think that if you repeat that enough, we'll believe it?"

"I'm repeating it because it's true and I'm scared."

"No. You're repeating it because it suits you."

"I don't know what you mean."

"It's simple. You would like Geoff to get the blame for killing Monty."

"What do you mean, get the blame? He *is* to blame."

"No. I don't think so," Greta said.

"Then who do you think is?"

"Guess," Greta said, leaning forward again.

Lexus pointed at herself. "Are you suggesting I had something to do with it?"

Greta smiled. "I'm more than suggesting."

Lexus put her hands to her heart. "How can you say something like that?" she protested. "I'm not the one who's disappeared. I'm not the one running around with a weapon."

"No. But you're the one that has the most to gain."

"No, Greta. You do."

Greta pointed to herself. "Don't be stupid. Monty was going to sell me half of his shares in the company, so his death was not a good thing for me. In fact, for me his death translates into a lost opportunity. That's why I don't need to forge a new will."

Lexus half rose. "And you think that I did that."

"Yes, I do. Most definitely. In short, you killed him because you got tired of waiting for him to die."

"I loved him."

"You considered him a meal ticket. Unfortunately, once you were married, he didn't turn out to be a very good one. Which is why you killed him. Oh, wait." Greta held up her hand. "Do something by yourself? Not your style. No. That's why you had Geoff do it, and now you want to finger him for it."

"That's absurd. Why would I want Geoff found, then?"

"So you can kill him."

Lexus glared at her. "You keep saying things like that, and I'm going to sue you for libel when we get out of here."

Greta took a sip of coffee and put her cup down. "Boy, that just terrifies me."

"It should."

Greta laughed. "If I were you, I'd stop talking about Monty's will and how it leaves everything to you. Frankly, dear, I find that impossible to believe."

"You do, do you?" Lexus said.

"Yes, Lexus, I do." Greta held out her hands and studied her manicure.

"And why is that, Greta?"

"Simple," Greta said, folding her hands back in her lap. "Monty told me, as he told Melissa and everyone else here, that he was going to divorce you, which would leave you on the street with nothing."

"God, you are such a liar!" Lexus cried. "He was most certainly not going to divorce me. He was going to kick you and those other two worthless bums out."

Audie half stood. "Are you talking about me and Bob?" he demanded of Lexus.

"You know what they say?" Lexus sneered. "If the shoe fits, wear it."

Bernie and Libby watched the two women from the other side of the room. It appeared as if they'd reached a standoff. There was a thirty-second lull in the conversation, then the arguing started all over again.

Lexus turned to Libby and Bernie. "Perhaps Geoff is down in the bunker," she said to them, as if the last five minutes of conversation hadn't taken place.

"There are no footprints going that way," Bernie told her.

"How can you be so sure?"

"We looked," Bernie said.

"Maybe they got covered up. I think you should look again," Lexus told her. "I think you should go out there and check."

"You're kidding me, right?" Bernie said.

"Not in the least."

"Don't be ridiculous, Lexus," Perceval said. "If Geoff is out there—which I doubt—let him stay there."

"Anyway, he definitely didn't go out the front door," Melissa said.

"How do you know that?" Bernie asked, stifling a yawn.

Much as she didn't want to admit it, she realized she was beginning to crash and would have to get some rest soon. She took a quick look at Libby. Her sister's eyelids were drooping, and she appeared to have trouble staying on her feet. It seemed as if the day had finally caught up with her, as well. On the other hand, Lexus seemed positively perky. She'd probably had a nap, Bernie thought, not without a certain amount of rancor.

Melissa tugged at her T-shirt, which had ridden up over her midriff. It didn't help. "I know because Bob and I were in the living room, cataloging the pictures."

"Ah, the vultures are circling," Lexus murmured sotto voce.

"That is entirely uncalled for," Melissa told her.

"Just remember," Lexus replied, "I know where every picture of any worth is in this house."

"And so do I, Lexus. So do I."

Lexus wagged a finger in Melissa's face. "If even a drawing goes missing, I'll speak to my lawyer."

"Not before I speak to mine," Melissa said. "And remember, they can tell about art forgeries these days."

Lexus shook her head. "You poor dear child, you must be so upset to say things like that."

"Get real," Melissa told her before going on with what she'd been saying to Bernie and Libby. "As I was telling you before we were so rudely interrupted," Melissa said, raising her voice, "Bob and I have been in the living room for the past hour and a half, and we would have seen Geoff if he went out the front door."

Lexus turned to Bernie and Libby. "So I repeat," Lexus said. "Where did he go?"

"He was beamed up to the mother ship," Libby snapped.

"Seriously," Lexus said.

"Well," Libby said, "it's as good an explanation as anything else."

"I'm not paying you to give me that kind of answer," Lexus huffed.

"You haven't paid us at all," Bernie pointed out.

"But I will."

"So you say," Libby told her.

Lexus shrugged. "I will."

"When? When are you going to pay us?" Bernie asked her.

"When this is over," Lexus replied.

"Don't believe her," Greta told Libby. "She never pays anyone."

"Do you mind?" Lexus told Greta. "I'm trying to find out something here."

"Like what?" Greta told her. "They"—she pointed to Bernie and Libby—"already told you they searched the house and they can't find Geoff. This is not complicated. There are only two possibilities." She touched the pinkie of her left hand with the pointer of her right hand. "Geoff is either inside or he's outside. And we've established that he isn't outside, which means he must be inside, somewhere in this house."

"That's no answer at all, Greta," Lexus snapped.

"I have a feeling it's the best you're going to get," Greta snapped back.

"Please." Melissa put her hands to her ears. "Can't we all just stop arguing? I can't stand it anymore."

Lexus ignored her and went back to talking to Bernie and Libby. "So what are you going to do about the situation?" she demanded.

Bernie didn't have to think about her answer. "I'm going to take a nap," she said. She was so tired that her teeth were hurting.

Chapter 30

There was a loud crack, and the lights in the living room flickered on and off for a few seconds. Then they came back on.

Perceval brought his hand up and smoothed his hair over the top of his forehead. "Must be a tree branch falling. Probably one of the elms down by the bunker."

Melissa shivered. "I hope the power doesn't go off in the house. That would be horrible."

"It would be cold," Audie observed. "That's for damn sure."

No one said anything else. It was as if, Bernie decided, they'd all run out of things to say. After a moment of silence, Greta lightly touched the gold chain she was wearing around her neck and rose.

"I, for one, have had enough of pointless arguing for the moment," she announced. "I'm going to bed."

Bob nodded. "So am I."

Ralph got up. "Me too. It's been a long day."

"That's one way of putting it," Melissa said as she levered herself out of her chair.

Audie stood as well. "Guess I'm going, too. I'm not going to be the lone duck."

"Lame duck," Greta corrected. "And that's a political term."

"Whatever," Audie shot back.

"Audie, how are you going to know you're doing something wrong if I can't tell you?"

Audie dug his hands into his pockets and rocked back on his heels. "Trust me. I'll be able to figure it out."

Lexus looked around the room. Everyone was standing but her. "I guess I'll go to bed, too, then. It's not as if I have a choice."

"Sure you do," Melissa said. "No one is forcing you to go upstairs. You can stay down here if you want."

"By myself?" Lexus put her hand to her heart. "And let Geoff attack me? No. I don't think so. Not that my bedroom is much safer. But I want you all to know that if I'm dead in the morning, my blood is on your hands."

"Oh, *puh-lease,*" Melissa said.

Perceval gave a derogatory snort, while the rest of the Field family pointedly ignored Lexus's comment. They were filing out of the room when Bob stopped short. Greta bumped into him and Audie bumped into her.

"I just thought of something," Bob said.

"Now, there's a novelty," Melissa murmured.

Bob glowered at her. "You're not exactly a font of ideas yourself."

Melissa was about to answer him when Perceval intervened. "Children, children," he said, putting both hands out in front of him and making calming motions. "Can we stop this nonsense?" Then, before anyone could answer, he nodded toward Bob. "Now, as you were saying?"

"All I was saying," Bob replied, "was how do we know that when we're in our separate rooms, one of us won't come down here and find the will?"

"Good point," Perceval said. "We don't."

Ralph rubbed the side of his nose with one of his knuckles. "Does it really matter? After all, how can anyone find it when Lexus already has it?"

"Yes, Bob," Audie said. "You forgot about that."

"You know, Lexus," said Perceval, "I think it's time we saw that will you keep talking about."

Lexus feigned a yawn.

"You don't have it, do you?" Ralph said.

"Of course I do," Lexus replied.

"Then show it to us now," Ralph demanded.

"Yes," Greta said. "I'm quite interested."

Melissa chimed in with, "So am I."

"We want to see it," everyone else said, taking up the cry.

"No, I won't," Lexus said.

"That, my dear," Perceval told her, "is because you haven't got it."

"That's not it at all, Perceval," Lexus replied.

Perceval smirked. "Then what is it?"

"It's simple."

"We're waiting," Ralph said.

Lexus put her hand to her heart. "If I did show it to you, what would prevent any of you from destroying it or even killing me to keep me silent?"

"So you don't have it," Melissa said.

"Of course I do," Lexus replied.

"Then let's see it," Ralph said.

"I already told you why I can't," Lexus replied.

"How about if we all went down to the bunker and put your precious will there and then locked the door, and we all stuck together till tomorrow night, or whenever it is that we can get out of here? How would that be?" Greta asked. "Would you feel safe then?"

"That's ridiculous," Lexus said.

"Why?" Ralph said. "It seems like a perfectly good plan to me."

Lexus didn't say anything.

"Just as I thought," Greta said to Lexus. "You don't have the will. You know, my dear," she continued, "you need intelligence to lie well."

"You are such a bitch!" Lexus screamed, taking a step toward Greta.

Ralph stepped between the two women. "Let's not do that here."

Lexus clenched her fists. Her face was turning red. "You're going to get yours," she told Greta over Ralph's shoulder.

Greta smiled. "Indeed I am, while you, on the other hand, are going to get nothing."

"Fat lot you know," Lexus spit back at Greta. "Monty promised me everything. The house. The business. The cars. All of it. He owes me. I deserve it."

Melissa laughed. "Spoken like the true queen of entitlement."

Bernie coughed. Everyone looked at her.

"From what I can gather, it seems to me as if Monty promised everybody everything," she said, interrupting the hostilities. "That's how he kept control over all of you."

Ralph said, "I keep telling all of you that."

"It's true," Melissa agreed. "Every time Dad got mad at someone, he wrote them out, and he got mad a lot."

"Not at me," Lexus said. "He never got angry at me."

"You most of all," Melissa told her.

"I was his perfect angel," Lexus replied.

Melissa made a gagging noise. "Remind me to vomit."

"Okay," Libby said, stepping into the breach. "Everyone, answer me this. Did Monty say he was going to change his will, or did he actually do it?"

"I think both," Melissa said after thinking it over.

"So there could be multiple versions," Bernie said.

Audie bobbed his head. "Without a doubt. Now you see the problem."

"Who witnessed the wills?" Libby asked.

"Alma and her son," Ralph said.

Perceval finished his brother's sentence for him. "Who are conveniently not here."

"He didn't use a notary?" Bernie asked.

"Not that I know of," Melissa said.

Libby bit her fingernail. "And I suppose it's too much to hope that he had a lawyer."

"He had one," Ralph said. "I'm just not sure he used his lawyer for this."

"I know he didn't," Perceval said.

"How do you know?" Libby asked.

"He told me," Perceval replied. "After all, lawyers cost money, money that my brother was loath to spend on something he was positive he could do as well as, if not better than, any lawyer in the business."

"What a mess," Bernie observed.

"Indeed it is," Ralph agreed.

There was another crack. Everyone jumped.

"We have to find that will," Melissa said.

"Yes, we do," Greta agreed.

This time Lexus said nothing.

"It's nice you agree on something," Bernie commented.

"Maybe Geoff's found it," Lexus said, ignoring Bernie's comment.

"Then we'll just have to get it from him, won't we?" Greta said.

Ralph nodded. "We have to look for it, anyway," he said.

"Agreed," Perceval said. "At least we know it's not in Monty's desk."

Or the bunker, Bernie thought. Or if it was there, she and Libby hadn't found it.

"I never really thought it would be in the desk in the study, anyway," Ralph said. "Too obvious."

"Why do you say that?" Libby asked him.

"Because my brother had a habit of hiding things," Ralph replied.

"Yes," Melissa said. "My dad was really good at putting things in unlikely places. I suggest we start looking now—as a group."

"I'm too tired," Greta protested. "I'm so tired, I can hardly stand up. Let's do it tomorrow."

"But then one of us can find it while the others are asleep," Melissa whined.

"I just said that," Bob told Melissa.

"And I'm just agreeing with you," Melissa told him.

Bob gestured around the room. "We can all sleep down here."

"Not me," Greta said. "I need a bed. Otherwise I won't be able to stand up in the morning."

"I second that," Perceval said. "We should start tomorrow, having had the benefit of a good night's sleep."

"Fine with me," Ralph agreed.

"Then how do we get everyone to stay in their rooms?" Audie asked.

"The honor system?" Libby said.

Greta snorted. "Is that your idea of humor?"

There was silence; then Melissa clapped her hands. "I know," she cried.

Everyone waited.

"The skeleton key," she cried.

"Skeleton key?" Audie asked. "What's that?"

"Something you're too young to know about," Perceval told him.

Melissa walked over to the desk. "I just remembered," she said as she opened the middle drawer and rummaged around inside it. A moment later her hand came out with a long, thin key. She held it up. "This fits all the keyholes on all the doors."

Lexus raised an eyebrow. "Not mine, Melissa."

"Yes. All of them, Lexus," Melissa said.

Lexus frowned. "Monty said the lock didn't work."

"Well, he was lying, unless he disabled it, and I don't think he did. Try it if you don't believe me. My dad used to lock all of us in at night," Melissa explained, catching the looks on Bernie's and Libby's faces.

"Why?" Bernie asked.

"So we couldn't come down and raid the frig in the middle of the night," Melissa said. "All the food was strictly accounted for, and Dad didn't want anyone to get more than he thought they should have."

Lexus smirked and patted her stomach. "Well, you do have to admit you do have a large appetite. Maybe your dad was trying to help you control your eating, dear. Have you thought about that?"

Melissa narrowed her eyes and glared at Lexus "My dad was a cheap son of a bitch who didn't want to spend any money on food if he didn't have to. If it hadn't been for Alma, we would have been living on rice," Melissa spat back. "When we had meat, he got all the good parts and we got the fat and the gristle."

"Let's not exaggerate, shall we?" Lexus replied. "You know you're prone to it."

"Actually, she's not," Perceval said, stepping in between the two women. "But I don't get why you're talking about the locks. That's old news."

Melissa puffed her cheeks out, then blew out a stream of air. "What I'm suggesting is that all of us get locked in for the night and let out in the morning."

"And who is going to be the key master?" Perceval asked.

Melissa nodded in Bernie and Libby's direction. "They will."

"We will?" Libby asked.

"Yes, you will," Melissa said.

Bernie blinked.

"I think it's a good idea," Greta promptly replied.

Lexus nodded. "At least that way I'll be safe."

Melissa rolled her eyes.

"What was that for?" Lexus demanded.

"Like anyone is going to go after you?"

"Need I remind you," Lexus said, "that someone put Monty's body on my bed?"

"If you ask me, I think you did that yourself," Melissa told her.

Perceval waved his hands in the air. "Enough, already."

Lexus favored him with a sly smile and adjusted her white fur scarf, which she was wearing even though it was now too warm for something like that. "You're right," she said. "I'm sorry. I was just trying to help."

Melissa opened her mouth to say something, thought better of it, and nodded.

"So we're agreed?" Perceval asked everyone.

Audie cleared his throat. "There is a problem," he said.

"What's that?" Perceval asked.

"How many keys are there?"

"One," Melissa said.

"How do we know that?" Audie asked.

"I remember Monty saying it," Ralph replied.

Bob shot the cuffs of his shirt. "Why should I believe you, Ralph?"

"Because otherwise we'll be here all night." Ralph turned to Libby and Bernie. "Unless . . ." he said.

"Unless what?" Bernie asked.

"Unless you two want to patrol the hallway after you lock us in."

"We will," Bernie said, even though that was the last thing she wanted to do.

"We will?" Libby said.

"Yes," Bernie said firmly. "We will. As long as you let us do things our way."

"And what way is that?" Lexus asked.

Bernie shook her head.

"What does that mean?" Greta demanded.

"That means I'm not telling you."

"That's absurd," Ralph said.

"That's the way it is. You can take it or leave it," Bernie replied.

Lexus turned to the other family members. "I'm not comfortable with this."

"Well, I am," Perceval said. "I move we vote. All in favor, say aye."

Everyone said aye. Except Lexus.

"There you go, Lexus," Ralph said. "You're outvoted. As per usual."

"Nothing will go wrong," Melissa said. "Bernie and Libby can let us out at six."

"Six?" Lexus shrieked. "That's the crack of dawn."

"Fine, then seven," Melissa said.

"Seven thirty," Greta said.

"But not a moment later," Melissa said, looking at Bernie and Libby.

Bernie shrugged. "Seven thirty is okay by me." Years of working at the shop had conditioned her to get up early.

"The time won't be a problem," Libby agreed.

"Good," Melissa said.

A moment later everyone was filing up the stairs. Bernie and Libby locked each person into their respective bedroom. The locks seemed sturdy enough, and fairly tamperproof, Bernie thought. Of course, if one was slightly talented, one could probably open them from the inside with something like a hairpin, but Bernie decided not to mention that possibility and get everyone going again. It was now blissfully quiet without the sounds of everyone yelling at each other. And at the very least, with everyone snug in their rooms, she and Bernie would get a good night's sleep.

"Good night. Don't let the bedbugs bite," Bernie called out to everyone once she and Libby had finished locking everyone in.

No one answered, but then Bernie hadn't really expected them to. "From caterer to jailer," she said. "Who woulda thunk it?"

"Who indeed?" Libby agreed as the lights in the hallway flickered again. "We're not really going to patrol the second floor, are we?" Libby asked.

"No," Bernie said. "Are you nuts?"

"Then why did you say we are?"

Bernie grinned and told Libby her idea involving the three bags of clear marbles she'd spotted sitting on a shelf in the garage.

"That way," she concluded, "we'll hear anyone coming down the stairs."

"Because they'll fall."

"Exactly."

"Brilliant!" Libby exclaimed.

Bernie smiled smugly. "I like to think so."

Chapter 31

"I wonder where Monty's will is," Libby mused as she and Bernie finished booby-trapping the stairs and walked into the living room.

Bernie shrugged. "He probably has his will in his lawyer's office, and he's left everything to some obscure charity," she said.

Libby pulled up her pants. She really had to get the waistband on them fixed. "You're probably right. All this hue and cry for nothing. Won't the Field family be in for a surprise if that happens!"

Bernie suppressed a yawn. "Especially the person that murdered him. Talk about wasted effort."

Libby started to yawn as well. "I'd think that whoever killed him had to be pretty sure that they knew where the will was."

"I agree. Otherwise why bother? Only, when they went to look—surprise—the will wasn't there."

"Jeez. Talk about not having your plans turn out."

"I'd say."

"Guess Monty really won."

Bernie chewed on the inside of her cheek. "I don't think getting your head blown up constitutes winning, unless you have a really fatalistic outlook on life, or you were dying and wanted to have the last laugh on someone."

"You'd really have to hate someone to do that," Libby said.

"Maybe Monty was a good hater. It certainly sounds that way."

Libby changed the subject. "On a more prosaic subject, I wonder if there are any extra pillows or blankets around."

"If there are, they'd be upstairs," Bernie said.

But she was too tired to check and so was Libby. Instead, she and Libby stopped by the living room window and looked out at the scene in front of them. The snow was still falling, but not as hard as it was before. It was coming down in shiny crystal flurries.

"It is pretty out there, isn't it?" Libby said to Bernie.

Bernie repinned her hair. "It certainly is." She sighed. "All that powder. It reminds me of the West. You know," she said, "it just occurred to me that if we had skis, we could get away from here."

"But we don't," Libby said, secretly glad that was the case.

As much as she wanted to get away from the Field family, the idea of skiing out of here seemed like a worse alternative. Bernie was a good skier, while she'd never gotten beyond the bunny slope. Mastering the snowplow had been beyond her. Maybe because she'd fallen down on purpose whenever she'd started going fast.

"Unfortunately." Bernie sighed again. "It looks as if we're stuck."

"I guess we should try and get some sleep," Libby said.

Bernie nodded her head in agreement. But as it turned out, *try* was the operative word.

Chapter 32

Libby and Bernie were attempting to sleep on the settees in the living room. This was proving to be next to impossible because the settees were narrow and hard and altogether inhospitable.

"I can't sleep on this sofa," Libby said, trying to get comfortable.

"It's a daybed," Bernie said as she tried to find a place for her feet.

"Whatever it is, it's built for midgets."

"That's because people in the fourteenth century were smaller."

Libby lifted her head. "What?"

"These are replicas of daybeds used in the court of Louis Quatorze."

Libby groaned again. "All I know is that my back is never going to survive. What is this thing stuffed with?"

"Horsehair," Bernie said.

"That's disgusting."

"That's what they would have used back in the day. Either that or straw. Now, from the feel of it, it's probably cotton batting or foam rubber."

"I hate this thing," Libby groused as she tried to get comfortable.

Bernie wasn't faring much better. While she was thinner than Libby, she was taller and her feet hung over the daybed's edge, and if she tucked them under her, she started getting cramps in her calves. She knew that this was a sign that she needed water, but she was too tired to get up and get some. "This thing is worse than the airline seats," she complained. "There's even less room, if that's possible."

"Tell me about it," Libby said as she shut her eyes and tried to imagine herself sleeping in her own bed. "I think these daybeds were meant for decoration," she said after another five minutes had gone by. "I don't think they're meant for people to actually sit on."

"Recline on."

"That too."

"I wonder if these daybeds are originals," Bernie said, sitting up and running a finger over the frame's ornate carving. "Because if they're not copies, these daybeds are probably worth fifteen to twenty thousand dollars apiece."

"Is that supposed to make me feel better? That I'm being tortured by something really expensive?"

Bernie laughed.

"But I guess if they're real, then they're another thing for the family to fight about," Libby mused.

"There's a lot of money up for grabs now that Monty's dead," Bernie said. "That's for sure."

"Yeah." Libby turned around again. No matter what she did, she couldn't get comfortable. "And there aren't a lot of good sharers in the bunch."

"I wonder what Monty wanted," Bernie mused.

"Peace and love and lots of money and total control of his entire family."

"Seriously."

"I'm guessing to be alive today and eating leftovers."

"I mean heir wise."

"He probably didn't know himself. I'm sure it varied with the day of the week. How often do you think Monty changed his will?"

"Way too often," Bernie said.

"That could get confusing."

"Well, it's going to give the lawyers some big, fat fees."

"If everyone here doesn't kill each other first."

"Which would also give the lawyers big, fat fees. I think it costs at least a hundred thou to hire a defense attorney for a murder rap, probably even more. Any way you go, the lawyers win."

"Which was exactly what Monty was trying to avoid. Ironic, isn't it?" Libby said.

"Life is ironic," Bernie noted.

"Waxing philosophic, are we?"

"I think the lack of sleep is finally getting to me."

"Me too," Libby said as she tried lying on her back. "The whole divide and conquer bit works every time."

"It's certainly worked in this case. Except for Monty. Maybe if he'd been a little looser with the purse strings, no one would have felt the necessity of jerry-rigging the turkey, and he'd be alive today, and we'd be home."

"Home would be a good thing." Libby sighed. "I miss my bed."

Bernie stretched. "I wonder how Dad's doing."

"Better than we are."

"I hope so."

"Me too."

Libby and Bernie were quiet for a moment. They lay in the dark, listening to the house creaking and the wind blowing outside.

"You know what you were saying before about Monty keeping everyone on such a tight string, and that if he hadn't, maybe whoever killed him wouldn't have gotten impatient and decided to try for the brass ring?"

Bernie turned her head. "Yes?"

"So you think this murder is all about the money?" Libby asked.

"Don't you? What else could it be about? It certainly ain't about love."

"Maybe it's about hate." Libby was going to say more, but before she could, she turned on her right side and rolled off the daybed and landed on the floor with a thunk.

Bernie burst out laughing.

"It's not funny. It hurt," Libby said, picking herself up.

"I just bet it did," Bernie said before going off in another gale of laughter.

Libby stood up and rubbed her shoulder. "That's it. We have to find another place to sleep. These daybeds aren't working for me."

"Me either," Bernie agreed and she got up. "My kingdom for a decent mattress," she said as she and Libby went looking for another place to stretch out.

Chapter 33

Bernie and Libby ended up in the study.

"Back here again," Libby said. Somehow, the lilac bookshelves didn't look so bad now.

"At least now we know why everyone hangs out here," Bernie said as she plopped herself down on the tweed-covered sofa.

Libby sat down on the flowered one. "Yeah, it's the only reasonably comfortable place in the house."

"I'd kill for an air mattress," Bernie said as she tested the sofa cushions with her fingers. They were lumpy.

Libby wadded up her parka to use as a pillow, placed it on the end of the sofa closest to the end table, and lay down. "Better," she said.

"Much," Bernie agreed after she'd done the same thing.

The sisters lay in the dark, listening to the whistling, whooshing noises the wind was making outside and the creaks and groans from inside. Every once in a while there was a noise that sounded like a shot being fired.

"It's an old house," Bernie said by way of explanation, even though Libby hadn't asked for one. "Old houses make noises. It's probably the wood beams cracking in the cold."

"Probably," Libby said. "But it's unnerving, anyway."

It was, but Bernie didn't want to say that. Because to say it would be to give in to a bad case of nerves.

Libby closed her eyes. After a moment, she opened them again. "God, this house has a lot of rooms," she observed. "Too many. It's like a maze."

Bernie turned on her back and stared at the ceiling. "Go to sleep."

"I'm trying," Libby said. She wasn't succeeding, she added silently, but she was trying.

Another five minutes went by. Bernie lay there wondering what everyone else in the house was doing. Whether or not they'd gone to sleep. Where Geoff was. How he'd managed to disappear into thin air like that. Surely there was something she was missing, but try as she might, she couldn't see what it was.

Geoff had to be somewhere. He could even be lurking out in the hall, by the door. She told herself that wasn't possible. She told herself she'd hear him or anyone else. She told herself to get a grip. But she couldn't. There was something wrong. Something wrong with the whole setup. But she couldn't figure out what it was. If she could relax and get her mind on something else, it would come to her.

So she tried thinking about recipes. Specifically about bread. About trying out a recipe for a yeast-risen sweet potato bread she'd read about last week. She pictured herself kneading the dough, feeling it smooth and satiny underneath her fingers, smelling the yeast and potatoes. But it didn't help. Her mind kept going back to Geoff. Finally she couldn't stand it anymore. She sat up.

"I need a drink," she announced, getting off the sofa.

Libby sat up, too. "Include me in."

"Will do," Bernie said as she marched out of the study. She came back a moment later with a bottle of Courvoisier and two glasses. "I couldn't find any snifters."

"I'm appalled," Libby said, taking the glass that Bernie had just filled. "Simply appalled."

"So I see." Bernie poured a couple of fingers into her glass and raised it. "To finding Monty's killer," she said.

"To getting out of here," Libby added.

"The sooner the better," Bernie said.

"Amen to that," Libby said.

They clinked glasses and drank. Libby savored the brandy on her tongue. Then she felt it slip down her throat, warming her as it worked its way down to her stomach.

"God, I needed that."

Bernie studied the amber liquid in her glass. "This is good stuff."

"Monty probably reserved it for guests."

"Probably," Bernie agreed.

"Important guests."

Bernie took another sip. "Well, he certainly wouldn't be pleased to see us drinking it. That's for sure. Us being common trades folk and all. I'm surprised Lexus isn't having us stay in the servants' quarters."

"That's because there aren't any."

"Which is surprising. I figured Alma for living here."

"For her sake, I hope not. That would be hell," Libby said as she took another sip of brandy. "I could really get to like this stuff," she observed, changing the subject.

"Sometimes you really do get what you pay for," Bernie observed. "Good chocolate. Good coffee. Good liquor. All cost money to make. And are worth every cent."

Libby ran her finger around the rim of the glass. Crystal made a high-pitched squeak. This made no sound at all. "Monty probably marked the bottle, you know, like Mom used to do when we were younger."

Bernie laughed at the memory. "And I kept on filling up the vodka bottle with water. . . ."

"And Dad kept on complaining to Mom that she was watering down his drinks. . . ."

"It was pretty funny."

"Until she came up and caught you red-handed."

"That wasn't so funny," Bernie said, picturing the expression on her mom's face.

"No, it wasn't," Libby said. She'd been in the bathroom at the time, but she'd heard everything through the door.

Bernie rubbed the side of her nose with her knuckle. "How was I supposed to know she'd forgotten her reading glasses? Boy, was she not happy. Neither was Dad, for that matter."

"But he wasn't as unhappy as Mom. In fact, I got the impression that he thought it showed initiative on your part. Not that he would have said that to Mom. How long did she ground you for?"

"Two very long months." Bernie intertwined her fingers, turned her palms outward, and stretched. "And don't forget, I had to wash all the pans in the shop as well. I think that was worse. Oh well, at least it was the winter. It would have been even worse if it had been the summer."

Libby kicked off her shoes and put her feet up on the coffee table. "How come you never told Mom I was drinking, too?" she asked.

Bernie shrugged. "You were her perfect little girl who never did anything wrong. I didn't want to disappoint her."

"I was insufferable, wasn't I?"

"Yeah. Pretty much."

"Did it bother you that you always got blamed for everything and I always skated?" Libby asked. She realized that they were both whispering.

Bernie grinned. "Once in a while, but mostly no. I got to have more fun."

"And I envied you for it. I think I was too scared to do anything," Libby reflected. "How come you weren't?"

Bernie shrugged. "I don't know, really. Maybe because I had less to lose than you. Or maybe because staying home never appealed to me."

"Well, I want to thank you."

Bernie inclined her head. "My pleasure."

"I never would have thought back in the day that we'd make a good team."

"But we do. Unlike the Field family."

"Exactly," Libby said.

"Let's drink to us," Bernie replied, raising her glass.

Libby did the same. "Love, health, and the time to enjoy them."

"Amen to that," Bernie said.

And they clinked glasses and drank.

"So do you think that Geoff killed Monty?" Libby asked Bernie after Libby had put her glass down.

Bernie took another sip from her glass and pondered the answer. "He is the obvious candidate," she said after a moment had gone by.

"Obvious is not necessarily true," Libby said.

"So you don't think he killed Monty?" Bernie asked.

Libby considered her answer for a moment before speaking. "I'm not saying he didn't, but I have problems with him as the perpetrator."

"How so?"

Libby thought about how to put what she wanted to say in words. Finally, she came up with, "I guess I don't think he's capable of orchestrating the whole turkey blowing up thing. Or maybe he's capable of it, but it just doesn't seem like his style. He's too emotional. Too impulsive. I think that if he were going to kill his father, he'd shoot him or hit him with something during an argument and then be scared and horrified and run away, not plan the murder out, then calmly sit there and wait for it to happen."

"Maybe you're right about that," Bernie said after thinking through what Libby had said. "But have you thought about the fact that he might have had help? Or more likely, Geoff was the 'helpee'. . . ."

"That's not a word," Libby protested.

"No, it's not," Bernie agreed. "But I like it, anyway. What I'm trying to say is that someone else might have planned the murder out and enlisted Geoff as a helper. He appears to be someone who could be easily led."

"And the person doing the leading would probably be Melissa," Libby said. "She seems like a likely candidate."

Bernie nodded. "Well, despite what Melissa said, they did look tight to me when we saw them when we first got up here."

"Boy, that seems like an eternity ago."

"I can't believe it's only been"—Bernie consulted her watch—"twelve hours. It feels like forever."

"It's certainly been a busy twelve hours," Libby observed.

"Too busy," Bernie said. She tapped her fingers against the sofa's arm. "The question is, how busy have Melissa and Geoff been?"

"Well, they were tight when we got here, you're right about that, but they've been arguing every since."

"Maybe they're turning on each other." Bernie stretched again. "We should try and help that along. See what happens."

"It's a definite avenue. Of course," Libby continued, "one of the other Field family members could have killed Monty as well, charming people that they are."

Bernie yawned. She could feel herself starting to relax. The brandy was finally working its magic. Soon she'd be able to sleep. "Like Lexus. She's a cold-hearted, money-grubbing . . ."

"Wow. Don't hold back with your opinion," Libby said.

Bernie laughed. "I guess that was a little over the top. But she has a definite motive. . . ."

"So does everyone else," Libby pointed out. "And I don't think she could rig the turkey by herself."

"We don't know that," Bernie protested. "For all we know, Monty could have taught her everything he knew about making fireworks."

"Somehow, she doesn't seem the type."

"I just have two words for you. Courting behavior."

"Maybe you're right," Libby said.

Bernie looked indignant. "Of course I'm right. I'm always right about male-female stuff. Premarriage, she was probably oohing and aahing over everything that Monty said and did."

"When you put it that way, I can see him taking her down to the bunker and playing the big man and showing her what he did. However, no way could she lug Monty's body to her bed. So please explain that to me."

Bernie smiled. "That's easy. Someone else did that. Which was why she was so upset. Obviously, she thinks it's Geoff, and she thinks the next step is going to be that he's going to try and blackmail her."

"Which is why she wants us to find out where he is. Then she can get rid of him."

"Maybe she already has. Or here's another possibility. Maybe she and Geoff were partners and had a falling-out. I mean, how else would he know that Lexus killed Monty?"

"*If* she killed Monty."

"Fine," Bernie acceded. "If she killed Monty. But Geoff's still involved whichever way you go."

Libby rubbed her forehead. "You're giving me a headache."

"I'm giving myself a headache," Bernie said. "The mathematical permutations are endless. Or maybe they're just thirty-six. Actually I think it's twenty-eight. It could even be sixty-four. Or maybe . . ."

Libby held up her hand. "Let's not go there, please."

"You're right. Let's not. That way madness lies."

"There has to be a way to whittle the possibilities down."

"There is," Bernie said. "We'll just keep on poking and prodding, and eventually something will shake loose. It always does."

"*Eventually* being the key word," Libby said.

"Do you have another suggestion?" Bernie asked her.

"Hey, I wasn't disagreeing with you. I was just making an observation." Libby took another sip of her brandy and ruminated on the situation at hand. "I think we should talk to Ralph and Perceval tomorrow about their trip . . ."

"And see if they have anything else to say. And let's not forget Bob and Audie. They always seem to be lurking around in the background."

Libby ran her finger around the rim of her glass again. "I don't think they'll talk if Greta is around."

"Agreed," Bernie said. "So we'll have to take care of that." She stifled a yawn. "You know, we really should have checked the bunker to see if Geoff was in there."

"He's not."

"He's most likely not."

Libby snorted. "Count me out of that one. And if by some chance he is, as far as I'm concerned, he can stay out there and good luck to him. I'm not taking that walk again."

"Maybe tomorrow," Bernie said. "Hopefully, it will have stopped snowing by then and we can see where we're going."

"Always a good thing," Libby noted. She glanced out the window. "It seems to be calming down out there a little." She turned to look at Bernie. Her sister's eyes were closed. "Are you asleep?" she asked.

Bernie's eyes flew open. "I guess I was," she admitted. She put her glass on the table, lay down on the sofa, and put one of the throw pillows over her face. A moment later she was sound asleep.

Libby drank the rest of her brandy and lay down as well. She started thinking about the Frosts' dinner party in four days and where she could get perfectly ripe pears for the pear-almond custard tart she was going to make. What had she been thinking? Good pears were hard to find, and she needed twelve for the two tarts.

And then she started thinking about Christmas and the gingerbread houses she was going to make for their window display. She figured she'd need twelve of them. This year she wasn't going to use a premade pattern. She was going to make her own. She'd make the usual two-story Colonials, but it might be fun to throw a ranch or two in there, and maybe a Spanish-style house as well.

They could have cacti in the yard. And maybe some gingerbread dogs and cats. And kids. They could do a whole village. It would be a lot of work, but worth it. Everyone would stop and look, and then they'd come in and buy things. She'd have to talk to Bernie and see what she thought, and on that note she fell asleep.

Chapter 34

El Huron waited ten minutes until El Huron was certain that Bernie and Libby were in a deep sleep. El Huron was tired. Exhausted, really. Standing on the other side of the door, listening to the two women talk had made El Huron furious. They didn't know what they were speaking about. They had everything totally wrong. They understood nothing. Absolutely nothing. They were ridiculous in their surmises. And so sure of themselves. They were stupid. Very stupid. That should have made El Huron glad. But it didn't.

El Huron wanted to explain to them. El Huron wanted to jump out and yell at the women and tell them they were missing the point. El Huron wanted them to admire the artistry of what El Huron had done and what El Huron was going to do. The rightness of it. The moral validity. El Huron wanted the sisters to understand the lesson El Huron was about to teach the Field family, a lesson the Field family richly deserved. Of that there was no doubt.

El Huron pictured the sisters listening to what El Huron had to say. El Huron pictured them agreeing with El Huron, telling El Huron that what El Huron was doing was correct, admirable even. That wrongs had to be righted.

That the universe demanded it. The sisters owed El Huron that.

After all, El Huron had spared their miserable little lives when El Huron could have locked the bunker door and left them to choke to death. But had El Huron done that? No. El Huron had not. El Huron had done the right thing. The correct thing. El Huron had left their lives in the hands of God, and God had chosen to spare them. For the moment. For this they owed El Huron. They owed him respect. And understanding.

But above all, the sisters owed El Huron silence. *Silencio profundo.* Profound silence. El Huron desperately wanted the sisters to shut up, to stop talking. All the words coming out of their mouths were hurting El Huron's ears. They were confusing El Huron, leading El Huron away from the path that had been settled on. The true path. The path of honor and of glory. But El Huron could not say that to them. Could not even hint at that. No. That would be a breach of discipline, something that El Huron never committed. El Huron could only stand on the other side of the door and remain absolutely still, even though every muscle in El Huron's body was crying out to move and El Huron desperately wanted to scratch the itch on El Huron's nose.

But no. One made a plan and stuck to it whatever happened. Of course, that said, one must always leave room for adjustments. Things did go wrong. Situations did change. So one must be committed but flexible at the same time. Watching Bruce Lee had taught El Huron that. In fact, that attitude, that ability to be both flexible and inflexible, was what made El Huron so good at what El Huron did. El Huron was like the bamboo. Strong but supple.

So instead of saying anything to the sisters, instead of setting them straight, which El Huron had so badly wanted to do, El Huron had followed the women from room to room, watching them while they searched for a place to sleep, wanting to tell them that there was only one place to go, but refraining.

And El Huron had done this shadowing so perfectly that they had not seen or heard El Huron. Not a single board had given out a crack or a creak as El Huron walked on them. That was because El Huron knew every inch of this house. Every nook and cranny. And El Huron had done this, had paid strict attention, despite being so tired that El Huron's eyelids felt as if they were closing by themselves and all of El Huron's muscles and bones and sinews were telling El Huron they wanted nothing more than to lie down.

But El Huron had persevered. And finally, as El Huron knew they must, the sisters had gone into the study, settled down on the sofas, and gone to sleep. El Huron peeked into the room and watched them for a moment.

Both of them were sleeping the sleep of the dead. The taller, thinner one, the one with the darker hair, had one of the throw pillows over her head, while the shorter, plumper one was using her parka as a pillow. Both were sleeping with their mouths slightly opened. They both looked peaceful, the result, El Huron supposed, of both brandy and exhaustion. Of course, El Huron knew what their names were, but El Huron preferred to think of them as the light-haired and the dark-haired ones, *la rubia* and *la morena*.

As El Huron's mother used to say, "Name something and it's yours," and El Huron did not want these two women. Not in any way. Not when they might become collateral damage, as the war movies that El Huron watched were fond of saying.

El Huron tiptoed closer. El Huron smiled. The darker-haired one had left her tote bag on the coffee table. Very, very carefully El Huron moved nearer. El Huron put El Huron's hand into the bag and felt around. El Huron heard a rustle and froze. The dark-haired one moved and mumbled something El Huron couldn't understand.

El Huron thought it had to do with mocha frosting and an attic, but El Huron wasn't sure and it didn't matter. Then she turned toward the back of the sofa, and the pillow she had over her face fell to the floor. That seemed to distress her, so very, very carefully, El Huron removed El Huron's hand from her bag. Then El Huron leaned over, picked the pillow up off the floor, and put it back where it had been. The thinner one sighed, lifted her hand up, brought the pillow down, and hugged it to her.

El Huron waited another moment, and when both women were resting comfortably, El Huron returned to the bag of the dark-haired one. El Huron carefully opened it and put El Huron's hand inside. A moment later El Huron had what El Huron was looking for. The dark-haired one's cell phone. El Huron deposited it in El Huron's pocket, along with the other ones El Huron had carefully collected from everyone's bedrooms a little while ago. It had been so easy. Now El Huron would put them in the bottom of the trash bags in the garage, where they would never be found.

The idea of locking everyone in was laughable. The locks were a joke. So was the booby trap the dark-haired one had set. El Huron had painstakingly picked up all the glass marbles on the steps and deposited them in a paper bag. At first El Huron had wanted to scatter them around the sofa the dark-haired one was sleeping on. The amusement value would have been considerable. But then El Huron had decided it would be better if they just disappeared, because uncertainty was always more unsettling.

Before El Huron had entered the rooms, El Huron had been worried that El Huron wouldn't be able to find the cell phones. That they would be buried in pants pockets. But that hadn't been the case at all. Everyone had left them out on their dressers or night tables. They were careless. And wasteful. As the rich tended to be. That was one thing El Huron had learned.

El Huron couldn't help smiling when El Huron thought about the scene that would ensue tomorrow morning, when everyone woke up and found their cells missing. There would be accusations. There would be fights. If El Huron was lucky, there would also be panic, and panic stopped people from thinking clearly.

Panic would distract everyone from what was to come. El Huron could hardly wait. The time was nearly at hand. But now it was time for El Huron to get to bed. El Huron had earned the right to sleep. And El Huron had to get up early. There was much for El Huron to do.

Part of El Huron wanted to keep going and fill the balloons with the gas now, but the other part of El Huron, the disciplined part, knew that sleep was essential. Sleep would ensure that no mistakes were made. Because if there were mistakes, all of El Huron's careful planning would be for nothing, and that was a thought that El Huron could not endure. El Huron had a responsibility, a responsibility El Huron would carry through until it was discharged. This El Huron had learned from El Huron's mother.

Chapter 35

It was two o'clock in the morning and Sean was lying in bed, staring at the ceiling, wishing he were back in his bedroom in Longely, instead of in Martha's condo in Florida. At least if he were home, he could turn the TV in his bedroom on. If he went out in the living room and tried that here, Martha would be up and on him like a tick on a dog, demanding to know what the matter was, wanting to make him tea, and generally driving him crazy. Why was it that some people couldn't understand that other people liked to be left alone? That was what he liked so much about Ines. She didn't fuss over him. It just annoyed him no end when people did that.

Here all he could do was lie in bed, listen to Martha's snoring coming from the next room, and think about what Joan had told him over gin rummy, and how that fit or didn't fit in with Monty Field's murder. And he had lots and lots of thinking to do.

It bothered him that for all these years he'd thought one person was guilty and that he could be wrong and it might turn out to be someone else. It was going to take him a while to wrap his mind around that. He'd been so positive that Monty Field had killed his wife Penny, and since he usually didn't make mistakes when it came to those kinds of things, Joan's comments had hit him hard.

And it wasn't as if he had been alone with his feelings. Clyde had thought so, too. Evidently so had Marvin's father. Or at least according to Marvin, he had. It was the conclusion that made sense. The obvious conclusion, and if there was one thing that Sean had learned from being on the force over the years, it was that the obvious conclusion was usually the correct conclusion. He'd thought that even though he'd never been able to prove that Monty had killed his wife. And that had eaten at his guts.

But maybe he hadn't been able to prove Monty had killed his wife, because it hadn't happened that way. Maybe he'd just attached the blame to Monty because he didn't like him after what had happened with Rose. Actually, he hadn't even liked him before anything had happened with Rose. He hadn't liked him, period, so maybe he'd just made the assumption that Monty was to blame and that had been that. Case closed. Sean didn't like to think that he worked off of personal biases, but maybe he did.

And maybe Marvin's father had felt the same way. Maybe it just irked him that Monty hadn't wanted to pay for a decent coffin for his wife and that he hadn't wanted a ceremony. That wasn't a crime. It was just mean-spirited. After all, nice people killed people, too. It happened more than people wanted to think it did.

Sean checked the time on the clock radio on the nightstand and then turned it around so it faced the wall. He didn't want to know what time it was. He'd fall asleep when he fell asleep. Then he went back to thinking about Penny's death. The truth was that he hadn't had a chance to conduct more than a cursory investigation. Not with the ME's ruling coming back the way it had. And that had rankled, too.

So even though he'd been furious with the ME at the

time for his decision, maybe it was a good thing that the ME had ruled Penny's death a misadventure/suicide rather than a homicide. It had been one of those borderline cases where the ME could have come down on either side of the fence.

After all, Penny *could* have taken too much insulin on her own. She *could* have made a careless mistake. That was within the realm of possibility. Even though everyone Sean had talked to had told him that she had had an abnormal fear of doing exactly that, so she was extra careful with her insulin, and he couldn't see how anyone could give themselves almost thirty units—or was it forty units?—by accident.

One or two extra, yes. But not thirty. He'd seen the insulin pen she'd injected herself with three times a day, and decided that that was a mistake that one couldn't possibly make no matter how befuddled one was. And then she'd had three ounces of Scotch on top of that, which kind of sealed the deal. Because, evidently, hard liquor reduced blood sugar levels, especially if you didn't eat anything as well.

And Penny hadn't liked hard liquor. That was another thing. Everyone except Monty had said so. But the ME hadn't wanted to hear about that. He hadn't wanted to hear about any of it. Neither had the ADA, for that matter. Jackson had told him, "Maybe something bad had happened and she'd needed a drink. Just because she usually didn't drink didn't mean that she wouldn't given the correct circumstances."

And nothing Sean could say could make him change his mind. Nor would Jackson agree with Sean that making that kind of mistake with your insulin wasn't suspicious. What Sean had pictured happening, what he'd told Jackson, was that Monty had come up to his wife when she was asleep and jabbed the insulin into her arm. Then he'd poured the Scotch down her throat and held her mouth shut until she'd swallowed it. After that it was just a matter of waiting for the insulin to take effect.

But Jackson had rejected Sean's hypothesis, pointing out that Penny would have woken up and would have had fifteen to twenty minutes before she went into a coma, and that she would have known her blood sugar was falling and either eaten something or called for help. In fact, there was a landline right next to her bed that she could have used. No, Jackson had continued, Penny's cause of death was either an accident or a suicide, but in either case she administered the insulin to herself. But despite the absence of hard evidence, Sean hadn't bought that. His gut had told him different. Aside from everything else, there was something off about Monty's reaction to his wife's death.

So Sean had put Penny's death in his unfinished business file, the file that he kept in his head. That, of course, was why he hadn't wanted the girls going out to the Field house, especially without him. Not that he was afraid that Monty would kill them. He wasn't, because in his experience, and statistics bore him out, most murderers were not repeat offenders.

However, that said, there were always exceptions to every rule, and you couldn't always tell who the nut jobs were. And it was the exceptions to the rule that bothered him. After all, he wouldn't be much of a father if he let his daughters get in harm's way, a thing he'd done his level best over the years to prevent, even though Rose had not approved of his methods. Like teaching the girls the three deadliest defense moves in the world when they were eight years old.

Sean smiled at the thought. Libby had been hopeless, but Bernie had proved to be an apt pupil, although in retrospect maybe teaching a kid how to tear someone's ear off hadn't been the best idea. Rose certainly hadn't thought so. She'd been apoplectic when Bernie had demonstrated the technique to her on her doll. She'd made him swear never to do anything like that again. Which he hadn't.

Sean took a deep breath and thought about Rose for a little while and their life together and about how much he missed her, and then, after a little while, his thoughts slowly drifted back to Monty's murder and his daughters and their current predicament.

When Clyde had called and told Sean he had heard that Monty Field was dead, part of Sean had been pleased that Monty had finally gotten what was coming to him after all these years, but a larger part of him had been worried there was a killer loose in the house, after all, and even though the person who killed Monty Field probably had a motive that didn't include his daughters, it didn't make Sean feel any better.

And then, when Clyde had told him his daughters were being looked at for the murder, he'd been furious at Lucy's temerity. The idea was ludicrous. And while he knew that everything would get straightened out eventually, he also knew that it could be a long, expensive process.

Which was why he'd advised Bernie and Libby to try and get to the bottom of this mess before Longely's finest came on the scene. Handing them a neatly wrapped package with all the i's dotted and the t's crossed would make life simpler for everyone. The police would be happy because they would have their perpetrator, and the girls would be happy because they wouldn't have to deal with the Longely police.

And now here was Joan telling him that it was Monty's brothers who were responsible for Penny's death, and he couldn't even get in touch with Bernie and Libby to tell them that. Even though the more he thought about the statement, the more he realized that it made no sense to him whatsoever.

Which was why he was lying in bed, unable to sleep, while he tried to figure out whether or not what Joan had said held even a slim chance of being true, whether her intuition was in any way valid. He had a tendency to think not. But maybe that was because he didn't want to believe what she was saying. He'd trusted her opinion before when she'd told him that she thought that Monty had killed his wife, but maybe that was because it confirmed his own. Joan obviously thought that what she was saying was true, and she had no reason to lie.

Of course, there was another possibility. Geoff could have been lying to her. Maybe Geoff had been making the whole thing up because he was angry with his uncles for something or other that they'd done. That would work. It was a fairly sick thing to do, but Sean had seen kids do things like that before. Take the Smith kid and his dad. The kid had accused his dad of killing his puppy, when the kid had done it himself.

Maybe that was why Geoff had said what he did to Joan. And then maybe Geoff had gotten embarrassed by what he'd done and started avoiding Joan at all costs, hence increasing Joan's level of concern, which increased Geoff's, which increased Joan's, and so on and so forth.

Then another thought occurred to Sean. Why would Perceval and Ralph kill Penny back then and Monty now? Why wait all this time? That was the question. *No,* Sean corrected himself. That was one of the questions. A subset really. Now he was allowing himself to get sidetracked from the other question, the more important one, which was, why would Ralph and Perceval kill Penny at all? How did Ralph and Perceval benefit from her death?

Monty got the company when Penny died. What did Ralph and Perceval get? As far as Sean knew, they got a chance to work in the company. Or maybe they got to own a part of the company. But still, Sean was sure it wouldn't be a big part. Monty was probably the chief stock owner. So what had Ralph and Perceval been doing before so that working in the company or even owning a piece of it was such a big step up for them that it was worth killing for?

Sean closed his eyes and tried to dredge up everything he remembered pertaining to Penny Field's death and Monty and Monty's brothers. He had vague memories of Perceval and Ralph.

There'd been a lot of drinking and smoking. A lot of dead-end jobs and a lot of getting fired from said dead-end jobs—mainly because Ralph and Perceval had been in the habit of not showing up for work—if Sean remembered rightly. But they didn't do anything criminal, unless you counted stupid stuff, like getting caught trespassing on the high school football field with a case of beer and a couple of girls.

Then their parents had been killed in a house fire started by a faulty electric heater, and that seemed to have sobered them up really fast. It had been the same summer that Penny had died. Everyone had had lots of sympathy for the Field boys. Which was another reason no one had wanted to touch Penny Field's death. Everyone had figured Monty had enough on his plate as it was.

Sean shook his head again. No matter how Sean figured it, he couldn't see Ralph and Perceval for Penny Field's death. They'd had no motive. Unless, of course, they'd colluded with their brother and all three of the Field boys had been in on Penny's murder and Monty had paid them off, as well as giving them a share in the company. That made a little more sense. And now maybe they'd had a falling-out and they'd killed Monty.

No. The theory that made the most sense was that Geoff had lied to Joan for reasons of his own and that Joan had believed him. That made Sean feel a little bit better, but not as much as he would have liked. Because what happened if he was wrong? God, he wished he were back in Longely. He sighed and rolled over and punched his pillow into submission.

He wasn't going to go there. He was going to tell himself that everything was fine and that his girls could protect themselves from anything that came along—at least Bernie could. After all, he'd taught her how. And he was going to keep telling himself that until he believed it. Otherwise he'd never get any sleep.

Ten minutes later he reached for his cell and tried Bernie's number again. It rang, so the network was back up. But there was no answer. He tried again five minutes later. Still no answer. *Plenty of reasons for that,* he told himself after he'd left a voice mail. She could have lost her phone. It could be dead. She was probably sleeping and didn't hear it. He was sure there was a perfectly reasonable explanation as to why she wasn't calling him back. Perfectly reasonable. But after ten minutes he caved and dialed Brandon's number. Sean let out a long sigh of relief when Brandon came on the line.

Chapter 36

Bernie woke with a start. For a moment she looked around, not knowing where she was, and then everything came rushing back. She groaned as she glanced down at her watch. The numbers on her watch dial were illuminated. They read 5:10. She looked across the way. Libby was sound asleep. Her lips were slightly parted. Bernie could tell from the way that her sister's eyelids were twitching that she was dreaming.

And it was still snowing, although not as hard as it had been. Hopefully, the police would be able to get here by this afternoon, and she and Libby would be able to go home. Finally. She didn't even want to think of all the shoveling she and Libby were going to have to do when they finally got back to Longely.

And then there was the shop, Bernie thought as she re-pinned her hair. The shop. They were officially closed today, so that was good, but they were going to have to get there by this evening, at the latest, so they could start baking. Otherwise, they wouldn't have anything to sell tomorrow morning. The store had never had an unscheduled closing, except for the week after her mother had died, and Bernie wasn't about to let that happen now.

Bernie rubbed her arms. It had gotten colder since she'd fallen asleep. Maybe the cold had woken her up. Or maybe she had woken up because she was hungry. She sat up and slipped on her boots and her jacket. Hopefully, she'd be able to find some leftovers in the kitchen.

If she remembered correctly, there was still some turkey and stuffing the last time she'd checked, as well as cheese, crackers, and nuts. And if worst came to worst, she could cobble something together out of that stash of camping food she and Libby had found. Then she'd go back to sleep until seven thirty, when she had to wake everyone up and get them out of their rooms.

Personally, she'd like to leave all of them in there—it was so much pleasanter not having to hear their constant arguing—but that wasn't a possibility. Bernie passed the stairs on the way to the kitchen, automatically checking as she did to make sure that the marbles were in place. But not only were they not in place, they weren't there.

She moved closer. The marbles were definitely not there. None of them. It was as if they'd never been. Someone had taken them during the night. She considered the implications of that fact. There were lots of them, and the more she thought about what they were, the angrier she got. Whoever was doing this was playing games with her, and she, for one, had had enough. Bottom line. She was tired of being jerked around. She was tired of being here. She wanted to get this settled and get the hell out.

She reached in her pocket and took out the skeleton key and weighed it in her hand before slipping it back in her pocket. For a moment Bernie debated going back and waking up Libby and telling her what had happened, but decided against it. She didn't want to talk. She wanted to act. She ran up the stairs and tried the bedroom doors on the second floor.

The doors that she'd locked last night were still locked.

Bernie stood outside of them, held her breath, and listened as hard as she could. She heard snores from Ralph and Perceval's and Melissa's rooms and nothing from the others. Next, she slowly opened the doors and peeked inside. Everyone appeared to be asleep. She carefully closed the doors and relocked them.

She checked out Geoff's and Monty's rooms next. They looked the same as they had last night. She sat on Monty's bed and thought about Geoff. Okay. So was he the one who had taken the marbles, or had someone else let themselves out of their room, collected the marbles, then locked themselves back in and crawled into bed?

Put like that, she was betting on Geoff. Bernie got off the bed and hurried down the stairs. She checked the first floor and the garage. No Geoff. She studied the snow piled up outside the front and back doors and the windows. It was smooth. There were no footprints. Geoff hadn't gone out. Frustrated, she headed for the kitchen to make some coffee. Even though she didn't want to waste the time, experience had taught her that she needed it to think. After it was done, she would wake up Libby. They had to talk.

In Libby's dream the snow kept on falling. And falling. It covered the houses and the sky. It smothered the air and weighed down the roofs of the houses. The houses collapsed slowly, each one breaking apart into shards of gingerbread, which melted in the snow, leaving terrible dark stains. She knew if she could get up to the attic, she could fix the leak. She could stop this. But there was no way up. The stairway was hidden. She needed the magic words. But in order to get them, she had to swim through the snow. Suddenly she was in a castle. There were snow flowers. Everything was glittering. Then something was shaking her. Her eyes flew open. She saw Bernie bending over her.

"Rise and shine, sunshine," Bernie said. "It's time to get up."

Libby groaned. "I had the worst dream. Except for the end."

"Tell me about it later," Bernie answered as she shoved a cup of coffee under Libby's nose.

Libby started to get up and groaned again. Everything hurt. Her back hurt. Her legs hurt. Her neck hurt. And her head. Her head hurt most of all. She had a throbbing headache right above her eyes. Or maybe it was behind her eyes. Or maybe it was both. And her mouth felt cottony and dry. And she had a bad taste in it. A very bad taste.

She looked at her glass, which was still sitting on the coffee table right where she'd left it. The smell made her want to throw up. And she hadn't even had that much to drink. Maybe four ounces of brandy at the most. Somehow it didn't seem fair to be so hung over after drinking so little. Now she remembered why she mostly stuck to beer and wine.

Bernie examined her sister. "You don't look good," she said. An understatement. Libby looked like Medusa with her hair going every which way, but she was trying to be polite.

"I don't feel good," Libby said.

"You have drool on your chin."

Libby wiped it away with the back of her hand.

"Have some coffee."

Libby squinched up her face. "Ugh."

"How about a raw egg?"

"That's disgusting."

"But effective."

"I'll take the coffee," Libby said, reaching for it. She took a sip, made a face, and took another sip. "What time is it, anyway?"

"Five thirty."

Libby grimaced. "I want to go back to sleep."

"You can't. The marbles are gone."

Libby gave her a blank look as she sat up and swung her legs over the side of the sofa. She felt as if she was in a stupor. "What marbles?"

Bernie snorted impatiently. Her sister always took forever to wake up. "The marbles I put on the stairs. Remember?"

"Oh, those marbles," Libby said.

"Like we had so many of them."

It was all coming back to Libby. Geoff. The Field family. The marbles Bernie had put on the stairs, which Libby had thought was an incredibly stupid idea, anyway.

"They're gone," Bernie repeated. "Vanished. Evaporated."

"I get it," Libby said as she wiped the sleep out of her eyes with the sleeve of her black cardigan sweater and patted her hair into place. Why did Bernie always look so good? She could spend a week sleeping in the back of a truck—and had—and still look perfect. It wasn't fair.

"Someone took them."

"Obviously." Libby took another sip of her coffee. "Couldn't you have waited another half an hour to tell me this?"

"No. It's not my fault if you can't drink and decided to, anyway."

"Sometimes you are beyond outrageous."

"Well, it's true."

"So you admit you are outrageous."

Bernie grunted. "Do you want to get out of here?"

"No," Libby snapped. "I want to stay here, because it's so much fun. Of course I want to leave. We have to get back to the shop so we can start baking."

Bernie nodded her head up and down vigorously. "Which is why we need to get this Monty thing sorted out, because if we don't, we're going to be answering questions from the cops forever when they finally arrive. And if we're really unlucky, they'll hold us over."

"I . . ."

"Which means," Bernie continued, "that we have to find Geoff and we have to find him now. He's the nearest thing to a lead we have."

Libby leaned forward. "I'm not disagreeing with you, Bernie."

"Good."

"You know, you're not exactly Little Miss Sunshine, either."

Bernie grinned. "That makes two of us."

Libby rubbed her temples. She felt slightly better after she had the coffee, but not by much. "How are we going to find Geoff?" she asked.

"I don't know," Bernie admitted. "I already looked through the house. He's somewhere, but I don't know where."

Libby drained the rest of her coffee and put the cup on the coffee table. "If that's the case, then I think we should do the next best thing. I think we should go back upstairs and wake everyone up. Maybe one of them isn't asleep. Maybe we'll learn something. At least it's something to do."

"As in if I'm up, they should be, too?"

"Precisely," Libby said. She got up and put her parka on. "It's gotten colder in here."

"Yes. It has." Bernie grinned. "Let's go and kick some butt. That should warm everything up."

"Let's," Libby said. For once in her life she was looking forward to it.

She followed Bernie up the stairs and down the hall. The floorboards creaked and cracked under the weight of their footsteps, and Libby wondered once again how anyone could walk on them without being heard. Bernie came to a stop in front of Bob and Audie's room. Libby did the same. She was watching Bernie fish the skeleton key out of her pocket when her dream flashed through her mind. Something occurred to her. She held up her hand.

"What?" Bernie asked impatiently. She was primed and ready to go.

"Wait a minute."

"Having second thoughts?"

"No. I just had an idea." Libby gestured to the hallway. "Remember how I said the layout of this floor struck me as odd?"

"Yes."

"Well, I think I finally figured it out. Something isn't here that should be."

Bernie's eyes flitted over the hallway. She wasn't getting it, and she didn't want to waste time figuring it out. "And that is?"

"This house has an attic, correct?"

"Correct," Bernie said, still not seeing where Libby was going with this. "We saw it when we came in. It's got three small windows and a fourth with a window fan in it."

"So where's the door to it?" Libby asked. "We have doors to the bedrooms. We have doors to the bathrooms, but that's it. No attic door." Libby pointed to the ceiling. "And the entrance is not one of those pull-down trapdoor jobbies with a ladder."

"There isn't any entrance," Bernie said, marveling at how she could have missed something that obvious.

"But," Libby continued, "there has to be one. Whoever built this house wouldn't have built an attic without some kind of access to it." She realized they were whispering. "That wouldn't make sense."

"And the logical place for it would be in this hallway,"

Bernie said, taking up where Libby had left off. "Which means someone closed the doorway up and covered it over with the wallpaper."

"Has to be," Libby said.

Libby and Bernie studied the walls. After a few minutes Libby thought she saw a raised line.

"I think it's here," she told Bernie as she ran her finger up the line. "I can feel it."

Bernie stepped in front of her and ran her thumbnail up the line. "Never underestimate the power of fingernails," she said as the paper split in two. She carefully tore off a little piece of the paper. "Look," she said to Libby. "Here's the wallboard and here's the plaster."

"Someone used wallboard to sheetrock over the doorway."

"So it would appear."

"It looks like a do-it-yourself kind of job," Libby noted. "They didn't use joint compound or tape. Plus, there's an eighth-of-an-inch difference between the Sheetrock and the plaster."

"Well, it was good enough. We didn't see it." Bernie was quiet for a moment, and then she said, "The question is, why did they do it at all?"

"More importantly," Libby said, "is Geoff hiding up there?"

"And if he is, how is he getting in and out?" Bernie chewed on the inside of her cheek while she thought. "If he is up there, that would explain why we haven't heard him walking around."

"Indeed it would." Libby licked her lips. They were dry. She needed her ChapStick, which was at home. "The entrance has to be on this floor. A closet would be the most logical place to locate it."

"Well, we were going to wake everyone up, anyway," Bernie noted.

"I know, but . . ."

"But what?" Bernie asked.

"I think there may be an easier way to find out what we want to know."

"Such as?" And then Bernie realized why her sister had said what she had. "The plans," she cried.

Libby nodded.

The women ran for the stairs.

Chapter 37

Bernie turned on the kitchen light, while Libby yanked open the bottom drawer of the kitchen cabinet and grabbed the manila envelope she'd seen yesterday. While Libby looked over her shoulder, Bernie opened up the envelope, shook the remodeling plans out, and spread them across the top of the kitchen counter. As she did, she noted that the date they'd been drawn up and the name of the architect, P. Bidwell, were stamped in the upper right-hand corner.

"You ever hear of him?" Bernie asked Libby.

Libby shook her head.

"Me either," Bernie said. "I wonder if Dad has."

"Probably," Libby replied. "Dad knows everything about everyone in the tri-county area."

"Too bad we can't ask him." For a moment Bernie thought about seeing if she could call him and then decided against it. It was too early, and she didn't want to alarm him, so she turned her attention back to the plans.

There were twelve pages in all. Nine of them had to do with four separate jobs: remodeling the kitchen and the downstairs bathroom, combining four of the smaller rooms at the back end of the first floor into one great room, and adding a sunroom onto the left side of the house. The tenth, eleventh, and twelfth pages contained what Bernie and Libby were looking for.

"The good news is these are what we need," Bernie said, pulling the pages out and setting them side by side. She smoothed out the creases with the side of her hand, while Libby squinted to get a better look. "The bad news is they're in really bad shape."

The print on the three pages was faded, making them extremely difficult to read, but Bernie managed to make out the labels on their tops. The first page showed the original position of the stairs, the second page showed the stairs' projected new position, while the third page showed sketches of the two rooms that were going to be built in the attic.

"If I'm reading these plans right," Bernie said to Libby, "the new access to the attic is through the closet in Monty's room. If that was Monty's room back then."

"Very odd," Libby said. "It's not where most people would choose to locate a flight of stairs."

"And it was probably quite an expensive undertaking even back then."

"Had to be." Libby indicated the other pages. "Note that none of the other proposals were implemented."

"The stairs might not have been, either," Bernie pointed out. "Maybe whoever did this just got as far as closing off the hallway entrance."

"That doesn't make sense. Then you couldn't get up to the attic."

Bernie shrugged. "Maybe whoever was paying for it ran out of money and figured they'd finish off the job later, only they never did."

"I bet Monty was the one who commissioned it."

"I bet you're right." Bernie rat-a-tatted her fingernails

on the countertop. "I wonder if Ralph and Perceval would know."

"I'm sure they'd know. We should ask them," Libby suggested.

"We will." Bernie looked at her watch. It was a little before six. "After we see if we can find those stairs."

The sisters left the kitchen. On the way, Bernie grabbed two pieces of bread and some Brie that had been left over from the night before and handed half to Libby.

"Eat," she said.

Libby made a face. "My stomach is still kind of rocky."

"Eat anyway," Bernie told her. "I have a feeling we're going to need all the energy we can get."

"What if Geoff is up in the attic?" Libby said as she chewed on her bread. It was slightly stale.

"What if he is?" Bernie asked. "In fact, I hope he is."

"He does have that sword."

"Yes, but we have truth on our side."

"Seriously."

"Seriously, you're right." Bernie turned around, marched back into the kitchen, and picked up the knife they'd used to carve the turkey with.

"This does not make me feel confident," Libby said when she got a gander at what her sister was carrying.

"Well, it makes me feel better."

"Boy, I'm so-o-o relieved."

"You know the problem with you?" Bernie said.

"That I'm sensible?"

"No. That you worry too much."

Bernie walked over to Monty's closet, opened the door, and stepped inside. She reached up, took the clothes that were hanging on the rod, and handed them to Libby, who laid them out on the bed. When the closet was completely empty, Bernie stepped inside. Libby joined her, but it was too crowded to see anything with her in there, so she stepped back out and waited while Bernie eyeballed the wall.

"I don't see anything," Bernie said after a moment had gone by. She rapped on the wall with her fist. All she got back were thuds.

"Maybe Monty never got around to changing the stairs," Libby said.

"We already discussed that."

"Well, I'm saying it again. Lots of people commission things but don't follow through," Libby said, thinking of the kitchen renovation they kept postponing. "I think we should wake up Ralph and Perceval and ask them."

"Give me another minute," Bernie said, turning back to the closet wall. She knew the opening was here, and she was damned if she wasn't going to find it.

She studied the wall some more. It was blank. There were no seams. Nothing to indicate a door. Maybe there was some kind of lever you had to push to get the door to open. That was a possibility, but a far-fetched one in her estimation. No. The door was here. It had to be. But where?

She turned and examined the right-hand wall of the closet, tapping lightly on the wall as she went. Then she turned to the left-hand side and that was when she saw it. The slight indentation in the wall. It was barely visible. She wouldn't have seen it if she hadn't been looking. She reached over and placed the tips of her middle fingers in the depression.

They just fit. She pushed. Nothing. She pushed harder. She could feel a slight movement. She tried again. More of a movement. On the third try, the wall slid away, revealing a dark space. A burst of cold air came rushing out. And a hint of something else, which Bernie knew but couldn't name. A moment later Bernie's eyes got used to the dark, and she was able to pick out a vague outline of the steps. She picked up the carving knife she'd left on the floor and started up them.

"Wait!" Libby cried.

But Bernie didn't.

Chapter 38

The stairs were so dark that Bernie had to feel her way up them. She counted seven steps, then a landing, then five more steps after that. She could hear Libby crying, "Come back," behind her, but she ignored her and kept on going. She was determined to get this squared away one way or another.

She tightened her grip on her knife, just in case Geoff was up there waiting for her, but she didn't think he was. The space felt empty, devoid of life. She wouldn't be able to explain to anyone why she felt that way, but she did, and by this time she'd learned to trust her instincts. It was when she didn't that things usually went wrong.

She heard Libby say, "God, I hate you," as she scrambled up behind her. By that time Bernie had reached the attic. It was lighter up there, the illumination coming from the moon shining through the window. It had finally stopped snowing. She moved over so Libby would have somewhere to stand.

"Welcome aboard," she told her when she made it.

"I'd rather be on a cruise ship."

"You get seasick."

"I'd still rather be on a cruise ship."

Bernie didn't reply. She was too busy looking around. The room looked like the storage area their dad had built in their attic for their winter clothes, only this area was intended for human habitation. The room had been framed out with two-by-fours and sheetrocked with three-quarter-inch brads, which held the Sheetrock in place.

The Sheetrock went only two-thirds of the way up the two-by-fours. The rest of the space was open, leaving a view of the underside of the rafters supporting the roof. Bernie noted that the Sheetrock hadn't been finished off here, either. It was down and dirty construction at its finest. Probably an amateur job, she decided. Certainly a professional would never want his name attached to something like this.

There were two pieces of furniture in the room. A twin bed and a small dresser with a lamp sitting on it.

"Home, sweet home," Bernie murmured as she walked toward the bed.

She touched the coverlet. It was a thin cotton chenille. She lifted up the coverlet and felt the sheets. They were thin from too many washings. The single pillow on the bed was lumpy.

"It's cold in here," Libby noted. There was no sign of a heater.

"And boiling hot in the summer," Bernie added as she went over to the dresser.

"You know how we said that Alma probably lived somewhere else and came in every day?" Libby said, taking in the surroundings. "I think we were wrong. Who else would be living up here?"

"The mad sister," Bernie said.

"What?"

"Obviously you're not up on your gothics," Bernie said.

"Not since I was thirteen," Libby answered.

She watched as Bernie pulled the top dresser drawer open. It was filled with neatly folded socks, cheap under-

pants, two old bras, and a couple of pairs of folded pajamas. There was a manila envelope sitting on the bottom.
Bernie pulled it out and opened it up. The envelope contained three birthday cards signed *Love, your son Roberto*,
a photograph, and a letter.

Bernie opened the letter and read, "'Alma, if you continue harassing me, I will have no choice but to turn the
matter over to the authorities. Your accusations re your
son are baseless, and I will not be blackmailed by you.' It's
signed 'Monty.'" Bernie passed the letter over to Libby.
"The letter is dated a little less than three weeks ago."

"I bet that's when he called the immigration on her."

"It's not too much of a stretch to make that assumption."

"I wonder what she was accusing him of."

Bernie studied Alma's son's photograph for a minute, "I
think I know." She tapped the picture with her fingernail.
"Look at the kid's chin. Does it remind you of anyone?"

"No."

"Look again."

"I still don't see it."

Bernie took the photo back. "The kid has Monty's chin."

"I think you're stretching it."

"He does," Bernie insisted.

"I think you're seeing that because of the letter. I can
think of lots of other explanations."

"But what if it is true?" Bernie insisted. "What if Alma
had a son with Monty?"

"Well, it would open up a load of possibilities," Libby
conceded. "I wonder what Alma wanted Monty to do."

"Obviously give her some money for the kid. That
would explain why she agreed to live like this." Bernie gestured toward the room. "He probably promised her he'd
take care of the kid. . . ."

"Like send him to college . . . ," Libby hypothesized,
going along with Bernie's scenario.

"And she kept asking him. . . ."

"And he kept putting her off."

"So finally she makes a threat—like she's going to tell everyone."

"And he calls immigration on her and has her taken away. Problem solved."

"Which, if true, makes Monty even more of a turd than I thought he was."

"Which is saying a lot."

"Well, it's certainly one way to get cheap labor."

"Slave labor, really. With the attic door positioned the way it is, she couldn't come or go without his knowledge."

"And approval. I don't think the door opens from the inside."

"Lovely." Libby sighed. "Good reason to kill someone. I wonder what the rest of the family will say when we ask about Roberto."

"Something snotty and unhelpful, no doubt." Bernie cocked her head toward the opening leading to the next room. "I bet that's where Roberto slept," she said, walking toward it.

"At least he had a room of his own," Libby said.

"I suppose that's something."

"But not a lot."

"Well, as Mom used to say, it's better than a sharp poke in the eye," Bernie replied as she and her sister stepped inside the second room.

It was very much like the first one. There was a narrow bed and a small dresser with a similar-looking lamp, but there was a thicker coverlet on the bed, a small area rug on the floor, and a small mammal cage shoved over into the far corner of the room.

Bernie went over and took a look. "I guess the kid had a ferret as a pet."

"How do you know that?"

Bernie made fanning motions in the air with her hands. "The vibes are strong with me."

"Seriously."

"Seriously." Bernie pointed to the box, half hidden by the cage, that said FERRET FOOD. "That's how."

"You don't have to gloat."

"I'm not gloating. I'm rejoicing."

"Let's just drop the subject, shall we?"

"Fine with me." Bernie couldn't help smiling as she turned and studied the walls.

Alma's son had nailed pictures of football and basketball players cut from newspapers and magazines up on three of the walls, while the fourth wall was covered with photos of Mexican beach resorts and ruins.

"I guess he's getting to see them now," Bernie commented as her gaze swept over them and onto the empty bags of food that were strewn by the bed.

"One can only hope," Libby said. She looked at the food on the floor. There were half-empty potato chip bags, empty soda cans, empty bags of dehydrated Hawaiian chicken and noodles, and a plate from downstairs with the remains of turkey, cranberry sauce, corn-bread stuffing, and green beans. "I guess Geoff was camping out here," she said as she spied a rolled-up sleeping bag in the corner.

Bernie went over and unrolled it and shook it out. It smelled of unwashed bodies, but there was nothing in it.

"What were you looking for?" Libby asked.

Bernie shrugged. "I don't really know. Anything."

Libby went through the drawers. Tees, shirts, pants, briefs, hoodies, and socks were all crammed in together in no particular order.

"Nothing." Libby straightened up. Her hands were cold, and she flexed her fingers, then rubbed her palms together to get the circulation going while studying the square cut in the Sheetrock that served as an entrance to what Libby presumed to be the rest of the attic. "I wonder what's in there."

"Only one way to find out," Bernie said. And she walked through the opening.

Libby followed a moment later. "It looks like our attic," she said, assessing the boxes of old clothes, the mattresses, bed frames, and rolled-up rugs. A persistent odor of mildew and decay hung over the room, probably, Libby reasoned, because there was a leak somewhere in the roof.

Bernie walked over to a large armoire. "I wonder what's in here," she said.

"Probably more junk."

"Let's find out, shall we?" And Bernie opened the door.

Chapter 39

Bernie blinked. She couldn't believe what she was see-ing. It looked like one of those Halloween tableaus her neighbor down the street liked to set up on his lawn. Only this was real. Geoff was pinned to the back of the armoire with his samurai sword.

"I guess we don't have to look for Geoff anymore," Bernie said when she got her voice back a moment later.

Libby didn't answer. She was still in shock. She just stared at Geoff, and he stared back at her.

Bernie frowned. "I'll say one thing. This has certainly been a morning of surprises. First Alma's son and now Geoff."

"I just hope this is the last of the lot," Libby said.

"God, me too."

"So when Geoff ran away . . ."

"He came up here. Which is why we couldn't find him."

"And someone was waiting for him."

"Or he discovered someone up here who didn't want to be discovered, or someone came up and found him here."

"So all the time we were looking for him, he was"— Libby pointed to the armoire—"in there."

Bernie chewed on the inside of her cheek. "Maybe.

Maybe not. I don't think it's possible for us to tell when he was killed. But one thing is clear."

"What's that?" Libby asked.

"I don't think this happened here. It would take a lot of strength to pin someone to the wall like this."

"Okay." Libby crossed her arms over her chest. "I can see that."

"And he wouldn't have died instantly. He would have struggled."

Libby forced herself to regard Geoff's body. "It doesn't look as if he struggled, does it?"

Bernie shook her head. "Not at all. I think whoever did this killed him first and then pinioned him to the back of the armoire. Either that or he was so close to being dead that he didn't have any strength left to fight. Otherwise, he would have pulled the sword out of himself. Or tried to."

"Why do it that way? Who was going to see it?"

"That is the question, isn't it?" Bernie said.

"I wonder if he was shot first."

"If he was, it certainly isn't anyplace we can see it." And Bernie picked up a T-shirt that was lying on the floor and stepped into the armoire.

"What are you doing?" Libby asked.

"Checking to make sure Geoff wasn't shot in the back of the head." And with that Bernie inserted the shirt between Geoff's head and her hand, and gently moved Geoff's head forward. "No bullet wound," she announced after she'd had a look. She withdrew the T-shirt. "And no blood on the shirt."

She regarded Geoff some more, while Libby regarded her sister with an expression composed of equal parts of awe and horror.

Bernie pointed to a bruise on the side of Geoff's throat. "I think maybe someone pressed on his carotid artery and cut off his blood flow. Then, when he was unconscious, they skewered him to the back of the armoire, closed the cabinet door, and left him to die. Want to take a look?"

"Thanks, but I'll pass."

"Thought you would," Bernie told her.

"I don't do windows and I don't do bodies. I don't think that's unreasonable," Libby said.

"So you've told me."

And Bernie began emptying Geoff's pants pockets and handing the contents to her sister. Bernie found a half-eaten pack of peanut M&M's, a wallet with Geoff's driver's license, two credit cards, a business card with the name of a lawyer on it, which Bernie palmed, and twenty dollars in cash in his right-hand pants pocket; and a nasal spray, two three-week-old ticket stubs to a movie house down in New York City, and a pack of cigarettes and a Zippo lighter in his left-hand pocket.

"I guess Geoff was telling the truth when he told us he smoked," Bernie commented as she started in on Geoff's jacket pockets.

The left-hand one contained three quarters and a couple of pennies, while the right-hand one contained a neatly folded piece of paper. Bernie unfolded it, noting as she did that the paper was the kind used in printers. Someone had cut out letters from a magazine and pasted them on the center of the page to form four words.

"Interesting," she said, passing the paper on to Libby, who read the words, *payback is a bitch,* out loud.

"It certainly was in this case," Libby commented as she studied the paper. "I didn't think people did this kind of thing anymore," she said as she handed the paper back to Bernie.

"Did what?" Bernie asked.

"Cut out letters and pasted them on paper. It's not necessary now that people use computers instead of typewriters."

"Guess our murderer is an old-fashioned kinda guy. Or gal." Bernie folded up the paper and slipped it into her pocket along with Alma's letter and the photo of Alma's son. "Then he should be right up your alley, you not liking technology and all."

"Speaking of which," Libby said, looking down at Geoff's belongings. "Where's Geoff's cell phone? Because it's not here."

"It isn't, is it?" Bernie said, peeved at herself for having missed something so obvious.

Libby grinned. Now they were even.

"He must have dropped it somewhere around here."

"It would be good to find."

"Yes, it would," Bernie agreed as she took the contents of Geoff's pockets from Libby and put everything back the way she'd found it. She started to close the armoire door.

"I take it we're leaving him for the police?" Libby asked.

"That's the general plan. Unless you have another idea."

"Not me." Libby was glad not to have Geoff staring at her anymore. It made her feel guilty.

Bernie and Libby spent the next fifteen minutes trying to find Geoff's cell phone and failing. Finally, they both decided to call it a day. The phone could be anywhere. But the effort hadn't been wasted, because during that time Bernie began to form a hypothesis about who the murderer could be. It was slightly far-fetched, but she reasoned that far-fetched was better than nothing.

"And now I think it's time to wake everyone up, don't you?" Libby said as they went down the stairs to Monty's room. She slid the door shut behind her and closed the closet door.

Bernie nodded. She was curious to see how everyone would respond to the news. So was Libby. They discussed what they were going to do and how they were going to do it as they walked down the hall. Then they began knocking on doors.

Chapter 40

It took ten minutes to get everyone up and down to the study. Bernie looked at the assembled crew. They did not look their personal best, but then she reckoned that she and Libby didn't, either.

Libby watched Bernie watching everyone. The men looked as if they'd had a rough night's sleep. None of them had shaved, and Bob and Audie were wearing pajama bottoms, T-shirts, and hoodies, as was Melissa, while Ralph and Perceval were wearing slacks and flannel shirts. Greta and Lexus, on the other hand, had both been dressed and had had their make-up on when Bernie and Libby had come knocking on their doors. In fact, everyone had been up except for Melissa, who had been sound asleep.

"So what's this about?" Perceval asked.

Ralph smoothed down his hair with the palm of his hand. "It better be important."

"It is," Bernie said. She moved to the center of the room and made the announcement she and Libby had agreed on. They'd decided to impart their information in stages. It seemed easier to control things that way.

No one keeled over or ran from the room or jumped up and cried, "The son of a bitch deserved it," when Bernie told everyone about Geoff. But then Libby hadn't expected they would. In her experience most people didn't do that kind of thing. Unfortunately.

"So Geoff didn't kill Monty," Perceval said.

"Probably not," Bernie allowed.

No one said anything for thirty seconds; then Melissa started to screech.

"Oh my God, oh my God," Melissa cried.

Talk about a delayed reaction, Bernie thought as she watched Melissa's lower lip quiver and her eyes begin to fill with tears.

"This is my fault," Melissa said.

"What is?" Bernie asked.

Melissa snuffled in response.

"What is your fault?" Bob repeated.

Bernie thought he looked annoyed.

"Everything," Melissa said. "The whole thing." And she covered her face with her hands and began to sob.

"For God's sake, Melissa," Lexus cried. "This is bad enough without you going off the deep end. Stop sniveling and talk to us."

This was met with a fresh bout of crying from Melissa.

"She probably has nothing to say," Greta said. "She's just doing this to get our attention."

"My brother is dead," Melissa managed to get out between sobs. "How can you talk to me like that?"

"We know what he is," Greta said.

Perceval absentmindedly fiddled with the top button on his flannel shirt. "I don't suppose you've found my cell phone, have you?" he asked Bernie.

Lexus turned on him. "What is the matter with you?" she snapped. "We've already established that someone has taken all of them and put them who knows where." She shuddered. "Probably the same person that killed Geoff." She glared at Libby and Bernie. "I thought you were going to protect us. Stand watch. Or do whatever it is you were supposed to do. Instead, look what happened. We all could have died."

"But we didn't," Greta shot back. She looked at Bernie. "Is there any coffee in this place?"

Bernie nodded. "I'll go make it."

She could certainly use some more, that was for sure, and she wanted to give everyone a chance to calm down before she made her second announcement. She went into the kitchen, while Libby stayed behind to keep an eye on the Field family. At least, Libby thought, it had stopped snowing. Which meant the police should be here soon. Hopefully, they'd have some answers for them when they arrived.

Bernie reappeared fifteen minutes later with a tray full of coffee things. By that time Melissa's sobs had been reduced to quiet snuffles. Bernie waited until everyone had helped themselves to the coffee and had settled down. Then she dropped her second bomb.

"Monty had a son with Alma," she said, watching everyone's reaction.

"That's ridiculous," Lexus said.

"Total nonsense," Ralph said.

"Absolutely," Perceval agreed.

"Why do you say that?" Greta asked.

Bernie took out the letter and read it aloud.

"So what?" Perceval said. "Alma was bothering him. That's all that letter says. The part about Monty mistreating Alma's son is absurd. How could you possibly get that he was Monty's son from that? No wonder he called INS on her. I would have, too."

Bernie handed him the photograph of Alma's son.

"What do I need to look at this for? It isn't as if I haven't seen the kid before."

"Notice the chin," Bernie said.

"So?"

"It recedes slightly."

"So do a lot of other people's." And he handed the photo to Ralph.

"I have to agree with my brother. Lots of people have chins like that," Ralph remarked before handing the picture on to Lexus.

"What's your point?" Lexus said.

Greta nibbled on her lower lip. "Do you think the kid killed Geoff and Monty?" she asked Bernie.

"Don't be an idiot," Ralph snapped. "The INS got both of them. They came to the house."

"Were you here?" Greta asked.

"No. I was down at the bunker, working, which is something that some of us do from time to time."

"Then how do you know?" Greta insisted.

"Melissa told me," Ralph replied.

Greta turned to Melissa. "Well?" she asked her.

Melissa opened her mouth and closed it and started sobbing again.

"Stop it!" Greta yelled.

"I can't," Melissa said. "I can't. I'll never forgive myself. Never." Which brought on a fresh bunch of sobs. Only now she was hiccuping as well.

Bernie knelt in front of her and took her hands. "Did you know that Alma's son was your half brother?"

Melissa raised her eyes. "Yes," she whispered.

"How did you know?"

"He . . . he . . . told me. It was our secret."

"Did he tell Geoff, too?"

Melissa shook her head. "He wouldn't do that. He hated him."

"Why?"

Melissa looked down at the floor.

Bernie let go of Melissa's hands, took out the note she'd found in Geoff's pants, and showed it to Melissa. "Do you know what this means?" she asked.

Melissa bit her lip and nodded.

"What?" Lexus screamed.

Melissa shrank into herself.

Libby held up her hand. "Lexus, give her a minute and she'll answer, won't you, Melissa?"

"I have to go to work," Melissa said in a barely audible voice.

"Please answer the question," Libby said.

Melissa stared straight ahead. "They need me at the hospital."

"I'm sure they'll be able to manage until you can get there," Bernie told her.

Melissa swallowed. "It was the ferret," she finally said. Everyone had to lean in to hear.

"What ferret?" Perceval said.

"The one that Roberto was keeping."

"Here? In this house?" Libby asked.

"Impossible," Perceval said. "I never saw it."

"You never saw lots of things. He had it upstairs in his room. We used to play with it."

"And," Libby prompted when Melissa fell silent.

"And then one day it bit Geoff and Geoff told our dad." Melissa stopped.

"So Monty got rid of it?" Libby asked.

Melissa nodded. "It was bad."

"How bad?" Libby asked.

Melissa bit her lower lip so hard that Libby could see the tooth marks on it.

"Go on," Bernie urged.

Melissa nodded again. "He stomped on it with his boot, and he made Roberto watch. Gracie was his most favorite thing in the whole world."

"What did Alma do?" Libby asked.

"Alma didn't do anything. She told him she couldn't. That he should have been more careful."

Bernie straightened up. "That's awful, but I still don't see how your dad's and your brother's deaths are your fault."

"Because I helped him."

"You helped Roberto?" Libby asked.

"Yes."

"What do you mean, you helped him?" Bernie said. "You helped him kill your father and your brother?"

"No," Melissa cried. Two small red blotches appeared on both of her cheeks. "I helped Roberto hide from the INS. I helped him all the time he was here. I brought him food."

"Even after he killed your father?" Libby said.

Tears fell down Melissa's cheeks. "I didn't think he did that. He told me he hadn't. I thought Lexus did."

"How could—," Lexus began, but Bernie shut her down with a stare.

Bernie turned back to Melissa. "Where is he now?"

"I don't know. I swear I don't know," Melissa cried, and she got up and ran out of the room.

Libby and Bernie ran after her.

Chapter 41

"Wait!" Libby cried.

Melissa kept going. Finally, Libby and Bernie caught up with her near the basement stairs.

Bernie grabbed Melissa by the shoulders and spun her around. "Where is Roberto?"

"I don't know."

"And I don't believe you," Bernie replied.

"It's the truth."

"We need to know," Bernie said, keeping her voice level.

"I can't."

"Why can't you?" Bernie asked.

"Because I love him," Melissa cried.

"If you love him, you'll tell us where he is before the police get here," Libby told her. "We'll be a lot nicer."

"I can't," Melissa said. "I just can't."

Bernie looked her in the eye. "You can and you will."

Melissa shook her head, avoiding her gaze.

"Is he hiding in the attic?" Libby asked.

"No."

"In one of the bedrooms?" Bernie asked.

"I told you, I can't tell you," Melissa cried. She covered her face with her hands and began sobbing again.

Bernie took Melissa's hands away from her face. "You don't have to say anything. All you have to do is nod."

Melissa blinked.

"Is he on the first floor?" Bernie asked.

Melissa looked straight ahead.

"Is he in the garage?"

Nothing.

"The basement? He's in the basement, isn't he? That's where you were going."

Melissa nodded ever so slightly.

Bernie dropped Melissa's hands. "Thanks," she said.

"He's wounded," Melissa said. "He's bleeding. Please don't hurt him."

"If he doesn't try to hurt us, we won't try and hurt him," Libby said.

"You swear?"

"Yes, we do," Libby said.

Melissa nodded again. "Because he's dopey from the pain pills I've been giving him." She looked at her watch. "I have to change the dressing on his wound."

"We'll meet you down there," Bernie said.

"No," Melissa cried. "You'll scare him. Let me just get my kit, and we'll go down together."

"It'll be fine," Bernie said, opening the basement door. She'd had enough of waiting.

She and Libby walked down the short, steep flight of steps to the basement.

"Do you smell gas?" Bernie asked as they descended. She held on to the railing, because the poor light made it difficult to see and the steps were uneven.

"Very faintly," Libby replied.

Bernie squinted, trying to see Roberto in the gloom. But she didn't. Maybe, she thought, Roberto managed to crawl away somewhere, so he couldn't be that badly injured. Then it occurred to her that Melissa could have lied about his whereabouts. That was a possibility, too.

"I don't see him," she said to Libby. "I don't think he's here."

Libby was just going to suggest that maybe Roberto was behind the hot water heater when she heard the snick of the lock on the basement door, which alerted her that the door had closed. She cursed and ran up the stairs and pushed on the door. It didn't open. Bernie joined her. The door didn't budge. It was locked. Libby started pounding on it and yelling.

"Save your breath," Bernie told her after a couple of minutes went by. "They can't hear you from the study."

"So we're locked in?" Libby said. She rubbed the sides of her hands. They were sore from beating on the door.

"Until someone comes to get us."

"I feel like an idiot."

Bernie sucked in air and let it out. "So do I, Libby. So do I."

"Dad would never have gotten himself in this situation."

"Don't remind me." Bernie repinned her hair. "God, Melissa is good. She played us like a champ."

"And we went right along."

"I wonder where Roberto is."

"Not here. So what do we do now?" Libby asked.

Bernie shrugged. "I guess sit on the steps and wait for someone to let us out and hope that it doesn't take too long." And she turned and walked down to the bottom step. "Or maybe not."

"Why the change of heart?"

"That." And Bernie pointed.

Libby followed her finger. There were large bundles of fireworks set a foot apart over by the wall on the left-hand side.

"And that." Bernie pointed to the wall on the right-hand side. "And that," she said, indicating the middle wall. Both of the other walls had fireworks lined up against them. The whole basement was ringed with fire-works.

"Right," Libby said. Her stomach began twisting into a knot. "They weren't there when we came down before."

"No, they weren't."

"So I guess they're not being stored here."

"I don't think so." Bernie pointed to the balloons lolling around on the floor next to them. "Just like I don't think those are for a party."

Libby's stomach did a flip. "The balloons are filled with gas, aren't they?"

"It would appear so," Bernie said as she moved toward them. The closer Bernie got to the balloons, the stronger the smell of gas. She picked one up. It was heavy. She put it down again very carefully.

"What are the balloons for?" asked Libby.

"When they go off, they'll trigger the fireworks, which will collapse the walls of the house."

Libby swallowed. "Are you sure?"

"I'm positive."

"Do you think Melissa knew about this when she locked us down here?"

"No. I don't think so. I mean, why would she blow up her own house with all that artwork in it?"

"That's true, but it must have taken whoever did this . . ."

"I'm thinking Roberto . . ."

"Okay, Roberto a while to do this."

"Evidently not that long," Bernie said.

"How can Melissa not know?" asked Libby.

"Maybe she hasn't been down here," Bernie responded. "Maybe she lied about Roberto being down here. Maybe she just said that to give Roberto time to get away. But it doesn't really matter, because what we have to be talking about is how to get the hell out of here before we're blown to kingdom come."

Libby's stomach did another flip. "How is Roberto going to light up the balloons?"

"My guess is that he's either going to use a remote detonator or he's going to fire a rocket in through one of those windows." And Bernie gestured toward the three small windows set high up on the left-hand wall. Each window was divided into six small panes of glass. They in turn were held in place by a metal frame.

"Then let's find the detonator," Libby said.

Bernie shook her head. "Remember, I said remote. As in not here."

"Let's try the door again."

Bernie shook her head again. She'd already thought about it and discarded that option. The door had a solid lock and a metal frame with hinges that were set on the outside. There was no way they were going to get it open without a pry bar and more muscle than either she or Libby possessed. "I think the windows are our best bet."

"I don't think we're going to fit."

"Oh yes, we will," Bernie said. "We have to." She walked over and carefully examined them. "At least the metal is rusted. So that's a good thing. But then we're going to have to dig our way through the snow."

Libby thought that they'd worry about that problem when they came to it. Right now they needed something to stand on. She looked around and caught sight of an old bike lying in the far corner of the basement. She went and got it while Bernie carefully moved the fireworks underneath the window to the other side of the basement. Libby stood the bike along the wall and went to look for something to break the window with. She found a spade buried underneath a pile of old newspapers, brought it back, and showed it to Bernie.

"That should work," Bernie said.

She climbed on the seat of the bike while Libby held it

steady. When Bernie was ready, Libby handed her the spade.

"Just don't cut yourself," Libby warned.

"I'll be happy if that's the worst that will happen to me," Bernie told her as she carefully used the end of the spade to knock the glass out of the metal frame. Then she handed the spade to Libby, grasped the metal edges of the window frame, and pulled. She could feel the frame start to move. She pulled harder. It began to loosen up.

"Let me," Libby said.

She and Bernie changed places.

Libby pulled as hard as she could. The frame popped out, and Libby fell backward onto the floor. "Ta da," she cried, holding it up.

Bernie got back on the bike and began to dig the snow away from the opening. By the time she was done, she was covered with the stuff and there was a mound of snow on the floor, but she could wiggle through to the outside. Once she was outside, she lay down on her stomach and extended her hand to Libby, who was balancing on the seat of the bicycle, and pulled her through to the outside.

"I'm going to kill Roberto when I find him," Bernie gasped out as they lay in the snow.

"Include me in."

Thirty seconds later Bernie managed to sit up. "We have to get everyone out of the house. We have to do that now."

Libby nodded. Her arms were aching, and her fingers were raw and bleeding, and she was feeling light-headed from breathing in the gas fumes. She wanted nothing more than to stay where she was, but she knew that she couldn't. They had to get back and warn the others. They were rounding the bend to the front door when they saw a figure in the snow. It was dressed in black and carrying a Roman candle.

"Roberto!" Libby cried.

She and Bernie moved toward him. He noticed and

began moving faster. Bernie and Libby picked up their pace. The snow was heavy and deep, and Libby felt as if they were wading through treacle, but they were closing the distance. They were a little less than a foot away when Bernie made a flying leap and tackled Roberto. They both fell in the snow. The Roman candle rolled away, and Libby grabbed it. She turned back to find that Bernie was straddling the figure. Libby went over and ripped off his mask.

Bernie blinked. "Melissa?"

"I am El Huron," Melissa replied.

"You are Melissa Field."

"I am El Huron." Melissa had lowered her voice almost a full octave.

"Why did you try and blow us up?" Bernie asked her.

Melissa licked her lips. "El Huron serves the cause of justice."

"Did you kill your dad?" Bernie asked.

Melissa smiled and said nothing.

"Your brother?" Libby asked.

"El Huron serves the cause of truth," Melissa said.

"Where's Roberto?" Bernie asked.

Melissa remained silent. Her hand crept toward her pants pocket. El Huron was prepared. El Huron was always prepared. El Huron had a gravity knife in there. It was an old but useful weapon. El Huron slowly brought it out of her pocket. *La morena* was not looking. It would be a simple matter of stabbing her. The stomach was best.

Bernie caught the movement of Melissa's wrist and saw the glint of something in her hand.

"Help!" she cried to Libby as she grabbed for the knife.

Libby leaned over and caught Melissa's hand and tried to pry her fingers off the handle, but Melissa was stronger than she was.

"I'm trying," Libby told Bernie, but she could feel herself losing ground.

"Try harder," Bernie said. She looked at Libby, and then

she looked back at Melissa and socked Melissa as hard as she could in the jaw.

Melissa dropped the knife and Libby picked it up. Then she grabbed Melissa's hands.

She was telling Bernie they needed something to tie Melissa up with when she heard the noise of a motor. She looked up to see a Sno-Cat racing toward them. It halted in front of them, and Brandon and Marvin jumped out.

Brandon bowed. "At your service, madam."

"The cavalry has arrived," Marvin added.

"Oh my God!" Bernie cried. "What are you guys doing here?"

"Your dad got worried when he couldn't reach you, so he called me, and I called Marvin, and he called a friend who had a Sno-Cat, and here we are," Brandon told her.

"So who is the woman you were just punching?" Marvin asked Bernie.

"This is Melissa Field," Bernie replied, "and she killed her father and brother and was just about to blow up the whole house with everyone in it."

Melissa looked up from the snow. "I am El Huron, the righter of wrongs."

"You're Melissa." Libby said.

"No. I have sought justice for my mother."

"Oh, shut up," Bernie said and punched her again.

Chapter 42

Sean looked at Bernie and Libby. They were sitting in the living room of their flat with his friend Clyde, drinking 100 percent Kona coffee from a press pot and eating the ginger cookies and lemon bars that Bernie and Libby had made the day before. It had been two days since the Field house debacle, and Sean was still filled with gratitude every time he looked at his daughters.

"She's crazy," Bernie said, referring to Melissa.

Clyde inclined his head. "Maybe. Or maybe she's just pretending. I guess that's for the psych guys to tell us."

"I don't believe in multiple personalities," Libby said.

"Well, one of her killed three people," Sean noted.

"Do we know that for a fact?" Bernie asked.

Clyde took a sip of his coffee and another bite of his lemon bar. "That's what she said, and I don't think there's any reason to doubt her confession. She said . . . okay, El Huron said . . . that she killed her dad to get back at him for killing her mom and she killed Geoff and Roberto because they got in the way."

"And she was going to kill everyone else, including us?" Bernie asked.

Clyde shrugged. "That was the general idea. She needed

the money. She had a lot of bad debts with some very not nice people. It turns out the artwork was heavily insured."

"So it might not have been about vengeance, after all," Libby said.

"No." Clyde took another sip of coffee. "It might have been about good old-fashioned moola, and this whole other person she made up is just a convenient excuse. Or not."

Sean leaned back in his chair. There really was no place like home. "She's the classic bad seed," Sean said to Bernie and Libby. "And she would have killed a lot more people if you two hadn't stopped her."

Bernie nibbled around the edge of her ginger cookie. It was slightly overbaked along the edges and a little bit underbaked in the center, which was the way she liked them. "Where did you find Roberto's body?" she asked.

Clyde pressed his thumb down on the crumbs from the lemon bar and conveyed them to his mouth. "Out behind the bunker. I have to say she'd done a good job of burying him."

Libby put another spoonful of sugar in her cup and stirred it. She watched the brown liquid swirling around. "So he was dead before we got there?"

"He was dead for two weeks, near as we can tell."

"INS never picked him up?" Libby asked.

Clyde shook his head. "I don't think they got the chance."

"And Melissa called the INS on Alma, not Monty," Bernie said.

Clyde nodded. "That's what their records show."

"But everyone thought it was Monty," Bernie said.

"Because that's what Melissa told everybody—in confidence, of course," Clyde said.

Libby took another nibble of her cookie. "So Melissa set everything up from the get-go. She made it appear that she was Roberto . . ."

"Because if he were around, he would be the natural one to blame," Bernie said, finishing her sister's sentence for her.

"And she wrote and planted the letter in Alma's drawer," Clyde said.

"So Roberto wasn't Monty's son?" Bernie asked.

Clyde shook his head. "Nope."

"And the ferret?" Libby asked.

"We located Alma," Clyde said. "According to her, the ferret was real. But she died a natural death."

"Poor lady," Sean said. "Losing your kid." He was silent for a moment. "I can't even imagine." He reached for another lemon bar. Of all the things his daughters baked, these were his favorite. Except maybe for their apple pies. And brownies. And chocolate chip cookies. He was unbelievably lucky.

"What about Monty's will?" Libby asked. "Who gets everything?"

Clyde reached over and snagged another lemon bar. "Evidently, he left everything to some distant cousin in the UK. The brothers are talking about challenging the will, so it's going to be tied up for years."

"And most of the money will go to the lawyers," Sean observed.

Clyde bobbed his head. "Exactly."

Everyone sat there for a moment, listening to the reassuring hum of business being conducted downstairs. It was Libby who broke the silence.

"I've decided we're going to have a late Thanksgiving this year," she announced. "On this coming Saturday. At four." She turned to Clyde. "It would be nice if you and the missus could come." She was going to invite Brandon and Marvin and Ines, as well. That would make eight. Eight was a good number for a dinner party.

Clyde grinned. "It would be my pleasure." He loved to

eat, and the food at the Simmons' house was his favorite thing to eat. It was always good, and there was always plenty of it.

"Because," Libby continued, "we have a lot to be thankful for."

"Amen to that," Bernie and Sean said at the same time.

Recipes

Thanksgiving is one of those holidays with a canonical menu. Everyone has turkey and stuffing and gravy and sweet potatoes and cranberry sauce and pie. But, to paraphrase an expression, as with so many things, the devil is in the details. The following recipes are loved variations on some of these themes.

Corn-Bread Stuffing

This recipe is the one I have used for years. It is adapted from one of Craig Claiborne's recipes and is enough for a twelve-to-fifteen-pound turkey.

3 cups crumbled day-old corn bread
3 cups *lightly packed good* white bread cut into cubes
1 cup butter
2 ½ cups chopped onion
2 ½ cups chopped celery
3 cloves garlic, finely minced
1 teaspoon chopped fresh thyme, or ½ teaspoon dried
⅓ cup chopped fresh parsley
1 tablespoon chopped fresh basil, or 1 ½ dried teaspoons
salt to taste
¾ teaspoon or more freshly ground pepper (freshly ground
   is important)
1 finely chopped bay leaf
Tabasco sauce to taste

Crumble corn bread into a large mixing bowl. Toast bread cubes in 375°F oven, and when brown, add to corn bread. Heat half the butter in a large skillet and add the rest of the ingredients. Stir over moderate heat for twenty minutes. Add remaining butter and stir until it melts. You can either stuff the turkey with this, or put it in a baking dish, dot it with butter, and bake it for an hour in a pre-heated 350°F oven.

Lois Renthal's Stuffing

This is another variation on stuffing.

1 cup pecans
1 cup cooked and peeled chestnuts
½ cup fresh mushrooms
½ pound chicken livers
2 tablespoons butter
1 cup finely chopped onions
2 minced garlic cloves
2 teaspoons fresh thyme
½ cup chopped parsley
salt and pepper
1 pound sausage meat
2 eggs
2 cups bread crumbs

Place nuts on a baking dish and bake until crisp. Let cool. Dice mushrooms. Cut chicken livers into small pieces. Melt butter in a large skillet over medium heat and add onions and garlic. Add mushrooms when onions are wilted. Cook until mushrooms give up their liquid and it has evaporated. Add liver, thyme, parsley, salt, and pepper. Cook until liver changes color. Add sausage meat, breaking up pieces with a spoon. Add eggs and bread crumbs and blend. Chop nuts and add. Cover and cook over low heat until sausage is done.

You can also eliminate the bread crumbs, and increase the liver and the mushrooms.

Pecan Pie

This recipe for Steen's Southern Pecan Pie comes from my good friend and neighbor Sarah Saulson and can be found in the pamphlet *The Story of Steen's Syrup and Its Famous Recipes.*

¼ cup butter
1 tablespoon all-purpose flour
1 tablespoon cornstarch
1 ½ cups Steen's Syrup
½ cup sugar
¼ teaspoon salt
1 cup pecans
2 eggs
1 teaspoon vanilla
unbaked pastry for 1 medium-sized pie

Melt butter, add flour and cornstarch, and stir until smooth. Then add Steen's Syrup and sugar and boil for 3 minutes. Cool. Add beaten eggs, nuts, and vanilla, blending well. Pour into pan lined with unbaked pastry. Bake in hot oven (450°) 10 minutes; then reduce to 350° and bake 30 to 35 minutes.

This recipe has nothing to do with Thanksgiving. It's a Pesach recipe, but I'm throwing it in because it's so simple and good. Thanks to Kate Rosenthal for this one.

3 eggs
1 16-ounce box of unsalted matzoh
butter
brown sugar to taste
cinnamon to taste

Beat the eggs thoroughly. Dip and cover matzoh in egg. Place in Pyrex baking dish. Layer with pats of butter, brown sugar, and cinnamon. Bake in a slow oven (275°) for about 45 minutes. Enjoy!